By

CURDS

OF

PREY

St. Martin's Paperbacks titles
by Korina Moss

CHEDDAR OFF DEAD
GONE FOR GOUDA
CURDS OF PREY

CURDS OF PREY

A Cheese Shop Mystery

BY

KORINA MOSS

St. Martin's Paperbacks

This is a work of fiction. All of the characters, organizations, and events portrayed in this novel are either products of the author's imagination or are used fictitiously.

First published in the United States by St. Martin's Paperbacks, an imprint of St. Martin's Publishing Group.

CURDS OF PREY

Copyright © 2023 by Korina Moss.

For information, address St. Martin's Publishing Group, 120 Broadway, New York, NY 10271.

www.stmartins.com

ISBN: 978-1-250-79523-6

Our books may be purchased in bulk for promotional, educational, or business use. Please contact your local bookseller or the Macmillan Corporate and Premium Sales Department at 1-800-221-7945, ext. 5442, or by email at MacmillanSpecialMarkets@macmillan.com.

Printed in the United States of America

St. Martin's Paperbacks edition / April 2023

10   9   8   7   6   5   4   3   2   1

For my siblings

ACKNOWLEDGMENTS

My gratitude goes to Madeline Houpt for making me a better writer by being an insightful and patient editor; to my fantastic agent, Jill Marsal; to Danielle Christopher and Alan Ayers, who designed and illustrated, respectively, another gorgeous book cover; to copy editor John Simko, grammarian extraordinaire; to my supportive publicity and marketing team, Sarah Haeckel and Allison Zeigler; to production editor John Rounds for making sure this book makes it to the finish line; and to everybody at St. Martin's who had a hand in bringing this book to life. I am very proud to be a St. Martin's author.

Continued thanks to Erin Moon for her brilliant narration of the audio version of this series for Blackstone Audiobooks.

I owe a huge debt of thanks to my trusted first reader, Caitlin Lonning, whose advice and enthusiasm for each of my books makes a considerable impact.

Thank you to Brian Kenney of *First Clue* for his positive review of the series and quote for this book. Once again, thanks to authors Carolyn Haines, Julie Anne Lindsay (Bree Baker), and Liz Mugavero (Cate Conte) for their continued support.

Thanks to the cheesemongers and cheese shops who give me inspiration and education.

A huge note of thanks goes to the independent bookstores who champion cozy mysteries, and to the bloggers, booktubers, and podcasters who read, review, and talk about cozy mysteries. You are a gift to authors and readers, alike.

To my readers who have been so enthusiastic about this series, including my family, friends, and fellow writers who support me in so many ways—I have a heart full of gratitude. That especially includes my dad, who reads my book the minute it arrives in his mailbox.

My heart is with my mom, who always made sure I knew how proud she was of me.

Cheese is my love language.

—Willa Bauer

CHAPTER 1

"Alp Blossom." I showed Olivia Harrington and her two grown daughters the beautiful cheese wheel coated in colorful trimmings of dried grasses and flowers. It looked plucked from a spring meadow. "This alpine cheese is made in Austria, but the edible flowers and herbs it's dressed in are from the surrounding meadows of Bavaria."

Olivia and her younger daughter Summer each nibbled at their samples as the four of us sat at the farm table in my cheese shop's kitchenette. Yes, we were up to our twenty-third sample (with no end in sight), but I wondered how they were even able to taste it with the teensy-weensy bites they took. Maybe nibbling was how they maintained their size-zero figures. The diamond on Summer's ring finger was way bigger than the bite she took.

Unlike Summer, her older sister Chloe ate the entire portion of whichever cheese samples she enjoyed and didn't think twice about wrinkling her nose and spitting out those she didn't. Chloe was just as svelte as her mother and sister, debunking my theory of how nibbling food sustained their figures. The sisters, both in their late twenties, also inherited their mother's aquiline nose, large blue eyes, and thick mane of brunette hair. Basically, Summer and Chloe looked like Disney princesses.

Summer waited for her mother's reaction before deciding her own, which always coincided with Olivia's. Olivia nodded at the latest cheese sample in satisfaction, thus Summer did the same. Chloe looked a little green in the gills from having enjoyed so much cheese—a girl after my own heart.

As maid of honor, Chloe was the official hostess of Summer's wedding shower taking place the following day, and had hired me to do a cheese bar. However, entrusting a cheesemonger to select cheese was apparently not in Olivia Harrington's comfort zone, so the last-minute call came yesterday for a cheese tasting with the Harrington women. Even though it was a little late (to say the least) to change my selections and accompaniments, of course I agreed.

The Harringtons had risen in the ranks as the wealthiest family in Yarrow Glen after the Lippingers sold their vast acreage of Sonoma Valley land twenty years ago. Not only were the Harringtons wealthy and influential, they'd also recently purchased *All Things Sonoma* magazine from the Lippingers. I knew Summer's wedding events would be highlighted in the magazine prior to a cover story for the six-figure wedding, which meant my shop would get a mention.

I was feeling slightly queasy from the déjà vu of being appraised by someone with the magazine. Guy Lippinger had been the magazine's food critic and had threatened to give Curds & Whey a bad review just before he was found murdered outside of my shop last year. I had to remind myself that his murder investigation was behind me and so were the Lippingers. I was looking forward to a fresh start with the magazine. This could mean big things for Curds & Whey.

The recommendation to use some of Yarrow Glen's local businesses came via our town mayor, as her nephew was Summer's fiancé. Not only was providing the cheese for Summer Harrington's wedding shower a big deal, but impressing Mayor Trumbull wouldn't hurt either.

I glanced at the clock again. It was a half hour past closing time. Mrs. Schultz and Archie, my two employees, were perfectly capable of closing the shop on their own, but I felt bad they were being forced to do so. Plus, I had a date tonight with Roman, who had been inching his way out of the friend zone for the past three months.

Excitement bubbled up like a fizzy drink when I thought about our first kiss outside my apartment door, and the way my security light clicked off in the middle of it like a movie screen fading to black after the happy ending.

I sighed. If I didn't get back to reality, I wouldn't get back to Roman.

"Are you satisfied with the cheeses I've selected for the shower tomorrow?" I asked the Harrington women with hidden crossed fingers.

Mrs. Schultz, who was "smack-dab" in her sixties, as she liked to say, tentatively approached the kitchenette where I was doing the sampling. "Excuse me. Willa? I'm sorry to interrupt." She displayed her usual toothy grin even after a full day of work. Her cheery disposition was matched by the bright colors of the dresses and scarves she always chose to wear under her Curds & Whey apron. "Archie and I are done closing the shop."

I excused myself from the Harringtons and walked with Mrs. Schultz to the front of the shop, where we met

Archie. I'd been mentoring twenty-year-old Archie since Curds & Whey opened last year. He was a lanky guy with a generous sprinkling of freckles across his face and a port-wine stain on his cheek. His love of cheese along with his work ethic and enthusiastic personality were assets to my shop. Both he and the equally loyal Mrs. Schultz had quickly become much more than employees. They were two of my closest friends.

"I'm sorry about this. I had no idea they'd still be here," I said in a hushed voice.

"No problem," Archie replied. "Do you need us to stick around?"

"Gosh no, you two get home. I know you have your poker night to get to, Mrs. Schultz. I hope I haven't made you late."

"It's at Sylvia's house tonight, so I've got plenty of time. No worries," she said.

"Thanks for the extra help." I let them out the front door and locked it behind them, wishing I was following them out. I returned to the rear of the shop, where Chloe seemed as anxious as I was to wrap up the evening. Thus far, Chloe was my favorite Harrington.

"I think we have enough choices, Mother. We're supposed to meet Nelson and the Trumbulls for dinner," Chloe said, although I couldn't believe she'd even be hungry for dinner.

Summer had taken out a compact mirror and was reapplying her lipstick, which was the exact shade of rose pink as her mother's. "You're supposed to be the one throwing me this shower, Chloe. You'd think you'd be a little more invested in it," she said, pouting her pink lips in the mirror.

"I've eaten so much cheese, I won't poop for a week! How much more invested can I be?" Chloe answered.

"Chloe, we don't use those kinds of words," her mother scolded.

Chloe continued, "What's the big deal anyway? It's not like this is your first wedding. We've gone through this routine before."

Summer snapped her compact mirror shut. "You're just jealous because you've never been asked."

"And you're just uptight because you're afraid this one will leave you at the altar like your last fiancé."

Oh my, this was spiraling fast. Cheese usually made people happier, not heated.

"Mother?" Summer pleaded with Olivia for backup.

"Girls," Mrs. Harrington admonished, although she didn't seem that ruffled. I got the feeling their squabbling wasn't new to her.

I, on the other hand, was mortified on everyone's behalf.

Thank goodness a knock on the door of the shop gave me an excuse to leave the table. It might've been a customer ignoring the Closed sign and dimmed front lights. I hoped it wasn't Roman. I was going to have to text him and tell him I was running late.

Through the paned-glass door, I saw the statuesque Mayor Trumbull. Her son Everett, and her nephew Nelson, Summer's fiancé, were with her.

Oh no, don't tell me there are going to be even more opinions about my cheese choices. I hoped my face didn't reveal my inner thoughts. I unlocked and opened the door.

"Mayor Trumbull. This is a nice surprise." I allowed them in, forcing a smile.

The mayor wore a power red blazer over a black sheath dress that landed just at her knee, and modest heels. Everett and Nelson were about the same age but that was where the similarities ended. The mayor's strong genes were passed onto her son, who had her wide nose and matched her in height. I'd met Everett before—Baz had been helping him transform the building on the other side of the alley next to Curds & Whey to open a bicycle shop. He always greeted me with a friendly "Hey, neighbor," and tonight was no exception.

In contrast, Nelson walked in and looked past me. Apparently, I was not someone he needed to concern himself with. I'd never met him before, but Summer had shown him off to me in photos. Sunglasses were perched atop his head, probably kept in place by all the gel in his hair. The sun had gone down an hour ago, so they must've been worn just to complete the look that he'd obviously worked hard on. He was a walking billboard for *trendy*.

I tried to introduce myself, but he talked over me: "Summer! We've got dinner reservations. You're keeping my aunt waiting."

"It's quite all right, Nelson," Mayor Trumbull said in a lowered voice. She turned to me. "This is such a lovely shop, Willa. I need to make a point to come in more often."

I beamed at the compliment. I was proud of how my French-inspired cheese shop had been thriving since I opened it almost a year ago. My shop's aesthetic was inspired by my brief time working at a *fromagerie* outside of Lyon where my passion for cheese blossomed. I wanted to bring the color, warmth, and romance of France into my shop with raised panel wainscoting and textured walls that resembled rich wallpaper. At the new year, I'd splurged on some crimson faux Aubusson rugs to warm up the hardwood floors, which made me love the space even more.

We sold charcuterie boards, cheese lovers' cookbooks, and anything you'd need for a cheese-perfect picnic: bo-

tanical tablecloths, picnic baskets, engraved cheese
knives, and plenty of sweet-and-savory cheese accompaniments. Curds & Whey was on the California cheese
trail, an online list of creameries and cheese shops for
cheese-loving travelers to visit, and we were a hit with
any who ventured to our small Sonoma Valley town.
Cheese was undoubtedly the star of the shop. Distressed,
turned-leg tables held stacked wheels of aged cheeses
from all over the world. Wrapped wedges at the front
windows revealed the shades and textures inside their
casings, luring customers inside the shop to inhale their
heady fragrances.

The kitchenette at the back of the shop was where I
held cheesemaking classes or hosted special guests, and
where our current cheese sampling was taking place.
Much to my relief, Olivia, Summer, and Chloe had collected their designer purses and rose from the farm table
to join us at the front of the shop.

Nelson slid his arm around Summer's waist and pecked
her on the lips. "Let's go get going," he said, giving her a tug.

"We'll go when Mother's ready," Summer muttered.

I was certain whichever restaurant it was would not
give up a reservation with Mayor Trumbull and Olivia
Harrington, no matter how late they were.

"It's only up the street. We'll make it just fine," Mayor
Trumbull assured him.

"Apricot Grille?" I said.

The mayor nodded.

"I'm heading there myself tonight," I said, immediately
igniting the belly flips that occurred when I thought of Roman.

I'd tried to tell myself tonight's dinner wasn't a special
occasion, but the nicest restaurant in town wasn't in our
usual rotation of dates. In fact, I'd only ever been there

a handful of times to sit at the bar to enjoy a drink and their truffle fries. Ever since Roman and I broke the ice with our harvest fair date last October, we'd been getting together when our busy schedules would allow. Neither of us were much for formal affairs, so his announcement that he'd made reservations for us at Apricot Grille was curious.

I thought maybe he was dodging the pressure of Valentine's Day next weekend by taking me out now. My best friend Baz was certain it meant Roman was going to ask me to be exclusive. I wasn't sure which scenario I preferred. Was I ready to go from dating to making it official with Roman, a known serial dater? Plenty of long talks allayed my trust issues with him and made me think I might be ready to take the next step.

Now that Nelson, Everett, and Mayor Trumbull were here to hurry the Harringtons along, I was feeling hopeful that I might have more than five minutes to get ready for the dinner. A rap on the door extinguished that hope. Roman stood on the other side.

"Will you excuse me for just a moment?" I said to everyone before scooting out of the shop.

I met him on the sidewalk under the light of the streetlamp. Our only spectator was Guernsey, Curds & Whey's lopsided bovine scarecrow. I'd made her last fall for the harvest fair, and, despite her shortcomings, she garnered a permanent position at the door as our mascot.

Roman was dressed in a blazer and smelling of fresh soap. He might as well have been wearing a tuxedo for the number of times I'd ever seen him in anything but a T-shirt. Normally seeing him and his slow grin that ended in a dimple on his left cheek left me atwitter. But since I hadn't even brushed my hair for our date, his presence left me less than thrilled this time.

"I'm early. I couldn't help it," he said, his grin stuck in place.

"I'm so sorry I'm not ready yet," I said.

He reached out and gently tucked a strand of my hair behind my ear. "Perfect. You're ready."

I felt myself drift into la-la land, where only Roman and I existed.

"Roman Massey? Is that you?" Chloe's voice broke the spell. She had opened the door wide and joined us on the sidewalk. She smiled for the first time that evening. "We were just talking about you."

The rest of the group filtered onto the sidewalk. Summer, her saucer eyes even larger than usual, said, "Roman?"

Conversely, Nelson's eyes narrowed at the name. "How did he know you were going to be here?" Nelson demanded of Summer.

"I-I don't know," Summer stammered.

"Roman's meadery is across the street. Is there a problem?" I asked, confused by the strong feelings surrounding Roman's appearance.

"Is that why you wanted to come here tonight? So you could run into Roman Massey?" Nelson raised his voice at Summer.

"Nelson," Mayor Trumbull implored, attempting to calm her nephew.

"We're in public, Nelson," Olivia reminded him, although we were the only ones on the sidewalk. As soon as all the shops closed for the day, our block emptied out.

"I just came to see Willa," Roman explained. "I had no idea Summer would be here."

"I can vouch for that. I think there's a miscommunication here," I said, hoping to calm Nelson. I had no idea myself what was going on. What did Chloe mean they were just talking about him? Why was I the only one in the dark?

"I don't want this guy anywhere near you or our wedding," Nelson said to Summer. He puffed up his chest and stepped in front of Roman, so they were chin to chin, challenging him.

"You can back off, buddy," Roman said without backing up.

"Hold on a minute." I stepped forward. This was getting out of hand. I didn't know what Nelson had against Roman, but this was my sidewalk and my almost-boyfriend.

"Leave him alone, Nelson," Summer said. She pulled her fiancé by the arm.

If she was hoping to stave off any further outbursts, her defense of Roman only served to do the opposite. As Nelson angrily pulled his arm out of Summer's grip, his hand flew up, his fist accidentally colliding with Roman's mouth. At least, I thought it was an accident. Nelson's initial surprise turned into a vengeful grin.

Stunned, Roman touched his fingers to his mouth. A trace of blood was left behind, now trickling from his lip. I lunged forward to get between them before anything else happened. Everett did the same.

From behind Everett, Nelson pointed his finger at Roman. "There's more of that if you come near Summer again. You had your chance with her, and you left her at the altar."

My mind reeled. When Chloe taunted Summer about her previous wedding, Roman had been the groom?

I looked to Roman, waiting for him to refute Nelson's claim. "Roman?"

Roman's disappointed eyes told me it was true. He directed his stern gaze at Nelson. "Don't touch me again, buddy, or you'll be sorry."

He turned and crossed the street to his apartment without looking back.

I wanted to go after him, but I had the two most prominent families in Yarrow Glen to contend with, not to mention my own confusion and anger. "I don't know what just happened here." I took a deep breath to help reel in my temper.

Everett kept a hand on Nelson's shoulder, likely to calm him.

"I can't believe you did that," Summer said to Nelson through clenched teeth. "You need to apologize to him."

"Summer's right, Nelson," Mayor Trumbull said. "That was uncalled for."

"I'm never apologizing to that guy," Nelson said. He rubbed his knuckles, reddened from connecting with Roman's lip.

"Nelson—" Summer started, but her mother broke in.

"You don't need to continue making a scene. Let it go," Olivia said.

Summer snapped her mouth shut, but it was apparent she was fuming inside.

"So are you and Roman together?" Chloe asked me like we were teenagers in a high school cafeteria. She seemed inexplicably excited at the prospect.

"He's a friend of mine," I said. I didn't want to say more. I felt protective of the relationship now that I discovered they all knew him and had their own history with him.

"I'm sorry this happened, Willa," Mayor Trumbull said.

Olivia readjusted the purse hanging from her forearm and fondled her diamond bracelet. "A little stress before the wedding is to be expected. Shall we go to dinner?"

"Mother! I'm not having dinner with him tonight after

what he just did. I'll be in the car." Summer stomped off down the sidewalk.

"Summer!" Nelson went after her, but she pushed him away and got into a BMW parked a few spots down from the shop. Nelson pulled on the handle, but she'd locked the car. He pounded on the window. "Come on, Summer. You can't be mad at me."

Olivia remained outwardly calm. "We'll expect you at the house tomorrow at two p.m. sharp," she said to me. "See you tomorrow, Kate," she said to Mayor Trumbull. She started down the sidewalk. "Let's go, Chloe."

"We're not getting dinner?" Chloe whined. Her mother continued to the car without answering. Chloe sighed. She seemed more upset about missing dinner than what had just transpired.

I watched Olivia speak into Nelson's ear before getting in the car. He gave up and stepped away from the car, allowing them to drive off. Hands in his pockets, he strolled back to us. He looked at his aunt a bit sheepishly. "Dinner for three then?"

Mayor Trumbull shook her head. "You have your father's short temper. I loved my brother, but he'd lose his cool in a heartbeat then be sorry for it almost as quickly."

Nelson looked down at his shoes. "I'll talk to her later. She never stays mad at me for too long."

"One of these days, she might get tired of forgiving you," Everett chimed in.

"You're going to have to help me find a good gift this time so she will. You're not my best man for nothing," Nelson said. He smiled at Everett and clapped him on the back. "Let's get some food." Everett waved goodbye to me as they headed to their car.

"Have a nice evening, Willa," Mayor Trumbull said

with an apologetic crinkle between her brows before joining them.

I went back into Curds & Whey alone and gladly
locked myself inside. *"Have a nice evening"?* I was supposed to be having a romantic dinner at Apricot Grille tonight with Roman, possibly taking our relationship to the
next level. Instead, I found out he'd almost gotten married to Summer Harrington. And he left her at the altar,
any soon-to-be-bride's nightmare. What possible reason
could he have had?

CHAPTER 2

I tidied up from the cheese tasting as I tried to process this bombshell about Roman and Summer. I was having a hard time even imagining him dating Summer. She just didn't seem his type. I had to remind myself there was a reason for his serial dater reputation—he had a lot of types. But engaged? That was the part that didn't fit. Even so, I could easily get past that he and Summer had been together, but he left her at the altar. Memories of my own broken engagement sprung forth and with it, all the old, ugly feelings I'd worked to keep locked away these past ten years.

Pearce was my college sweetheart. He and my best friend and I were the three musketeers, always together and forever making plans. We were all entrepreneurs at heart. Once I returned from my semester abroad in France, fully realizing my passion for cheese, the three of us knew our future would be to open a cheese shop together. But while I was studying to be a cheesemonger with cheesemakers and shops across the Northwest, they were falling in love behind my back. The heartbreak of that blindsided broken engagement and betrayal still lingered in my DNA. I could only imagine how much worse it would've been had he not broken it off until our wedding day.

I had to remind myself that Roman wasn't Pearce. There had to be a reason he did what he did. After all, Summer stuck up for him tonight. I doubt I'd do the same for Pearce. Maybe Summer had wanted to call off the wedding but was afraid of her mother's wrath. It was easy to see that Summer didn't often go against her mother. Maybe Roman took the fall for both of them. My brain was working overtime trying to make this new information fit the good guy I was dating. Still, it left a really bad taste in my mouth.

I'd just finished cleaning up when a knock on the door brought me to the front of the shop. It was Roman again, changed from a blazer to his usual T-shirt and jeans. My stomach twisted with uncertainty. I unlocked the door and let him in.

He said nothing at first. Neither did I. Arms crossed, I waited for an explanation.

"I'm sorry about what happened tonight," he finally said.

Even in the low lights of the shop, I could see Nelson's fist had left a small welt on his lip. I didn't like seeing him hurt. "Is your lip okay?"

"It's nothing. Look, I'm sorry I didn't tell you about Summer." The words darted out of his mouth.

I nodded and stayed silent, leaving space for him to say more. His gaze left mine and he said nothing.

I filled the silence with questions. "Did she want to call off the wedding? Were you doing her a favor?"

"No." His eyes stayed fixed on the cheese wheels on the table next to me.

There had to be an explanation. "Did you find out

something horrible about her? Is that why you didn't go through with it?"

"No. Summer was great. It wasn't her fault."

I waited once more for something further, some reason that would make it okay.

He finally looked at me. "There's nothing else I can say. I'm sorry again about tonight."

He walked out, leaving me feeling even worse than the first time he left. Where did this leave us?

I locked up for the last time and turned out the lights, grabbing some Manchego I fully expected to polish off tonight. I walked out the stockroom door to the alley and continued upstairs to my apartment. Once inside, I kicked off my Keds and headed for the bedroom to exchange my work khakis and blouse for yoga pants and an extra-large T-shirt. I returned to the living room/kitchen combo and plopped on the love seat. I wrapped myself in my grandmother's knitted throw blanket with my betta fish Loretta close by on the low, backless bench I used as a coffee table. It was as close to snuggling as we could get. I turned on *Rebecca*, my go-to movie whenever I wanted to be whisked away. But I could hear my mother in my head: *Problems are like gophers—if you ignore them, they'll just keep popping up.* She was right, of course, but for now, this one was getting pushed as far away as possible. I had a wedding shower tomorrow that needed my cheese bar.

I spent the next day at work keeping as busy as possible, hoping that fussing with my cheeses would work their magic. Focusing on cheese was the best meditation for me. Eating it worked even better, so it was lucky—or maybe not—that we got our weekly cheese curd delivery from the local Daybreak Creamery. I nibbled my way through the morning.

Doing last-minute preparations for the upcoming shower made for an extra-busy morning and before I knew it, I was in my old CR-V with a considerable amount of cheese on my way to Roman's former fiancée's wedding shower. *Ugh.*

Mrs. Schultz was holding down the Curds & Whey fort, so Archie could help me out. He and I were both dressed in white button-down shirts and black slacks, as required by Olivia. Baz offered to also help haul the items from my car to the cheese bar once we got there, so he followed us in his pickup truck.

When we arrived at the address, I drove through the open gate to an expansive European-Spanish-style home that elicited a "Holy camoly!" from Archie.

I pulled through the circular drive to the pavement in front of the three garage bays on the left wing of the house where I noticed two catering vans and a few other vehicles were parked. Baz parked next to me and emerged from his truck with three gorgeous cheeseboards he'd carved for such an occasion. Chloe met us outside dressed in leggings and a T-shirt but glammed from the neck up. She greeted us cheerfully.

Given the arguments in the shop yesterday, I wasn't expecting cheerful. In fact, I'd checked my phone throughout the morning to make sure the shower was still going forward as planned.

"My mother decided we should have the shower in the garden instead of inside," Chloe said.

"It *has* been warmer than usual lately," I said. Today the temperature hovered in the low seventies.

"Thank goodness for global warming," Chloe replied

without sarcasm. "Bring your stuff around the house and you'll see where everyone's setting up."

"Is there any particular place you want the cheese bar to be?" I asked.

Chloe's laughter burst forth. "My mother will be sure to tell you. I have to finish getting ready. Toodles!" She strode back into the house.

I turned to Baz and Archie. "Great. Momzilla will be giving orders." I was relieved that there was at least no mention of Roman.

A lime green car pulled up beside the catering vans.

"Hey, that's Hope," Archie said, his smile widening by the second.

Archie and Hope had been crushing on each other since I'd known them. I found their friendship adorable and hoped their blossoming romance would be less bumpy than mine and Roman's.

Hope, who had inherited Rise and Shine Bakery from her mother, emerged from the compact car with a large paper bakery bag. I was used to seeing her behind the bakery counter in pastel overalls, but today she wore the required white and black uniform. I couldn't put my finger on what else was different about her.

"Here are the bagel crisps you ordered," she said, handing the bag over to me.

I opened it and inhaled the aroma of the buttery crisps. They'd go perfect as an alternative to the various crackers I was also serving.

"Thanks so much. Are you by yourself?" I asked.

"Jasmine was supposed to help me, but when Mrs. Harrington came by yesterday, she said she refused to have Jasmine here because of her tattoos and her nose ring."

"That's just plain stupid," Baz said.

Archie and I echoed the sentiment.

"She didn't like my hair either," Hope said.

Now I knew what was different about her. Her pixie-style blonde hair was missing its usual streaks of color to match her nail polish.

She continued, "I wanted to tell her to go you know where, but getting my cupcakes into *All Things Sonoma* will really help promote my cakes."

When Hope's aunt ran the bakery, it was mostly known for its breads, but now that Hope was in charge, she wanted to change it into a cake bakery. She was even taking courses at Sadler Culinary School to improve her baking and decorating skills.

"Do you need help carrying your cupcakes to the house?" I asked her.

"I can help you," Archie volunteered.

"That would be amazing. Is it okay with you, Willa?" Hope asked.

"I've got Baz to help me. Go ahead, Archie. I guess we're not allowed to go through the house. Chloe told us to walk around to the backyard," I said to Hope.

"It's in the *gahhden*, *dahhling*." Baz did his best socialite impression, complete with imaginary cigarette, which made us laugh.

"Thanks so much. You're a life saver." Her stress turned into a relieved smile as she opened her hatchback. "This car is okay for the bread deliveries, but I might have to get a bigger one for cakes."

"It's the price of success," Archie said.

Hope's smile grew even more. "That's a good way of looking at it."

She and Archie managed the bakery boxes from her car and started around the house while I decided the best way to carry all the cheese and accompaniments from mine.

"So . . . ?" Baz said as I loaded his arms with containers of cheese.

"So . . . what?"

"How was the big date with Roman? You don't want to tell me I was right—he wants to make it exclusive?"

I'd told Mrs. Schultz and Archie the surprising news this morning but hadn't gotten around to telling Baz. It was hard to ignore things that you had to keep talking about.

"We never made it to the restaurant," I said.

Baz's eyebrows shot up. "Okayyy. TMI. I don't need to know that much information," he said, misunderstanding.

"I don't mean we hooked up. The furthest thing from it. In fact, I don't even know if we're dating anymore."

"What?"

I told Baz what happened last night.

"Wow. I'm sorry. Are you okay?" Baz asked.

"Not really. I know I wasn't his girlfriend officially, but I was starting to get used to the idea. Now I'm not sure how I feel about him."

"I wouldn't have figured Roman to be the kind of guy who would leave someone at the altar," he said.

"No kidding."

"We know Roman's a good guy, right? Did he explain how it went down?"

"No. I gave him a chance, but he didn't say anything, which made me feel even worse about it. I can't help but think he might've been having an affair during his engagement, like Pearce was."

"Maybe that's why he didn't explain what happened— he knew it would only make you more upset."

"Maybe. Do you think that's why he never told me about it?"

Baz shrugged.

I grasped a cooler in each hand and shut the back of the CR-V. We began our trek to the garden.

"Being blindsided about it when we've been friends for a year is what makes it even worse. That's why I was being careful and taking my time to get to know him. He has a pattern of not being transparent with me, but these last few months, I felt he was opening up more and we were getting closer. But maybe not. I mean, Summer Harrington obviously didn't really know him, and she was going to marry the guy. Maybe I don't know him either." I hated to think it. "Am I being unreasonable? You and Ginger are getting closer—when would you tell her something important from your past?"

Ginger was the barista at the used bookstore café on our street. She and Baz developed a friendship last autumn while they were working on a parade float together for Yarrow Glen's harvest festival. Now that she was single, Baz was considering asking her out.

"Something that big? I don't know, but then again, I don't have any big secrets to tell," he said.

"I know there are things from my past that I don't share with everyone right away, but I've shared them with him. I guess we weren't as good friends as I thought."

"Now don't go saying that. You and I both know that's not true."

I wished I was as certain as Baz. I didn't want to talk about Roman anymore. "All I know for sure is we have to get to the garden and start concentrating on my cheese bar."

"You got it, boss." Baz winked.

At the side of the house, a golf cart was parked near the end of a dirt trail. My gaze followed the trail to a horse stable and an empty paddock.

As we walked around to the back of the house, my eye followed the level property that eventually turned into brush and a smattering of trees as far as I could see. On the back lawn, a neat horseshoe of tall hedges blocked our view of the garden. We walked through an opening that hid a striking patio with an inground pool. I admired the house's romantic arches and the second-story terrace with a beautiful wrought-iron railing. Through the arches I spotted an outdoor kitchen, but no one was here.

"Where is everybody?" I asked, confused. I was used to lifting cheese wheels, but my arms were starting to tire from the coolers' loads.

A woman with her hair pulled back into a bun and wearing a simple black sack dress uniform that hung on her exceedingly thin frame, appeared from the other side of the covered patio. She motioned for us to join her. "Over here. I'm so sorry. I was showing the others where to go." She seemed harried. Upon closer look, she didn't appear too much older than me. I could only imagine what working for Olivia Harrington would be like.

"No problem," I said, wanting to allay her concerns that we'd complain to Olivia. "I'm Willa from Curds and Whey, and this is Baz."

"The cheese shop lady? I heard about you from Lou after your shop opened last year," she said.

"Yes! You know Lou?"

"My mom has always shopped at his market. Now I order groceries from him for the Harringtons. I'm their housekeeper, Polly."

"Nice to meet you."

"I'm allergic to dairy or I would've come by."

"That's okay. Stop by to say hi sometime. I promise, I won't feed you cheese."

Now smiling, she led us around the outside of the

house, the white and gray speckled patio tiles showing us the way like the yellow brick road to Oz. "It's been hectic since the party planner quit."

We'd now managed to walk three quarters of the way around the house to get from our cars to where the shower would be. It might've been nice of Chloe to mention the best way to get to the garden.

We arrived at the portico to another expansive patio at the side yard—the garden. An arbor stood in the middle of the patio where a well-dressed man, likely the florist, was perched on a ladder attending to the roses draped on it. A long table was centered beneath it with matching flowers among the elaborate centerpieces. White-gloved workers were carefully placing silverware beside the beautiful place settings for at least fifty or sixty, by my eye. To the side, an ice sculpture was being propped on the champagne table. Hope was stationed under the shaded portico, beginning to unpack her cupcakes. We sidestepped a bartender carrying a box of wine bottles to the bar we were inadvertently blocking. I couldn't help but notice the wine was Enora's—Roman's family's brand.

As Chloe had said, Olivia Harrington—already in full spring luncheon regalia in a silk floral caftan—was directing everyone. She noted our arrival and immediately strode over.

"Is he with you?" Olivia looked down her nose at Baz, giving him the once-over. "Why is he dressed like that?"

Baz self-consciously smoothed his Carl's Hardware work polo over his slight beer belly and hitched up his jeans. We'd both assumed he wouldn't need to wear the required white shirt and black pants just to haul cheese.

"He's helping me carry what I need for the cheese bar. He'll be gone long before anyone arrives," I assured her.

I didn't give her the chance to protest further. "Where should we set up?"

Like Hope, I was also given a table under the covered section of the patio, a good thing for my cheese. Luckily, Olivia was an equal opportunity micromanager, so her attention was divided.

She called to the housekeeper, "Polly!"

"Yes, ma'am," Polly replied, scurrying up to her.

"All the staff seem to be here, so you're the point person. I'm going inside and getting dressed before the guests arrive."

I'd thought she was already dressed. What I considered dressy enough for a wedding shower was apparently her party-prep outfit.

Baz and I made another trip, this time walking the more direct route across the front lawn to the driveway. When we got to my car, I handed him the bags and baskets of accompaniments and garnishes. I carried the table-cloth, draping cloths, and the small wooden crates to use underneath the tablecloth as risers. Elevating some of the items would add interest to the cheese bar.

I needed to make one more trip to the car to bring back all the extras I didn't need and fetch a final bag of odds and ends. As I rounded the corner to the front of the house, two of the catering trucks were pulling out of the driveway. Chloe, now in a vibrant cocktail dress and heels, was on the wide front steps doing multiple poses for a photographer as if she were in a photo shoot on *America's Next Top Model*. The photographer, who from my vantage point looked like he could've been a model himself, was laughing and clicking shot after shot. Chloe noticed me as I passed behind him.

"Willa!" She removed her heels and scampered over to me on the grass in bare feet. "I was supposed to tell everyone before that you have to move your car when you're done unloading so the guests can park here."

She put her hand up to the photographer, who was continuing to snap photos of her. "Marcos, give it a rest." She smiled when she said it and rolled her eyes in mock exasperation.

He took the camera away from his face. I was right— he *was* good-looking. He looked about my age—early thirties—with perfectly coiffed thick black hair and a smoky stare. He wore a crisp white shirt, tight black trousers, and expensive-looking leather shoes.

"I can't help it, Chloe. The camera loves you," he said with a hundred-watt grin.

"Yeah, but my mother won't if you have more pictures of me than Summer."

"Aw, these are just for fun until Summer's ready." He scooped up a satchel near his feet and slung it over his shoulder.

I stopped drooling over Marcos and waited to be told where to move my car while they enjoyed their flirty banter. *Hello! Person working your event over here!*

"Where should I park then?" I finally interjected when my patience had run its course.

"Oh." Chloe seemed to have forgotten I was there, not that I could blame her. She turned her attention back to me. "Take three lefts and you'll come to a dirt driveway. There's a shed and a little parking area next to it that's used by our landscapers. If you reach the entrance to the stable, you've gone too far. The horses don't like all the noise of cars, so that gate won't be open. Once you park at the garden shed, you'll see where to cross the lawn to get back to the house."

"Sure, no problem." If I were being honest, it *was* a bit of a problem. I was already sweating and hadn't started arranging my cheese boards and platters yet. I wasn't looking forward to this extra trek.

"Did you happen to see Summer while you were in the garden?" Chloe asked before I walked away.

"I didn't, but there was a lot going on."

She sighed dramatically. "She knows we're supposed to take pictures for the magazine before the guests arrive. It's just like her to go off while the rest of us run around like chickens with our heads cut off."

I wasn't too sure Chloe could be grouped in as one of us headless chickens, but perhaps driveway duty was more work than she was used to.

The remaining bag in my car was light, so I drove out to the remote lot so I wouldn't have to make an extra trip. As Chloe had directed, I found the dirt driveway where a manual gate had been pushed open and continued to the small lot. The shed was almost like a doll house cottage, certainly bigger than some studio apartments I'd lived in. It had one second-story window and wide garage doors that looked like they opened to the sides. I pulled next to one of the catering vans and hoped I wouldn't have to trek across too much of the Harringtons' expansive property to get back to the house. Maybe I should've asked Baz to follow me and drive me back. Too late now.

I got out of my car with the last of my supplies. Once on the other side of the catering trucks, I could see beyond the shed to more of the property. A well-worn dirt trail wound from a meadow of scrub brush dotted with trees past the shed and continued to the paddock and stable on the other side of the property. I was relieved to see the house was closer than I'd thought.

I continued toward the shed and heard voices. Perhaps the caterers were taking a cigarette break before traipsing back to the house? I was brought up short when I recognized one of the voices. It was unmistakably Roman's.

I looked back at the parking area. His white convertible Mini Cooper was tucked beside the catering vans, hidden from my view when I'd parked. There was no doubt it was his car—it was the old Roadster model with black stripes on the hood and MEADMAN on the license plate.

I reached the other side of the shed, but he wasn't there either. Was I imagining his voice? I began to walk the length of the shed but stopped when I noticed a woman sitting on the ground, half-hidden by the building. I could see her mane of brunette hair cascading down her back. It was Summer.

"It's just the caterers," she said.

They must've heard my car pull up.

The shed hid Roman entirely. "Your mother would kill both of us if she knew I was here," I heard him reply.

"Don't worry about Mother. She doesn't hate you anymore. Neither do I. In fact, I never did. How could I? You were my first love."

I froze. What did I walk in on?

"You were mine too. I haven't forgotten what we had together, you know," he said.

I forced my feet to move and tiptoed back to the opposite side of the shed. As soon as I was far enough away, I took off across the lawn toward the house before I'd be discovered. The last thing I wanted was to be caught listening in on their renewed feelings for each other.

I speed-walked across the lawn and hoped they couldn't see me. I wasn't sure what I felt, but I knew it wasn't good. Were Roman's feelings so easily swayed by seeing an old love? I couldn't compete with that nor would I want to.

I hated the pit of jealousy that had suddenly lodged itself in my stomach. I reminded myself I had no dibs on him, but I still felt the blow. I think more than anything I felt disappointment. What was Roman doing here? Summer was engaged. It was the day of her wedding shower! I wasn't a fan of Nelson in the brief time we'd crossed paths, but no one deserved to be duped. And if I was being honest, I felt a little duped, myself.

CHAPTER 3

As I approached the garden, I took a deep breath, wiped my sweaty forehead, and stuck my short hair behind my ears in hopes I didn't look as frazzled as I felt. I had to put Roman out of my mind. Marcos the photographer had left Chloe's side and was taking shots of the beautiful table. I panicked when I saw Mayor Trumbull. Were the guests arriving already? Was it later than I thought?

I looked around, but there were no other guests. Olivia and Chloe weren't out yet either. Baz was unpacking the containers of accompaniments, and Archie had left Hope's side and had started unpacking the cheese. My full-blown panic attack was averted.

"Sorry, I had to move the car," I explained when I finally got back to our table. I purposely said nothing about Roman and Summer. I had to concentrate on why I was here.

"We got ya covered," Baz said.

"Hope's set, so I'm all yours. Thanks for letting me help her," Archie said.

I looked over to Hope's table, where she was carefully placing her silver luster–dusted cupcakes dotted with candy pearls onto a tower. They looked perfect for the occasion.

"What's Mayor Trumbull doing here already?" I asked under my breath so as not to be overheard.

The guys shrugged.

I put all other thoughts aside, Roman included, and concentrated on my cheese bar. Lucky for me, arranging cheese was the best stress reliever, aside from eating it. All stray thoughts vanished as I fussed with my cheeses on the three beautiful charcuterie boards Baz had hand carved for me to use. Tartufo, a truffle-infused Italian cheese, went on the board with the Brie and Manchego. Archie added the accompaniments—roasted red peppers, olives, dried salami, and spicy honey for this board. We'd add the garnishes at the end. We managed to complete the next two boards while Baz carefully stacked the empty containers and coolers.

Chloe came out of the house in black muck boots instead of heels. Growing up on a dairy farm, I practically lived in muck boots. She stuck her hands on her hips and surveyed the patio with a sour look on her face. Uh-oh. What now? Was she here to pass along more instructions from Olivia?

Marcos's camera lens left the tablescape and focused on Chloe.

"Not now, Marcos," she said. This time she wasn't pretending to be annoyed. "Where's Summer?"

"Haven't seen her. I figured she was inside getting primped," Marcos answered.

"We've been waiting for her. She hasn't been in the house or out front. Mother even made me check the stable. Do I smell like horse?"

"Only if horses smell divine."

Even Marcos's charm didn't change Chloe's mood. "Well, where is she?"

"Runaway bride?" Marcos said in jest.

Chloe arched an eyebrow, seeming to consider this possibility.

I knew where Summer was. I wrestled with whether to get involved, but if Summer didn't turn up, there would be no shower. No wedding shower meant no magazine photo spread. I looked over and saw Hope admiring her shimmering cupcake tower. Archie was adding the garnishes to our cheese boards. Whether Summer and Nelson should get married or not wasn't up to me, but I wanted this wedding shower to go on as planned. I walked over to Chloe.

"Can I talk to you for a second?" I whispered. "It's about Summer."

Chloe shooed Marcos away. "Go photograph those cupcakes before they melt."

He strutted over to Hope, and Chloe took me aside.

"I saw Summer next to the garden shed," I told her.

"What is she doing there?" she groused.

Olivia stepped outside, now in a sleeveless dress embellished with a multitude of silk roses that could've come straight off the runway or been made in a crafts class. Since she was Olivia Harrington, I assumed the former.

"Mother's not blaming this one on me," Chloe said, turning to tattle on Summer.

I grabbed ahold of her arm. "I wouldn't tell your mother."

"Why not?"

I was hoping not to have to mention Roman, but it looked like I'd have no choice.

"Well?" Chloe said, looking down at my hand still gripping her forearm.

I released it. "She was with Roman."

"What?" Realizing she'd said it too loudly, her eyes darted about. Luckily her mother was immersed in giving more instructions to Polly.

"I don't know what they were talking about, but I think you should go get her before your mother finds out," I suggested.

"You're right." Her spirits appeared lifted. "Thanks so much. I'll be back in a jiffy."

She trotted back into the house. When I looked out into the yard a short time later, I saw a golf cart racing across the lawn toward the shed. I kept my fingers crossed that Roman would be gone by the time Chloe arrived.

I went over to my table, where Mayor Trumbull was chatting with Baz and Archie.

"The cheese bar looks lovely, Willa. You did a great job," the mayor said graciously.

"Thank you. I'm very proud of my cheese. I think it'll be a hit. Did you notice these three gorgeous cheese boards? Baz hand carved them."

Baz took a step back, embarrassed by being singled out.

"I should've known. I always admire your handywork at the farmer's markets," Mayor Trumbull said to him.

Baz sometimes showcased his woodcarving hobby at our local farmer's market, selling wine racks, keepsake boxes, birdhouses . . . you name it. I wanted to make his help worthwhile by also being named in *All Things Sonoma* when it covered the shower.

Mayor Trumbull continued, "I'll be sure to tell Marcos so he can give you a mention in the magazine photo spread. When he comes over, ask him to get a close-up of one of them."

Despite his embarrassment, Baz seemed chuffed.

"I'm thrilled my nephew is happy with Summer, but I have to say, I'm also excited at the prospect of having Yarrow Glen on the good side of the magazine for a change," Mayor Trumbull said.

The community's relationship with the Lippingers had been contentious, and it showed in the way our town was treated—or more often ignored entirely—in *All Things Sonoma*. With the Harringtons as the new magazine owners soon to be related to the mayor, the town was sure to be more advantageously featured.

Olivia Harrington approached us. "Hello, Kate." She said her name as if she'd just gotten a whiff of cooked cabbage.

Mayor Trumbull greeted her in return, but the warmth she'd had in her voice was gone. They made exceedingly polite small talk. I wondered if the fake friendliness was from what happened last night with Nelson at my shop, although I hadn't sensed much chumminess between them yesterday either.

"Did you come early to check on your people? I'm taking quite a chance on using the untried establishments you recommended for my daughter's wedding shower."

"They're hardly untried. *You* may not have used them before, but they're all successful businesses. I'm certain you'll be very pleased. No, I simply came early to be available if you needed an extra hand with anything."

"I've got it covered. I only rely on myself to get things done right."

Especially when your party planner quits.

"You're certainly good at taking care of things, Olivia," Mayor Trumbull said.

Olivia raised a brow. "I'm rarely disappointed that way. Now, if I could only find my daughters." She looked around before stopping to stare at the lawn. "What the . . ."

I followed her gaze to where it landed, as did Mayor Trumbull, Archie, and Baz. Marcos, Hope, and the rest of the staff on the patio also turned once they heard the galloping. I knew I thought Summer looked like a Disney princess, but were my eyes deceiving me or was Prince Charming on a horse riding our way?

The horse stopped on the lawn just before reaching the garden patio. Now I could see it was Nelson, dressed in an elaborate costume to look like a prince—belted royal jacket, white gloves, and all.

"Summer, my love?" He scanned the patio then looked up at the house and shouted to one of the second-story balconies. "Summer?"

"They're doing Romeo and Juliet!" One of the caterers said, sighing as if watching the play.

The mention of the romantic-tragedy was more apt than she knew if Summer had run off with Roman.

Marcos left the patio for the lawn and began to take pictures of the scene.

"Summer?" Prince Nelson called again. Everyone looked around, expecting her to appear.

I swallowed hard. Would she come when Chloe found her? Or did she leave to be with Roman?

Olivia and Mayor Trumbull approached Nelson.

"Nelson, why are you here? It's Summer's shower," Mayor Trumbull said to her nephew.

"I came to propose to Summer again. I don't want what happened last night to ruin her party," he said. "Where is she?"

Mayor Trumbull visibly relaxed, as did Olivia.

The whir of a golf cart sounded, and relief flooded me when I saw both sisters in the front of the cart. Nelson turned his horse around to face them when Chloe stopped the cart far enough away to keep the horse from being startled. She hopped out of the driver's seat, and my relief was drained. Roman was in the back seat.

CHAPTER 4

Roman and Summer got out of the cart after Chloe. Did they come to call off the engagement? One look at who was on the horse and Summer turned on her sister.

"Chloe!" Summer said angrily.

"I didn't know," Chloe said in her own defense.

"Massey again? What are you doing with him?" Nelson yelled at Summer.

"It's-it's not what you think," Summer stammered, approaching Nelson and the horse.

"I told you to stay away from her!" Nelson yelled at Roman. He kicked his heels into the horse's sides, causing the animal to charge toward Roman.

Roman dove just in time to the screams of those of us witnessing the spectacle from the patio. Nelson and his horse missed Roman by mere inches.

I left my spot behind the cheese bar and ran toward Roman. Summer got there first just as Nelson turned his horse around to make another pass at him. Roman got back on his feet after the hard fall.

"Leave him alone, Nelson. If you hurt him, you'll have to hurt me too," Summer said, standing between the two men.

"Summer, come away," Olivia called.

"Listen to your mother, Summer," Nelson said. His horse's nostrils flared and snorted, as if mimicking Nelson's feelings. They were both ready to charge again.

Mayor Trumbull's son, Everett, walked up from the back of the house looking bewildered. "What's going on?"

"Your cousin is trying to trample my friend," I said to Everett. I no longer cared about what the Harringtons or Mayor Trumbull would think of me. This was the second time Nelson had tried to hurt Roman.

I could see Everett assess the situation. "Well, this went sideways," he said. He sauntered over to Nelson on the horse. "Come on, bruh, you're going to hurt the horse. Maybe it was a bad idea. Let's go back to the stable."

"Mind your business, Everett. I'm not letting this guy get away with this. He's trying to get between me and Summer." As Nelson spoke, his horse was in constant motion, obviously agitated.

"Roman's not doing anything!" Summer cried. "Please, Nelson. Listen to me."

"I did all this to show you how much I love you and you ruined it!" he shouted at Summer.

"I'm sorry!" Tears streamed down her face. "I didn't know."

Nelson turned his focus to Roman. "You got off easy this time, Massey." He kicked his heels into the horse again, but this time he steered the animal away toward the stable behind the house and out of sight.

Summer stuffed her face in her hands and continued to weep. Chloe stared at her without patience, as if Summer was being melodramatic. I wasn't sure how to comfort a woman I didn't know, but I went to her side anyway and patted her back. Olivia strode to her daughter, pushing me aside without a word, and coaxed her toward the house. Chloe followed.

Summer stopped before reaching the house and looked around, as if noticing the rest of us for the first time. "You can all go home. I'm canceling the shower. I can't celebrate like this," she said.

"Summer?" her mother questioned.

"Oh Summer, you're making too much of it. You two do this every other week. Just let him cool off. It'll be fine," Chloe said with exasperation.

"Why is nothing ever a big deal to you?" Summer screamed at Chloe. She ran inside ahead of her mother before Chloe could answer.

Olivia turned and pierced Chloe with a withering stare.

"It's not my fault," Chloe insisted matter-of-factly.

Her mother ignored her and went inside after Summer.

Chloe didn't follow. She turned from the house, facing us, shoulders drooped, hands on her slender hips. Everyone stared at her, not knowing what to do or say.

"Well don't look at me!" she yelled at everyone before stomping toward the golf cart, where Roman and I were standing. "I'm sorry, Roman. I didn't know Nelson would be here."

Roman had his arms crossed. "Are you sure about that?" He didn't sound convinced.

"Now *you're* mad at me too? What were you doing here with Summer in the first place?" She didn't wait for an answer. She hopped in the golf cart and floored it, zipping across the backyard and disappearing behind the house.

"Are you okay?" I asked him.

His shoulders dropped and his voice lost its angry edge. "She's not wrong. I knew I shouldn't have come when Summer asked. Sorry, Willa," he said.

I watched him walk down the lawn toward the garden

shed. Part of me wanted to run after him and comfort him. The other part just wanted answers.

Mayor Trumbull and Everett had been standing to the side of us. "Do you know why Roman came here, Willa?" she asked.

"I have no idea," I answered, truthfully.

"Do you want to explain what *you're* doing here?" she said to her son.

Everett shrugged. "It was supposed to be a surprise. Nelson felt bad about last night, so he was going to ride in like a prince and swear his undying devotion to her. It sounded like a good idea at the time," he said.

"This is a disaster. Let me see what I can do to help." Mayor Trumbull went into take-charge mode. "Everett, come with me. You should stand guard in the driveway to stop any guests from coming through."

Mayor Trumbull and Everett walked through the patio to go inside.

"What should we do?" Hope asked her.

"I'm afraid there's not going to be a wedding shower. I know all of you put a lot of effort into this event. I'm sorry it turned out this way, believe me," she said.

They proceeded into the house, leaving the rest of us awkwardly on the patio.

A snapshot would show an opulent spread: an ice sculpture dribbling champagne, a long table set for sixty with flowers bursting in a line down the middle beneath a ceiling of roses, Hope's tower of shimmering cupcakes, my resplendent display of cheeses. It was a flawless scene for a magazine photo, but behind the façade it was anything but picture perfect. No wonder the photographer was no longer in sight.

"Are we really packing up?" Archie asked.

"We might as well," I answered.

The disappointment around the patio was palpable. I knew I'd feel the dismay later, but right now all I could think about was Roman. What was he doing here? He looked so defeated walking away. I hated to see him that way, even if it was perhaps because he was still in love with Summer.

We began packing up the cheese. I wouldn't get a mention in the magazine, but at least I wasn't left holding the bag—Olivia had already paid the bill. Still, my pleasure comes from people enjoying my cheese.

"Archie, you should help Hope. She's got a lot of cupcakes to pack up."

"Thanks, Willa," he said, lumbering over to her, disappointment apparent in his body language.

Archie's long face always hit me the hardest. He had such a positive nature—when *he* was down, it was truly a bad day.

Baz and I dissembled the gorgeous cheese board arrangements, carefully separating the cheese accompaniments—the charcuterie, fruits, nuts, and crackers—so everything remained as fresh, and edible, as possible. It took almost as long to take apart as it did to put together.

"What do you want me to bring back first?" Baz said.

"Olivia already paid for the food, so it's hers. You can take anything else you can carry to the truck and I'll go in and see if Polly can tell me where she wants all this cheese. Maybe they can use it for another occasion."

Toting two large bags with containers of cheese wrapped in butcher paper and their accompaniments, I entered through one of the glass doors. It led to a vaulted room with white walls and dark wood flooring. I walked past a grand piano through an arch into a sophisticated, contemporary living room with a marble fireplace. A swooping staircase with a decorative wrought-iron railing curved upstairs to a balcony hallway overlooking the room. Underneath it, more wide arches separated the more formal living room from a casual family room. Floor-to-ceiling glass doors made up a good portion of the back wall, revealing the backyard patio and pool.

I continued straight through the formal living room only to come to a hallway that led to a mudroom area where a side door was, possibly to the garage. I was already holding the cheese—why did I feel like a rat in a maze? I hoped my good intentions were enough that navigating through the entire first floor wouldn't be considered trespassing. I walked back through the hallway to the living room. Where was everybody who'd come inside?

"Willa?" It was Polly, carefully stepping down the stairs, balancing a pitcher and glasses on a tray. "Can I help you with something?"

"Hi, Polly." I met her at the bottom of the staircase. "Here's everything from the cheese bar. Mrs. Harrington already paid me for it, so I wanted to leave it here."

"Follow me to the kitchen. I'll take care of it."

We walked toward the front of the house. I glimpsed a formal dining room with a butler's pantry attached. I knew the kitchen had to be the next room.

A couple of the caterers were at the center island, which was as big as a king-sized bed, transferring their food into aluminum containers. Having done parties in large homes before while I was working at other cheese shops across the country, I'd come to the conclusion that the less the owners cooked, the bigger their kitchen was. I was impressed with the sleek black cabinetry and white marble countertops, but the brick pizza oven was what really won me over.

Polly set the tray down with some relief. It must've been heavy with an almost full pitcher. The pitcher and glasses looked to be crystal, which would've made me supremely nervous to be transporting them on a tray. She dumped the watery remains of one glass into the sink and put the other glass back in the cabinet alongside identical ones.

"I'll make some room in the fridge." She took my bags and opened the double-wide refrigerator, which was hidden behind a cabinet door.

I eyed whatever intense berry-colored beverage was in the pitcher. It looked so refreshing, especially after traipsing across the lawn and lugging cheese back and forth.

"What is this? It looks wonderful," I said after she'd safely stowed the two bags.

"It's homemade hibiscus tea," Polly said brightly. "It's my mom's specialty, handed down to me. It takes me about a half hour to make, but Mrs. Harrington and Summer will only drink it freshly made."

"That seems like a lot of work."

"I don't mind. I'm happy to make it for people who enjoy it so much."

"It looks very refreshing." I tried not to smack my lips as I salivated over the drink.

"I would offer you some but . . ." She motioned for me to join her at the fridge and opened the door. She leaned closer and whispered, "It's got a special ingredient in it." She slid a bottle of vodka out from the lowest shelf.

"Ohhh," I replied.

She handed me a water bottle and whispered, "Mrs. Harrington likes me to disguise it. She thinks it looks unseemly to drink hard liquor during the day."

"I see. I thanked her for the water as I left the kitchen.

I navigated my way back to the living room and was surprised to see Marcos walk in from the mudroom hallway, his Nikon still hanging from his neck and a satchel over his shoulder. He looked a little peaked, although his hair was still on point. My presence apparently surprised him too.

"What are you doing here?" he barked.

"What are *you* doing here?" I returned.

He looked down at his shoes, now dusted with dirt from the outdoor photo shoot, and massaged his forehead. "Sorry. I'm just bummed about what happened. This was going to be my first big shoot for the magazine," he said.

I let my guard down too. "Believe me, I get it. It was going to be a big deal for all of us."

He pointed a thumb over his shoulder. "I forgot that my car's not in the driveway."

I nodded. We were both going in the same direction, so we walked in awkward silence until we reached the side garden. He continued across the patio and then the lawn toward the shed parking lot.

When I got to my cheese table, I saw that Baz must've already made a trip to his truck. Almost everything was packed up.

"Sorry to waste your time, Baz." I offered him the water before we finished with the last of the items I'd brought.

"Where else would I experience something like *that*?" He made a *yikes* face, which made me chuckle. Getting through this with my best friend was the only way. "What do you think Roman was doing here?"

"I don't know. I feel awful. I was the one who told Chloe where Summer was. I saw her and Roman by the garden shed."

"Doing what? Or should I not ask?"

"They were talking. I didn't stick around to listen to their conversation. That reminds me, I gotta get my car at the shed," I told him.

"We'll put the rest of this in my truck and I'll drive you to your car."

"Good idea."

We told Archie what we were doing, and we agreed that Hope could drive him back to the shop when they were finished.

"Let's just go through the house, it's quicker. Nobody seems to be around anyway," I said to Baz, leading him into the house. At least I knew my way through this time.

Marcos had the right idea—going through the house to the side door nearer the driveway was a more direct route than going around the house from either way.

Baz lagged, as he craned his neck to gape at the manor-like house. "This is sweet."

"Come on." I led him to the mudroom hallway, and we went out the side door. The golf cart was once again parked by the path to the stable.

"I wonder if Nelson really left," I said, looking toward the stable. "I feel bad for Mayor Trumbull. I think she was counting on having a family connection with the Harringtons. It wouldn't have been a bad thing for Yarrow Glen."

"Don't count the couple out yet," Baz said, as we made our way around to the driveway.

"I don't see them getting past this."

"Some guys like to play games and some women like the drama."

"Since when did you become a relationship expert?" I asked him.

"I'm no expert, but I'm learning a little about dramatic women."

"Oh?"

"Ginger can be that way sometimes. We're not even dating and she's kind of possessive."

"Uh-oh."

"Maybe I'm reading her wrong. I like her—she's gorgeous—and I'm glad she's interested in me too. Kinda surprised, but glad."

"Surprised? Why? Everybody likes you."

Baz cocked his head in thought. "True."

I shook my head and chuckled.

"But I'm a handyman with a dad bod. Not exactly her type. And I don't have a regular schedule. She doesn't seem to get that," he said.

"It sounds like she wants some time with you. Maybe you should go on a real date with her. She might just want reassurance that you're interested."

"You think she's over Chet?" he asked.

Chet was Ginger's last boyfriend. He was no longer in the picture, but the breakup was hard on her.

"There's only one way to find out. The F.U.N. dance is next weekend. You'd better ask her to go before someone else does. Weren't you the one poking fun at me for not making a move with Roman for the longest time?"

"Yeah, but you finally did and look how that worked out."

"Hey!"

Baz cackled and knocked my shoulder with his. I bumped him back. Only Baz could make me laugh after such a bad day.

Baz's truck and Hope's car were the only ones left in the driveway, except for a Prius, which I assumed belonged to Mayor Trumbull.

"At least none of the guests have arrived yet," I said. Now that the shower being called off had sunk in, I was anxious to leave. I felt bad for Polly having to stick around until the bitter end. I wouldn't want to be around Olivia Harrington right about now.

We put the empty coolers and boxes of containers in the bed of Baz's pickup and hopped in his truck. I directed him to the garden shed. He pulled past the open gate. The catering trucks were gone, but Roman's sporty Mini was still there.

"What is Roman's car still doing here?" I said.

"Oh man. What is he doing?" Baz said, his head falling back on the headrest.

Baz pulled the truck up beside Roman's car.

"He's not in it. You don't think he went to confront Nelson, do you?" I asked.

"I sure hope not."

Suddenly the thought panicked me. "Let's go to the stable," I told Baz.

He put the truck in reverse. We pulled out of the space, bumped down the dirt drive, and took a left onto the main road. Just when I thought we must've missed it, we came upon the entrance to the stable. It would've been quicker to have hoofed it there. Luckily, the gate was open. One car was in the lot—probably Nelson's or Everett's. That didn't make me feel better. We got out and immediately walked into the stable, where the mixed odors of pine oil, hay, and horse manure permeated the space.

"Roman?" I called.

A horse's neigh was the only response. Three horses stuck their heads out of their stalls. One of them shook its mane, clearly agitated. It looked like the horse Nelson had ridden.

"I've got a really bad feeling," I said to Baz.

We walked farther into the shadowy stable. I stopped short when I saw a pair of boots sticking out of one of the empty stalls at the far end. Someone was lying prone in the stall, and they weren't moving.

"Oh no." My mouth went dry, and my stomach dropped as if the floor had opened up beneath me. The ringing in my ears almost drowned out Baz's words.

"Let me look," he said, putting an arm in front of me so I wouldn't continue on. He walked toward the unmoving pair of legs while I stayed behind.

Every fiber in my body was vibrating like blaring sirens for fear that Roman was hurt . . . or worse. It was the same sensation I had when my parents told me my brother had been killed in a car accident. My system didn't know how to handle the shock of a reality so unreal.

Baz stopped at the body and stared into the stall. His hand went over his mouth, and he stumbled backward at the sight. A horse neighed again, propelling me forward. I couldn't take it. I knew the loss would be no easier to bear hearing about it secondhand.

I ran to the stall and looked down at the body. My brain didn't register the shovel by his head at first. A pitchfork stuck straight up out of his stomach where blood had pooled and run down his sides, darkening the hay he was lying on. It was a dead body, but it wasn't Roman's. Nelson Trumbull had been murdered.

CHAPTER 5

Baz and I sat on a log in the parking area near the stable to await the police. Officer Shepherd—Shep to those who knew him, which was just about everyone—arrived first, with two other officers in a second patrol car.

"Hey guys," he said, plodding over to us.

Shep was a great town cop—always fair, able to de-escalate an argument or make the drivers of a fender bender walk away shaking hands. Behind the friendly personality was a deceivingly dogged cop who'd become Detective Heath's right-hand man.

He sighed, his gentle brown eyes studying us. He pressed his lips together and twisted his face in commiseration, making his nose appear even more crooked. "In there?" He indicated the stable.

We nodded.

He turned to one of his colleagues, Officer Melman. I'd seen him at other crime scenes, a squat, doughy guy probably in his mid-thirties, same as Shep. They often arrived together, bringing up an image of Abbott and Costello in my mind, although Melman was surely more competent than Costello was in the old movies I'd seen.

"Melman, cordon this whole area off," Shep instructed,

then turned to us. "You two will have to wait here. Please don't cross the tape."

"We know," I said, sticking my elbows on my knees and placing my chin in my hands in anticipation of the long wait.

"This ain't our first rodeo," Baz said.

I gave him a weary look.

"Sorry, I say stupid things when I'm stressed out," he explained.

"It's okay." I patted his jiggling leg, another nervous habit he had when finding dead bodies, which was all too often.

Shep went into the stable and came out about fifteen minutes later when the forensics unit pulled up. The coroner, Ivy Reynolds, and her team hopped out of the big white crime scene unit van. I'd seen her a few months ago when we'd found celebrity chef and reality star Phoebe Winston drowned in her bathtub. We thought it was an overdose, but it was Ivy's skills that determined she'd been murdered. A striking woman with lips colored deep red that offset the white jumpsuit uniform she wore, she appeared no-nonsense. Laser focused, she barely noticed us as she allowed Shep to guide her into the stable where the body was.

We stood up and sat back down periodically while we waited—there was no comfort to be had. The question remained: Where was Roman? We'd looked in the other stalls, my heart in my throat, and around the stable, but there'd been no sign of him.

I checked my phone again—I'd called him but he hadn't answered, and there were no messages or texts from him now.

Then, with a ding, his name suddenly appeared on my phone as if I'd willed it. I scrunched my eyes shut and opened them again to make sure I wasn't imagining it. His text was still there. I tapped his message, which simply said, *No need to worry. I'm fine.*

Nelson's been murdered! I typed.

Another car pulled into the lot, the car I'd been dreading. I hit *send*, clicked off the ringer, and tucked the phone back into my pocket just as Detective Heath emerged from the unmarked Dodge Charger. Even his dark good looks couldn't loosen the pit from my stomach. It wasn't my fault that I'd happened upon another dead body, but I always felt scolded by Heath as if it were otherwise.

He came over to us first. As usual, his face revealed no signs of what he was thinking. "Are you okay?"

I'd built up my wall of defense in the minutes before he arrived, so I was unprepared for his question. He must've been informed that it was us who'd made the call, so he wasn't surprised. Or maybe he was being gentler because he and I had gotten a bit closer over the last few months. I saw him around town more often than I used to, and I never minded that our casual chats delayed wherever I was going.

"We're okay," I answered.

"Relatively," Baz added.

Shep came out of the stable and approached his boss. "Ivy's inside. She hasn't moved anything. There's no doubt it's murder. She estimates he's been dead about an hour. Baz and Willa identified the victim as Nelson Trumbull."

Shep stepped aside and Heath turned back to us. "What were you two doing here?" He reached into his suit jacket pocket for his trusty mini notepad and pen.

I cringed inside but tried to play it cool on the outside. I knew this was coming. "We thought Roman might be here."

"Roman Massey? Why would he be here?"

"Well, uh . . ." How was I supposed to tell him and open the floodgates to questions about Roman? I had my own questions for Roman, but the one thing I knew for certain about him was that he was no murderer.

"He was at the house earlier," Baz finished for me. He knew how bad I felt the last time I gave Detective Heath information about an investigation, only for it to be used against a friend. I hated being forced to do the same to Roman. "We were picking up Willa's car at the garden shed—that's where they told the people hired for the party to park—and we saw his car was still there. We thought he'd left way before, so we stopped here." Baz made it sound like a casual pursuit.

Heath ignored his little pad and stared at me instead. I tried to meet his gaze, but he had a habit of being able to get more information out of me than I wanted to give. I found myself looking anywhere but at him.

"Have you spoken to anybody other than the police since discovering the body?" Heath asked us.

"Nobody," Baz said.

"And you?" he asked me.

"I called Mrs. Schultz because she's alone at the shop. And Roman, of course, since he wasn't here," I emphasized the last part.

Heath's skeptical stare returned to me. "Okay," he said, surprising me. He flipped his notepad closed. "Shep's going to take you back to the house, where one of my officers has everyone gathered. I'll meet you there shortly." He walked away toward the cordoned-off stable.

As soon as we got into Baz's truck, I checked my phone. There was a text from Roman.

Roman: *OMG. Is everyone ok?*

I replied: *We're ok. Police are here.*

I waited. No reply.

We followed Shep's police car back to the house, where an officer allowed us in. His tall stature, broad shoulders, and humorless eyes reminded me of *The Addams Family*'s Lurch. Shep, who was taller than both Baz and me, was only chin-high to this imposing police officer. It was no wonder Heath had assigned him, and not Melman, to watch over everyone at the house.

"This is Officer Ferguson," Shep informed us.

"Fergieeee," Baz said with swagger, extending his hand to give him a bro-handshake.

Officer Ferguson left Baz's hand where it was between them. His steely face was unchanged.

Baz used the hand to rub the back of his neck, embarrassment no doubt creeping in. He should've felt lucky Officer Ferguson didn't shake it—it could've been crushed. They steered us ahead of them.

"Told ya I say stupid things when I'm stressed," he whispered to me.

I patted him on the shoulder. I didn't want him to feel worse, although I would've preferred to deal with the jiggling leg.

We walked through the foyer with its own grand staircase and worked our way to the living room I was becoming familiar with. It was hard to believe it was only an hour or so earlier that I'd been wandering around this house looking to store the leftover cheese. So much had happened.

All three Harrington women were there. Olivia was seated in a high-backed chair by the cold fireplace, the only chair that wasn't identical to the rest of the furniture. She'd changed into clothes that looked designer-casual, but still not comfortable by my standards. Summer was slumped in one of the chairs facing the sofa and the living room staircase, wearing yoga pants and a T-shirt, one knee pushed under her chin. Chloe was seated in the identical chair next to her sister, stroking her ponytail. She was now in a casual yellow maxi dress, the high slit showing off one tanned leg crossed over the other. Mayor Trumbull and Everett were stiffly seated across from them on the sofa. Archie and Hope were on an upholstered bench with untouched glasses of lemonade in their hands, looking anxious.

Our appearance seemed to rouse everyone from a shocked stupor. Chloe tossed her hair over her shoulder, and Summer sat up and turned to address us.

"Is it really him? They said you found him," Summer said to us.

I nodded and started to say more, but Officer Lurch stopped me.

"No discussion about the case until Detective Heath arrives," he said firmly.

Summer stuffed her face in her hands.

I noticed the absence of the caterers and the florist. All the cars had been gone, so they all must've already left before they were told about the body. I'd watched Marcos leave earlier too, so he wasn't present either.

Polly entered with a tray of her *special* hibiscus tea, the vibrant reddish-purple color unmistakable in its glass pitcher. She set the tray on the coffee table and proceeded to pour a tall glass of it for Olivia and another for Summer, with a wedge of lime on the rims. Olivia sipped hers, allowing a slow sigh to escape.

Summer took hers and drank from it immediately, then rested it on her knee as she silently sobbed, causing the dark liquid inside to slosh from side to side.

"How many of these have they had you make today, Polly?" Chloe asked.

"I don't mind." Polly replied in a quiet voice.

"Hibiscus tea has a relaxing property," Olivia stated.

So does vodka. I recalled what Polly had told me about the drink.

"Would you like a glass, Chloe?" Polly asked.

Chloe lengthened her legs and propped her bare heels on the coffee table. "Sure, why not? But skip the tea, keep the vodka."

Olivia's focus left her own drink, already half-drained, to glare at Chloe. She gauged everyone's reaction, but nobody but me seemed to pick up on Chloe outing the tea. Or if they did, they didn't care. Olivia's façade of not imbibing during the day was unnecessary under any circumstances, but especially today. Her daughter's fiancé was dead in her horse stable—a drink was practically mandatory.

With a look from her mother, Chloe took her feet off the table.

Olivia held out her glass for a refill and Polly obliged. "That'll be all, Polly," Olivia said.

Polly picked up the tray and started out of the living room.

"Don't leave the premises. The detective will want to speak to everyone," Officer Ferguson said to Polly.

Polly's eyes widened. I thought she might drop her tray. She nodded and scurried off to the kitchen.

"How long do these people need to stay in my home, Officer? We're grieving," Olivia said.

"Detective Heath will be here shortly," Shep answered.

Amid the silence, it felt like an interminable wait, but in fact, it wasn't too much longer before we heard Heath's footsteps in the hallway.

Mayor Trumbull stood when Heath entered the room. "Is it true, Detective?" she asked.

"I'm afraid so. Willa and Baz have identified the body

as your nephew, Nelson Trumbull. I'm very sorry for your loss," he said to both families.

Mayor Trumbull stoically returned to sitting on the sofa.

Heath said to her, "As next of kin, we'll need you to come down to the morgue after he's been moved to confirm the identification."

She nodded and put a tissue to her nose. Her other hand found her son's and she squeezed it.

"We've ruled it a suspicious death, which means we'll need to question all of you about your whereabouts in the hour between the time Nelson returned to the stable and the time his body was discovered."

"Suspicious? You mean like murdered?" Chloe said.

"Yes," Heath replied simply.

"I don't understand!" Summer wailed. "Who would want to murder Nelson?"

Olivia went around to the back of Summer's chair and placed a hand on her shoulder. "Detective Heath, you're upsetting my daughter. Can't this wait until tomorrow?"

"I'm afraid it can't. We'll do this as quickly as possible," he assured her, dissuaded.

"I can tell you right now, Detective, that my son and I were keeping guests from arriving," Mayor Trumbull said.

"And I was upstairs consoling Summer," Olivia said.

"We'll take everyone's statements in a moment. I'm sorry to have to keep you waiting. Mrs. Harrington, are there a couple of rooms we can use for private preliminary interviews?" Heath asked.

Olivia reluctantly conceded. "The study is through the arch and down the hall." She pointed to the rear of the house. "Across from it on the other side of the family room is Chloe's art room."

"Not my art room, Mother. That's private," Chloe said.

Olivia sighed. "Fine. Use the dining room."

"Thank you. I'm sure Officer Ferguson has instructed all of you not to discuss anything about what happened today with each other," Heath reminded us sternly, as if any of us would defy Officer Lurch. "Shep, start with those who were working the party. I'll speak with the families and Willa. Willa, you first."

Olivia spoke up, "Detective, I should go first."

Heath hesitated for a moment, then acquiesced with a wave of his arm for her to proceed to the study. I was glad for a chance to get my thoughts together.

Shep brought Hope into the dining room, and Heath followed Olivia into the study. The door closed behind them.

Baz gestured to Olivia's chair, but I couldn't bring myself to sit in it. It would be like sitting on a queen's throne in her absence. I went over and sat next to Archie, since Hope was in the dining room with Shep. Baz had no problem taking Olivia's seat.

"You okay?" I asked Archie.

"Sure," he responded without enthusiasm. "You?"

I shrugged. I couldn't say what I wanted to in a room full of people, half of whom loved Nelson. I felt guilty about my first thought upon seeing Nelson's dead body. After the initial slap of disgust, relief had washed over me. I couldn't help it. I was thankful it wasn't Roman, and I felt horrible for feeling that way. I was itching to check my phone, but Officer Lurch's eagle eye didn't let up. I kept it in my pocket.

Eventually, Hope came out of the dining room, having finished her interview with Shep, and told Archie he was next.

In time, Heath and Olivia emerged from the study. Baz stood from Olivia's chair. Heath beckoned me from the bench, and I met him on the outskirts of the living room as Olivia stepped away from us. I tried to hold everything that had happened today in my memory so I could be useful in the interview, but Heath was fixated on something else.

"Did Roman tell you where he was when you called him?" he asked me without continuing to the study.

"No, he didn't answer so I left him a message," I said. Why was he asking about Roman again?

"What was the message?"

I thought back. "I asked him to call me. I wanted to know that he was okay."

"Why wouldn't he be okay?"

"Because his car was still at the garden shed and I-I didn't know where he was."

"Did you tell him you found Nelson's body?"

"I told him Nelson had been murdered, yes."

Heath's poker face slipped, revealing his annoyance with me. His hands went to his hips, flaring his suit jacket behind him. "You know better."

It was then I realized Olivia must've told him all about Roman and Nelson's fight, putting suspicion on Roman.

"Roman's not guilty of anything," I added hastily. "I only called and texted him because I was worried about him. I thought something bad had happened to him." It registered that my voice was raised, but I couldn't help it.

"Because his car was still on the property?"

"Yes!"

"It's not there now, which means he left at some point between the time Nelson Trumbull was murdered and when you told him you'd found the body."

"Were you giving him a heads-up?" Chloe accused, having overheard.

I turned to see she had sidled up against the archway to listen in.

"Giving who a heads-up?" Summer put her drink down and sat at attention.

Everyone's eyes were on us. At this point, I didn't care who heard.

"No, I wasn't giving him a heads-up! Roman didn't do anything wrong. I'm sorry if this sounds insensitive, but Nelson was the aggressive one."

"He's also the one who's been murdered," Heath responded. "Shep, put out an APB on Roman Massey. We need to bring him in for questioning ASAP."

CHAPTER 6

It was another hour before Detective Heath and Shep finished interviewing Baz, Archie, and me, and we were able to go home. Of course, we didn't go home, we went to Curds & Whey—our safe haven where we were able to discuss what had happened.

Mrs. Schultz had just closed the shop when we arrived. I told Baz and Archie I'd meet them inside, and I trotted across the street to Golden Glen Meadery to check on Roman. The lights were still on, but the door was locked. I spotted Angela inside—Gia to her friends, which I was not. That much she'd made clear. She used to work at Apricot Grille along with her former boyfriend Derrick, the restaurant's manager. Last year, while I was trying to clear my name of Guy Lippinger's murder, I'd openly suspected him. Now she was the manager at Roman's meadery, which unfortunately put us in fairly regular contact.

She strode over to the door on very high heels, calling out "We're closed," as she got closer.

"I know. It's me. Willa," I called through the door. I knew darn well she could see it was me.

She stopped directly behind the door and put her fist on one of her slender hips. "We're still closed."

We had a bit of a staring contest, which she must've

realized she wouldn't win, as she finally unlocked the
door. I opened it, but she didn't back up so I could enter.

"What do you want?" she snapped.

"I want to talk to Roman, obviously."

"He's at the police station. I'm surprised you didn't
know that."

"I wasn't sure. I just wanted to make sure he was okay.
I'll catch him later."

"Seriously?" she said before I let go of the door.

"What does that mean?"

"You make a habit of this, Willa. It's all a game to you,
but not for the people around you. I've only been pleasant to you for Roman's sake.."

"I didn't ask Roman to be at Summer's shower." This
wasn't my fault.

"But you were there and lo and behold, so was another
dead body. I don't think he needs you to check on him. If
you care about Roman, stay away from him."

I didn't have a comeback for that. Maybe a part of me
even believed she was right. I released the door handle,
allowing it to shut between us, and walked back to Curds
& Whey.

I stood for moment on the sidewalk to collect myself
before going into my shop. My feelings for Roman were
so jumbled. I was disappointed in him, but I still felt protective. He was still my friend.

I needed to discuss the case with a clear head, which
meant I needed sustenance. None of us had gotten a
chance to eat dinner. I ran upstairs to my apartment for
some extra food stuffs. I had ham, eggs, and milk, so I
knew just what I'd make.

When I returned to Curds & Whey's kitchenette, Baz
and Archie were filling Mrs. Schultz in on what had transpired. I accepted Mrs. Schultz's big hug.

"Thanks. Sorry I took so long." I lifted the bag of food I'd pilfered from my fridge. "Dinner." I put the bag on the counter and opened a container of the fresh curds we'd gotten in that morning. "Have some squeaky cheese while I whip up some dinner." Cheese curds were Baz's favorite, partially because they make a squeaking sound when you bite into them.

"Thanks for dinner, Wil. We could've grabbed something at The Cellar," Baz said, immediately digging into the curds.

"Cooking something cheesy relaxes me, especially if I'm going to be eating it. I need some time to decompress."

"What can we help with?" Archie asked.

"Nothing this time. Sit at the table and enjoy the curds. This will be ready in no time."

They got themselves water from the fridge, and I concentrated on the ingredients in front of me, combining eggs, milk, and grated cheddar before whisking in flour to create a batter. I used my heavy cast iron skillet to crisp chopped ham, then swirled butter into the pan and added the batter. I sprinkled more cheese on top before sticking the skillet in the oven. I joined the others at the table while I waited the fifteen minutes for it to bake—as simple as pie . . . or pancake, as was the case.

"Thanks again for taking care of the shop, Mrs. Schultz," I said, dusting flour off my blouse.

"Of course. How is Roman?" she asked me.

"Angela said he's at the police station. He must've told her what happened."

"You think they suspect him?" Archie said.

"I don't think they put out an APB on just anyone."

"It's not good that everyone saw him and Nelson going at it," Baz said.

"But Nelson was the one making the threats." I was starting to get exasperated that I had to point this out again.

"Roman obviously hasn't run off, so the police ought to be second-guessing themselves if they think he's a person of interest," Mrs. Schultz said.

"I still don't know why he didn't leave right away. Where was he from the time he walked off until he finally got in his car and left?" I wondered.

"I'm sure he'll tell the police. I feel bad for the guy, though. I know what it's like to be in the hot seat, and it ain't fun," Archie said, obviously thinking back to when he was the prime suspect in the last murder investigation.

"Hopefully someone can corroborate his alibi," Baz said.

"Heath always says not to put too much stock in alibis," I recalled, unable to put a positive spin on Roman's predicament.

"You think Roman killed Nelson?" Archie exclaimed.

"No! Of course not. I just mean I don't think he'll be taken off their suspect list so easily, alibi or not."

My timer sounded and I hopped off the bench. I used two mitted hands to pull out the heavy skillet. The pancake was puffy and golden brown, just as I'd hoped it would be.

"Ooh. Is that a Dutch baby?" Mrs. Schultz asked, getting up from the table.

"Yes! A savory one." I watched the pancake collapse as it cooled. "I made it with cheddar for you, Baz, but if you're ever feeling adventurous, I'll make it with fontina and parmesan. Or how about smoked Gouda?"

"Nothing's better than cheddar," Baz replied, fork in hand, ready to dig in.

I cut into it, and Mrs. Schultz helped me serve hearty

wedges of the cheesy egg dish. With everyone served, I sat down at the farm table to a round of applause.

"Just eat," I said, embarrassed at the fuss.

We were quiet for the first few minutes as we all tucked in. The pancake part was light like a popover but crispy at the edges, making a perfect foundation for the egg infused with melty cheese sprinkled with salty bits of ham.

Archie was the first one to speak. "Who else do you think Detective Heath is looking at?"

"It depends on who had opportunity. I sure would've liked to have been a fly on the wall while Heath and Shep were interviewing everybody," I replied.

"Well, we know what questions they asked. Same ones they asked us, right? 'Where were you at the time of the murder?'" Baz said.

I swallowed a forkful of my Dutch baby. "You're right. Maybe we can narrow it down based on where everyone went after Nelson rode away on the horse."

"Should we do a reenactment?" Mrs. Schultz's hazel eyes widened in excitement. Being a former drama teacher, she enjoyed a good reenactment.

"Too many people. I think it might get confusing. How about a map instead?" I suggested.

I put one of our cheese boards in the middle of the table. "Let's pretend this is the house. The stable is at the back of the house toward this side, and we were all here on the other side of the house on the patio." I put an apple on one side of the cheese board to indicate where the stable was supposed to be and the container of curds on the opposite side to represent everyone who was there.

"This curd is Nelson. He rides off around the back of the house to the stable." I transferred one of the curds to the apple.

"We all saw Olivia take Summer into the house," Baz

said, taking two more curds and putting them on the board.

"So that leaves them out," Archie concluded.

"Not necessarily. They could've gone out the back door or the side door by the garage. From our vantage point on the garden patio, we couldn't see anyone who walked from the house to the stable."

"How would you know if they left the house?" Mrs. Schultz asked.

"We wouldn't. Let's keep Summer and Olivia as possibilities." I plucked their curds and dropped them by Nelson's.

"Don't forget about Chloe. She took the golf cart around the back of the house. She could've driven it to the stable," Baz said.

"We saw the cart when we left, but she could've been back by then. Okay, so she's a possibility." I also put her curd by the apple.

"You said Mayor Trumbull was there," Mrs. Schultz reminded us.

"She said she was going to find Olivia, so it's possible she was with one or both of them. But when I brought my cheese into the house, I didn't see any of them," I said.

Baz took the curd representing Mayor Trumbull and placed it by the apple too.

"And Everett?" Mrs. Schultz asked.

"The mayor sent him to the front of the house to stop any guests from coming in," I said.

Baz's forehead wrinkled. "He wasn't there when I took your stuff back to my truck."

"You're right. He wasn't there when we left the house either."

Archie plucked the Everett curd and put him with the others.

"Was there anyone else there?" Mrs. Schultz asked.

"Everyone who worked there, but we were all pretty much waiting together at the time he would've been murdered. The coroner said he was dead at least an hour by the time we found him, so it had to have been pretty soon after he rode back to the stable."

"What about the photographer?" Archie said.

"Marcos. That's right. He disappeared right after the confrontation between Nelson and Roman. I saw him come back into the house from the side door. That's where the trail is to get to the stable."

"Would he have had enough time to kill Nelson?" Mrs. Schultz asked.

I looked to Baz and Archie as I calculated the timing in my head. "Let's see, I went inside the house, what, about thirty or forty minutes after the whole thing went down with Prince Charming and Roman?"

Baz and Archie nodded.

"It seems like it would only take five minutes or so to walk to the stable, if you were in a hurry." I took another curd to represent Marcos and stuck it with the others.

We looked at the six curds by the apple and Nelson's curd. One piece each for Olivia, Summer, Chloe, Mayor Trumbull, Everett, and Marcos.

"That's a lot of curds," Archie said.

"Too many suspects. Can we narrow it down by motive?" Baz suggested. He'd been eating his Dutch baby while we were calculating suspects and had almost cleared his plate.

"After what happened, I'm sure they were all upset with Nelson, except for maybe Everett," I said.

"Upset enough to kill Summer's future husband?" Mrs. Schultz sounded skeptical.

She had a point. "Maybe he was going to call off the

wedding. Summer or her mother could've gone to speak with him, and if he told them he was calling it off, it might've upset one of them enough to do him in."

"So it could be Olivia or Summer," Archie reiterated.

"But Mayor Trumbull seemed stoked about getting in good with the Harringtons and *All Things Sonoma*. Maybe she's the one who talked to Nelson. If he told *her* he was calling off the wedding, Yarrow Glen could be in the doghouse again with the magazine," Baz said.

"Would she kill her own nephew over it?" Mrs. Schultz was once again not convinced.

"What's Marcos's and Everett's connection to this theory? Neither of them would've cared if he called off the wedding," Archie added. "And Chloe?"

"Her relationship with her sister seems pretty strained. I doubt she'd have killed Nelson on her sister's behalf," I admitted.

We were all quiet in contemplation. Our discussion yielded possibilities but nothing conclusive. We all stared at the curds surrounding the apple.

"Where's Roman's curd?" Archie asked. "I don't think he did it, but where was he when all this was going down?"

"Good question," Baz said. "What the heck was he still doing there?"

"He said he shouldn't have come when Summer asked. So he must've been there in the first place because she called him. He was mad at Chloe after the argument with Nelson went down, so I wonder if she had anything to do with Roman showing his face at the shower. I don't know why he wouldn't have left afterward, though." I thought about it some more. "Do you think they set him up?"

"There's only one way to find out." Baz looked at me expectantly.

"Are we investigating this one?" Archie brightened.

Suddenly they were all staring at me.

"I may not be on great terms with Roman right now, but I'm not willing to let him go down for a murder I know he didn't commit," I said.

"Looks like we're investigating." Archie declared.

"Not so fast," I replied. "Let's wait to see what Detective Heath has to say. Maybe Roman has a rock-solid alibi for where he was when Nelson was murdered. If he's not a person of interest, I'm happy to let the police handle it."

Archie looked disappointed.

"I thought you wanted to be a cheesemonger, not a detective," I said to him.

"Cheese is my first love, but I wouldn't mind a side gig. I kinda like feeling like the Scooby gang."

"The Scooby Gang?" Mrs. Schultz laughed.

"You *know* which one of us is Scooby Doo then." I looked pointedly at Baz.

"Hey, Scooby's cool. The whole show's named after him," Baz replied, stealing the cheese curd "suspects." "Scooby snacks," he declared with a smile as he popped one in his mouth.

It was nice to feel a smile on my face, even briefly. "Unfortunately, Archie, we're not after ghosts."

"I know, but it makes life a little more exciting," he replied.

"Sometimes too exciting, especially for your mother."

"But I'll be moving out soon. I've been saving up to rent my own place, but I don't have wheels except for my skateboard."

"Do you really need a car? My bike gets me most places I want to go," Mrs. Schultz said.

"Everett's opening up that bicycle shop right next

door," Baz said. "Maybe you could get one of those electric ones. It would be cheaper than a car."

"That's a good idea," Archie said.

My ringtone sounded—*Sweet Dreams Are Made of Cheese*—indicating an incoming call. It was a number I didn't recognize. I answered and hit *speaker*. "Hello?"

"Willa? This is Kate Trumbull."

My eyebrows shot up. The others' surprised faces mirrored my own. "Mayor Trumbull. How are you doing? I'm so sorry about your nephew."

"Thank you. Would you mind coming to my office tomorrow afternoon at twelve thirty? I'd like to speak to you."

"Sure."

"Please don't tell anyone you're coming here. I'd like this to stay between us."

My gaze darted to the three others, who were already listening to the conversation. Oops. "Of course. I won't tell anyone." It wasn't a lie. *I* didn't tell them.

"See you then," she said and hung up.

"What do you think that's all about?" Baz asked.

I felt bothered by the phone call. "I have no idea, but please don't tell anyone about it."

Of course, they agreed. I knew I could trust them. It was something else that was troubling me about the phone call. Why would Mayor Trumbull ask to keep our meeting a secret?

CHAPTER 7

I awoke Monday morning, not sure of the time. I usually set my alarm even on my weekly day off because I have a thing about wasting the morning hours. Growing up on a dairy farm, we never got a day off to sleep in, so it took years to adjust my internal clock not to awaken at five a.m. When I finally had to start setting my alarm, it felt ridiculously indulgent to sleep past seven. I had a hard time getting to sleep last night, however, and turned my alarm off when my last check of the clock read 2:47.

I reached over the side of my bed to lift the blinds on one of the two tall, arched windows facing Pleasant Avenue that flanked my bed. I pushed them up as far as I could from my vantage point, stretching my arm to reach around my bedside table lamp to get to the window. Yes, it would've been easier just to step out of bed and push the blinds all the way up, but once even one foot hit the floor, there was no going back to my cozy nest under the comforting weight of my grandmother's handsewn quilt. I wasn't ready to face the day yet.

Seeing a dead body is something that doesn't leave you right away. It was easier to focus on the logistics of the investigation than on the reality that someone's life had been snuffed out. Someone from that shower killed Nelson while we were packing up to leave. But who?

The muted light coming in through the six inches of window beneath the blind told me we weren't going to have a repeat of yesterday's sunny day. It didn't do anything to improve my mood, but we could use a break from the drought we'd been having. I picked up my phone from the bedside table. It was almost ten o'clock! Even though my parents were still in Oregon and would have no possible way of knowing I was in bed at this late hour, I nevertheless felt their admonishment by osmosis. Two phone calls to them this week instead of one might relieve my guilt. But first I wanted to call Roman. Maybe now that some time had passed, he'd be more willing to have a real conversation about him and Summer. Plus, I wanted to know how his interview went with Detective Heath. I needed to know if he was being considered as a person of interest. I called, but his voicemail picked up.

I considered going over to his apartment to talk to him face-to-face since he wasn't answering my calls or texts. Angela's words played in my head. She could be right— maybe Roman just wanted me to stay out of it. For all I knew, he'd already moved on to rekindle a romance with Summer. I hadn't heard from him and he didn't pick up just now, so maybe he did want his space. I decided to honor that.

I made myself get out of bed only because my flashy red and blue betta fish Loretta was probably starving for her breakfast by now. I slipped on a pair of yoga pants— which had never experienced a moment of yoga in their well-worn years—and a comfy, oversized *It's Gouda to Brie Me* sweatshirt. After a quick trip to the bathroom, where I purposely avoided the mirror, I shuffled into the kitchen/living room combo that was the rest of my apartment (except for a small second bedroom that stored some of my unpacked boxes) and fed Loretta.

"Good morning!" I said to her while I dropped bits of food into her round fishbowl. She swam around her SpongeBob house excitedly—or maybe angrily, seeing as how breakfast was three hours late. "I know, I'm sorry." I hit the remote, and Food Network's *Chopped* automatically came on, already queued up on my streaming device. "I'll keep Ted Allen on the TV for you all day today. Will that make up for keeping you waiting? You're getting your food before I get my coffee, so no complaining, okay?"

She settled in, staring at the television as Ted itemized the mystery ingredients in the basket for the contestants. I rounded my small kitchen island that separated the two living areas and made myself an espresso. I usually make a more leisurely coffee drink for my day off, like a cappuccino or a latte, but I needed a swift kick to get myself going today.

I downed the drink as soon as it cooled. I prepared a second and then decided the best way to clear my head was to start the day right—with some cheese. Much to my surprise, I was also in the mood for something on the sweet side—gosh, I was really not myself this morning.

I looked through my fridge and spotted some tortillas. I knew just what to make—a twist on a breakfast quesadilla. I took out some cranberry-walnut goat cheese, which would be perfect for what I had in mind. The one Fuji apple left in the bowl on my counter would be enough. I sliced it paper-thin, spread the goat cheese on half the tortilla, then topped it with the apple slices and drizzled it with honey. I folded it in half and heated it in a buttered skillet. Minutes later, I was munching on a crunchy, gooey, sweet-and-savory breakfast.

I reminded myself that I was going to have to shower and look presentable for my meeting with Mayor Trumbull. I had a bad feeling she wanted information from me about the scene of the crime that Heath must've refused to give her, which made me uneasy. If there was something about the body or the manner of murder Heath didn't tell her, it was for a reason. I didn't want to get him on my bad side or make his investigation more difficult. But saying no to the mayor was also not something I relished. She'd always been nice to me, but powerful people were used to getting their way. Would our meeting ruin our cordial relationship?

There was no getting around it. I popped in the last bite of my quesadilla and got ready for the day.

CHAPTER 8

I left Loretta in the apartment watching *Chopped* and locked the door behind me, sticking the key in the small purse I wore across my body at my hip. I descended the deck stairs and walked through the alley between my shop and where Everett's new bicycle shop was going to be. I was already sorry I wore my dressy shoes instead of my Keds. They were cute, but I rarely wore them, and now I remembered why. My feet have gotten spoiled always living in comfortable shoes.

I forced myself to go left instead of walking across the street to Roman's apartment. As I rounded the corner, I was pleasantly surprised to see two fellow members of the Good Neighbor Committee in front of Everett's shop window. Frank was in his sixties, with thinning reddish-blond hair, parted in the middle, and a face that looked sweetly malleable, like putty. He was always ready with a smile.

Mrs. Schultz had introduced me to Frank, whom she knew from her teaching days. This was Frank's last year as a teacher before retirement. He was overseeing the high school seniors who were caught stealing decorations from our parade floats last fall. In lieu of any charges being filed, the teens had been tasked to "volunteer" on the

Good Neighbor Committee until graduation. The F.U.N. (Friendly United Neighbors) dance was the first event they were helping out with.

One of the students, Trace, was with Frank now. I'd crossed paths with Trace a handful of times since being on the committee together. I'd been surprised to learn he was one of the harvest float vandals, as he looked younger than the seniors—although he wasn't—and kept his distance from the others.

Three pints of bright paint were lined up on the sidewalk. Looking through his long bangs, Trace brushed blue onto Everett's shop window, making the letter *N*. He was spelling out *F.U.N. Dance*.

"Looking good," I said.

Trace continued to paint.

"You can say thank you," Frank instructed.

"Oh, thanks. Sorry," Trace mumbled.

"No worries," I replied.

"Politeness is a habit, not a skill," Frank said. "Right, Trace?

"Yes, Mr. Coogan," Trace replied.

"It's going to be a while before Everett opens his bike shop, so he offered to let us use his windows to advertise the dance," Frank explained.

"That's nice of him." I peered inside the shop to look for him, but the lights were off. There were some questions I wouldn't mind asking him about where he was yesterday at the time of Nelson's murder.

I moved aside when I heard footsteps behind me. It was Lou from the market.

"Good morning, Lou," I said. We usually exchanged pleasantries while he was sweeping the walk in front of his shop, which he did regularly. His sidewalk was cleaner than my apartment floors.

"Afternoon, Willa." Lou was polite but unsmiling, which was expected. His overarching personality trait was grumpy.

"Oh right, it's afternoon already."

"You're not having him do that to *my* windows," Lou told Frank.

"Just Everett's. He gave us permission. It's not permanent," Frank replied defensively. He pulled back his shoulders, trying to stiffen his doughy frame. He was still several inches shorter than Lou.

Lou glanced around. "Where are the other vandals?"

"Lou!" I gave him my sternest look.

Frank answered without addressing the label Lou had used. "Strictly speaking, this isn't part of the program. Trace was the only student who volunteered to paint."

"I'd rather do it on my own anyway." Trace dipped his brush into the paint again. It was obvious he took the painting job seriously, or maybe he just wanted to get it done.

"They'll be at the hall later today, helping with the decorations. That's mandatory. Don't worry, Lou. I'm in charge." Frank crossed his arms and puffed out his chest some more as if to prove his point.

"The hall's starting to look good," I said.

The event hall in the historic Town Hall building was being used for the dance. It was just a large room with white walls, but the beautiful row of floor-to-ceiling arched windows facing the park gave the room potential. We were hoping our decorations would transform it for the dance.

"How about you, Mr. Pimbley?" Trace asked. "Will you bring some radishes and carrots so we can try to make those vegetable flowers?"

"It's Lou. Mr. Pimbley is my father," Lou answered.

"What vegetable flowers?" I asked.

"Sometimes I carve flowers out of vegetables for the market and stick 'em in the produce section or on the deli counter. He saw them the other day," Lou explained.

"It'd be cool to make them to decorate the tables," Trace added.

"I've seen those. That's a great idea, Trace. I bet the committee could reimburse you for the produce," I said to Lou.

"We'll see if I get there today. Not everybody's shop is closed on Mondays. Why are you out of school?" he barked at Trace.

"It's winter break," Trace answered, unaffected.

"When I was your age, I was working at the market whenever I wasn't in school."

"My mom doesn't want me biking home at night and it's hard to find a job that'll let me out before dark. My dad works the night shift, so he sleeps during the day. Believe me, I'd rather have a job than have to tiptoe around the house all afternoon."

I felt for him. "I'll keep my ears open about an afternoon job for you, Trace."

Trace looked my way and gave an appreciative nod.

"Will the Curds and Whey folks be at the hall later too?" Frank asked me.

"As far as I know," I told him.

"It looks like rain. You'd better finish up," Lou said to Trace before heading back to the market.

He was right. The clouds looked like they might finally decide to give up what they were holding. I'd put on a nice blouse and a buttoned cardigan for meeting with the mayor—it would be just my luck to get there looking like a drowned rat. "I'll see you at the hall later. I gotta run."

I continued up Pleasant Avenue and rounded the corner

at Main Street on my way to Town Hall. I was a little
early, but I hoped I'd be able to see the mayor right away.
My curiosity now outweighed any anxiety I had about
why she wanted to see me.

I pulled on one of the heavy double doors at the entrance to the historic stone building. If I went right and
then turned down another hallway, I'd eventually end up
at the half-decorated event room where our F.U.N. dance
was going to be held. I'd been in Town Hall plenty since
joining the Good Neighbor Committee and knew Mayor
Trumbull's office was in the opposite direction, to the
left. I entered the plain outer office with a small seating
area made up of two chairs. An empty coffeepot sat on
a short table against the wall. The reception desk had
no one behind it. I wasn't sure if I should sit and wait or
knock. Before I could make the decision, the mayor's door
opened, and A. J. Stringer emerged.

A. J., with his mop of curly black hair and wearing
his usual green Salvation Army jacket over a T-shirt and
worn jeans, was the editor of the *Glen Gazette*, our free
town newspaper. We'd become unwitting cohorts several
months ago when we were both looking into a murder.

"Willa!" he said, more in surprise than greeting.

I felt the same. "Hi, A. J."

"What are you doing here?"

I saw Mayor Trumbull at the door, dressed in a navy-
blue pant suit. She stiffened when she saw me. I was early,
and she wanted to keep our meeting a secret. Oops.

"We've got the dance on Friday," I said noncommittally.

"Oh yeah. I've got Deandra on that story," he replied.

Deandra was a longtime *Gazette* writer.

"You can come in now, Willa," Mayor Trumbull said.

A. J.'s curiosity was worse than mine, and his sense for
sniffing out the truth was pretty keen, so I avoided further

eye contact as I walked past him into the mayor's office. She shut the door behind us and crossed to her desk.

"Thank you for that. I'm leaving for the day after our meeting, so I let my administrative assistant go home. I just needed to take care of a few things here. I wasn't expecting A. J., although I suppose I should've been. He always seems to pop up," she said.

I had the same experience with him. He was like a jack-in-the-box without the music.

This was my first time in the mayor's office, and I was surprised at its large size compared to the tiny outer office. The far side of the room consisted of a seating area with a couch and two chairs around a low coffee table. Against the wall nearer the door was a buffet cabinet. I couldn't help but admire a bronze eagle sculpture that was perched on it. It had to be a foot tall, and it was exceptionally detailed.

"It's beautiful, isn't it?" she said, noticing.

"Yes, it is. I admire artists so much. It's something I have absolutely no talent in."

"My brother got the artistic genes in the family. That's his sculpture."

"You're kidding! Wow."

"His pieces are quite sought after, especially now that he's passed."

"I'm sorry. I didn't know you'd lost him."

"It was a private plane crash. Both he and his wife—Nelson's parents. Nelson was an only child."

"How tragic!" It was traumatic enough when I'd lost my only sibling. I couldn't imagine losing everyone in my family, especially at once.

She continued, "I wasn't ever very close with my brother. I became the black sheep of my family after I had Everett my junior year in college and decided to raise him on my own instead of marrying his father. But after my brother and sister-in-law died, Nelson moved to Yarrow Glen to be near me and Everett. He was twenty-two, but he still needed family and we were the only ones he had."

"I'm so sorry about Nelson."

"Thank you." She sat at her desk and gestured for me to take a seat in the chair opposite her. For some reason, I felt like I was sitting in the school principal's office.

"I like to think they're all together again." She shook her head and opened a drawer to pluck out a tissue. "I'm sorry," she said, dabbing at the corners of her eyes.

"Please, don't be."

She took a few moments before continuing. "I felt Nelson was just starting to blossom and mature. He'd been angry since his parents died, and a little reckless and wild with all the money he'd inherited. I was excited at the thought that he was going to marry and settle down, even if it was with one of the Harrington daughters."

I was frothing to ask what she meant by that, but decorum kept me from doing so.

She went on, "I suppose I should belatedly apologize for my nephew's actions in your shop the other night."

"Not at all. It's not worth mentioning now."

She gathered herself and threw away the tissue. "How's your shop doing by the way? I've been so impressed with it. As you can see, I keep copies of all the awards our town businesses have won through citizens voting in the 'Best of' editions."

I was surprised and feeling suddenly proud to see a copy of my certificate framed on the wall along with awards for other Yarrow Glen businesses.

"Winning 'Best New Business' was one of the highlights of last year. We've been doing well bringing in the cheese trail tourists and holding steady with the locals," I said, hoping she'd be pleased.

"It's easy for Yarrow Glen to get lost amidst the vineyard towns. It was nice to get recognition despite Guy Lippinger's attempts to keep us down in years past. Everett's very excited to be opening his bike shop next to your shop."

"We're all excited to have him downtown with us." I briefly wondered what the relationship would be between the town and the magazine now that Nelson wasn't around to marry a Harrington daughter.

"I'm sure you're wondering why I asked you here and why I asked you to keep it confidential," Mayor Trumble said. "Did you? Keep it confidential?"

"Of course. I didn't tell anyone." It was the truth. Mayor Trumbull inadvertently told my friends, I didn't. However, over this past year, I'd trusted my three best friends with a lot more than a secret meeting with the mayor.

"Good. And you skirted A. J.'s question expertly." Mayor Trumbull clasped her hands on her desk and leaned forward. She looked me in the eye. "I'd like you to look into my nephew's murder."

Of all the things I might have been expecting her to say, this wasn't it. I recovered from my surprise quickly and asked, "Why?"

"I know about your involvement in helping to solve the last two murders that occurred in our town, and . . . I know the Harringtons. They're by far the wealthiest people in town, and they wield a lot of power with that wealth."

"You don't trust the police?"

She hesitated before answering, "Of course I trust our police department. Detective Heath has been an asset to the department. But Chief Jeffers won't want to cause waves if the Harringtons complain about any police intrusion, and I'm not in a position to . . . push back."

I would think as mayor, she was exactly in that position. The chief of police was the face of the police department, but the mayor had jurisdiction over him. There was more to this than Mayor Trumbull was telling me.

She continued, "You seem to be able to find a way to speak with people under the radar. That's what I'd like you to do. I could be underestimating Detective Heath, but I feel the investigation will stall without somebody getting answers the police won't be able to get."

"Do you think the Harringtons have something to do with Nelson's death?"

She splayed her palms as if to say "Who knows?" but the skeptical expression on her face told a different story. "I'd just like more assurance that all the pertinent information will make its way to Detective Heath. You can feed it to him however you like, as long as you don't mention my involvement. Will you do it for me, Willa? I'd consider it a personal favor."

I didn't know what to say, so I stayed mute. I'd jumped headfirst into the last two murder investigations to save myself and my friends. I was willing to do the same for Roman, so why was I hesitating about saying yes to Mayor Trumbull's request? Something wasn't sitting right with me. I wasn't sure how I felt about her insinuation about the Harringtons, but she obviously wasn't allowing me to be privy to whatever history was between them.

Mayor Trumbull spoke again. "I've heard the police consider Roman Massey a person of interest."

My stomach tumbled. "Has Detective Heath told you anything?"

"Just that Roman doesn't have an alibi and he seems to have the most motive. What I'm afraid of is that the

Harringtons will make sure the police stay focused on him."

Now she had me worried. I spilled what I knew. "He said it was Summer who told him to go to the garden shed yesterday. And it was Chloe who somehow convinced him to show his face at the shower. Do you think this was planned and they set him up for the murder?"

Mayor Trumbull leaned back in her high-back leather chair. "Who knows? But if they did do something, they're likely to get away with it."

I didn't like the sound of that. I knew he was innocent. When it came to this case, I didn't care that my relationship with Roman was in shambles. He'd shown himself to be a good friend since the day I met him. "Okay, I'll do what I can," I promised.

"Thank you." Mayor Trumbull stood, effectively ending our meeting. "Now that it's settled, this conversation never took place."

"O-of course," I stuttered.

By the time I stood, she'd already opened her office door to see me out.

CHAPTER 9

I walked down the hallway feeling uneasy, and it wasn't just because my shoes were causing a blister on my pinky toe. I exited the building in my own thoughts and jumped when A. J. tapped me on the shoulder.

"Why are you always lurking?" I said, putting a hand to my rapidly beating heart.

"I wasn't lurking, I was waiting for you."

"Why?" I asked, continuing down the wide stoop.

A. J. followed. "That's the question I wanted to ask you. Why were you meeting with Mayor Trumbull?"

It wasn't a surprise that A. J. didn't buy my earlier excuse, but the mayor wanted me to be discreet and telling the editor of the *Glen Gazette* the truth would most certainly not be discreet. I was sticking to my story. "I told you. I'm on the Good Neighbor Committee and we had a meeting set up to discuss a few things about the F.U.N. dance. She didn't want to cancel. You know how dedicated the mayor is."

"Uh-huh." He walked in step with me toward the corner of Pleasant Avenue.

He looked behind him. I looked too. There was a sprinkling of pedestrians on the sidewalk but nobody nearby.

He leaned in and whispered, "Okay, so tell me why you were really there."

"That *is* why I was really there," I whispered back.

"You weren't asking her questions about the murder?" He returned to his normal voice now that he wasn't getting any scoop.

"It was her nephew who was killed! How insensitive do you think I am? Is that what *you* were doing there?"

"Of course not. I was taking a statement from her and getting his obituary. You were my next stop, but here you are. Serendipity. I heard you found the body."

"I can't talk about it with you. I have to be sensitive to Mayor Trumbull."

I started to round the bend onto my street when he held me back by my arm. "You're not curious at all what happened?"

"Not this time, A. J."

I shook my arm out of his grasp.

"Even though the police have their eye on your boyfriend?" he called.

He knew exactly which button to push to get me to stop. I hated to give in, but I had to know. "Do you know anything?"

"You know how this works."

I rolled my eyes. "Quid pro quo."

"Exactly."

"How do I know you really have anything worthwhile? The fact that Roman might be suspected isn't a surprise to me."

"Aw, come on, Willa. We're kinda bonded now, aren't we? Doesn't being held at gunpoint together mean anything to you?" he said. His green eyes softened, and he held his arms out, as if we should hug, which neither of us would ever do.

I couldn't deny he was right. Even though A. J. was annoying as heck, I had a soft spot for him after what we'd been through together. "Fine. But if I'm going to give you details about what I know, you have to have something else for me besides the obvious."

His lips curled into a grin. "The photographer at the wedding shower—Marcos Navarro? He used to be part of the paparazzi in L.A. He didn't have the right personality for the job, but we got to be friends. He owes me a favor. Since he's now working exclusively for *All Things Sonoma*, he's got an inside track to the Harringtons."

"He could be a good resource," I agreed.

"He knows about the *Case Closed* feature articles I published after the last two murder investigations. I told him I'm starting to write another one for Nelson's murder. We're meeting in my office in about five minutes."

I had no choice. It looked like I'd be working with A. J. again. "What are we waiting for?"

The pedestrian signal gave the okay, so we crossed to the other side of Main Street. I hobbled the rest of the way to the cinderblock building that was the *Gazette*, wishing again I'd worn my Keds.

I waved to Deandra, the *Gazette*'s longtime local events reporter who was working in her cubicle, as we made our way to the back of the building and into the stairway vestibule. Instead of going straight up to his office, A. J. pushed on the bar of the back door to open it and stuck his head out. Marcos came inside. I was starting to get used to his look of surprise every time he saw me.

"I know you," Marcos said to me.

"Yeah, I was at the shower yesterday. Willa Bauer."

"She's the cheese lady," A. J. said, starting up the stairs.

Marcos caught up with him and said in his ear, but loud enough for me to hear him, "Why is she here?"

"She's my sidekick," A. J. replied. "Don't worry, you can trust her."

My jaw dropped like it had come unhinged, and I halted on the third step. *Sidekick?*

When they got to the second floor, A. J. leaned over the railing. "Keep up," he called down.

They continued on while I stewed a few seconds longer. I had a mind to turn around and leave, but Marcos could be a good ally. He could also be one of the suspects. What's that they say about keeping your friends close and your enemies closer? A. J. was treading perilously close to the enemy camp if he kept calling me his sidekick.

I resumed climbing the stairs to A. J.'s office loft. It was a good thing I was still ruminating on my annoyance with him—I didn't have time to feel anxious about being in this space again where I'd been held against my will. It didn't hit me until I was already upstairs, and by then Marcos was at the large monitor bringing up his photos from Summer's shower. I shook off the willies the memories were bringing up and joined the guys.

Marcos scrolled through the shots. Most of them were of Chloe. I remembered their flirty banter and wondered if there was anything more to it than that.

"How did you meet Chloe?" I asked him.

"I took photos for her portfolio when she had her sights set on being a model. She only did it until it became too much like a job, but we got close. It was because of her that her mother hired me at *All Things Sonoma*. She's a good friend."

"What about Summer? Have you ever been close with her?"

"Summer? No." He looked me up and down. "Listen, I'm flattered that you want to know if I'm unattached, but . . ."

I coughed and sputtered, "N-no! That's not why I'm asking." I looked to A. J. for backup, but he was holding back his laughter. *Thanks a lot.*

"Why are you asking then?" Marcos said.

"I just wondered how well you know them." *Somebody's* got an ego. "Do you think Summer and Nelson were really in love?"

"As far as I know. He was definitely her type—rich. I'm not rich enough for either Summer or Chloe. Chloe likes to be friends with regular folk, though. Sometimes I think it's just to annoy her mother, since she kind of collects us, like a hobby. I don't mind. She's not like her sister, who only hangs out with the upper crust."

"Summer was engaged to Roman, and I wouldn't say he's upper crust," I said.

"He's one of the Masseys, isn't he? They don't have Harrington-level wealth, but they're a wealthy family. The working class is fine for them as long as there's family money behind them. Olivia's always got her eye on rich men for her daughters."

A. J. took control of the mouse and started scrolling, apparently not interested in my questions to Marcos. The photos moved from Chloe to the elaborate patio decor.

"I'm happy to show these to you, but I don't think you're going to get too much information from the pictures I took," Marcos said.

I was starting to think he was right until the photo of Nelson on horseback came on screen.

"Here's when the fun started," Marcos said to A. J. sarcastically. "Now remember, I never showed you these. Right?"

"My sources are always anonymous," A. J. assured him.

"Did you know Nelson was going to be there?" I asked Marcos.

"I had no clue, but when I saw him, I thought it was going to be a romantic moment I should capture. Sometimes photographers need to think on their feet." He took over from A. J. and slowly scrolled through the rest of the pictures.

The final photo was after Summer and Roman got out of the golf cart. A. J. leaned over and hit one of the keys to zoom in. Summer looked distraught, but Chloe's reaction was the complete opposite.

"Chloe's all smiles," I noted. *Just like when Roman showed up at Curds and Whey.*

"She probably thought it would be a nice surprise too," Marcos said.

She was there the night before at my shop, so she had to have known how Nelson would react once he saw Roman. She may have even orchestrated it. I kept my thoughts about Chloe to myself.

"Did Roman go to the shower with you?" A. J. asked me.

"No, he was there to talk to Summer. I didn't know," I said.

"A love triangle that ends in murder. This is going to be a good story."

"That's not what happened." I stopped looking at the screen to face A. J.

"He almost married her, didn't he? Like six years ago? That's what I read. And now at her wedding shower, he shows up to confront her fiancé? I'm just laying out the facts." A. J. splayed his hands out as if there were no other conclusion to come to.

"Who said he was going to confront her fiancé?

Supposedly nobody but Everett knew Nelson was going to be there to make that grand gesture," I pointed out.

"So what was Roman doing in the golf cart?" he said. "Were he and Summer going to make an announcement?"

I hated when he asked a good question. Journalists! "I don't know, but it doesn't necessarily mean anything was going on with Summer. And it sure as huckleberry doesn't mean he killed Nelson."

"How sure is a huckleberry?" Marcos asked.

He and A. J. exchanged glances, like I was strange. Both seemed amused at my annoyance.

"It's just a word I picked up from my friend, Baz. His mom used to use it in place of any curse word, and it's stuck with him. I guess it's stuck with me too."

"We're just teasing you, Willa," A. J. said.

"I can handle the teasing, but you need to take me seriously about Roman. He had nothing to do with Nelson's murder."

A. J. shrugged it off. I knew he didn't believe Roman killed Nelson. "So who killed him? Any other pictures that might give us a clue?" he asked Marcos.

"Sorry, that's it. Once I realized it was turning bad, I stopped shooting," Marcos said.

"Where did *you* go after Nelson left?" I asked.

Marcos shrugged one shoulder. "I was just hanging around with everybody else."

"I didn't see you until I ran into you in the house."

"Oh right. I had to make a phone call, then I went looking for Chloe."

"Did you find her? I heard she went after Nelson," I bluffed, hoping he'd confirm it.

"Where'd you hear that? She was in her art room when I saw her, hiding from her mother and Summer. She told me I should just go home, so I went out to the driveway thinking my car was still there."

"Did you run into anybody else? Summer or Olivia?"

"Nobody was around." His prior amusement had vanished. "You got a problem with that?"

"No. I was hoping you saw them so I could place where they were."

He peered at me for a few long seconds. "I'm going to go. I've got a job to get to." He took his flash drive out of the computer.

"Can I have a copy of those?" A. J. asked.

"No way. They won't be going in the magazine anymore, but I'd be fired if they showed up anywhere else. I agreed to show them to you, not give them to you."

"You can't blame a guy for trying. Thanks for bringing them by." A. J. and Marcos did the handshake/shoulder bump goodbye. "And you don't need to worry. I never reveal my sources."

"I trust you." He then turned to me. "But can I trust *you*?"

Taken aback, I managed to spout, "Of course."

He was standing close to me now. "You'd better hope so."

I said nothing in return.

His sudden smile coupled with his movie-star good looks made me question what had just happened.

He turned to A. J. "Good luck with your story, man. See ya later." He descended the stairs. The *thunk* of the back door announced his departure.

"You two got off to a good start," A. J. said sarcastically.

I sat in the chair Marcos had just vacated and opened my purse in hopes that I hadn't yet used my emergency bandage. *Aha—found it!* I wrapped it around the raw patch of skin on my toe. "He was very defensive. He obviously didn't like that I questioned where he was at the time of the murder."

"Ah, don't worry about him. He's got a lot riding on that job. He's an excellent photographer, but he knows he got lucky. He always wanted to be on the other side of the camera—be one of the rich and famous, not taking photos of them. That's why he couldn't handle being part of the paparazzi. He hated how celebrities treated him. They'd act all friendly when they wanted their picture taken, then scoff at him whenever they didn't. With this gig, he's in good with the Harringtons. It's as close as he's gotten to being on the other side. Plus, he doesn't have to go into debt for his wardrobe anymore."

"He *is* a snappy dresser, but that sounded a little like a threat."

"Trust me, I know him. He's not going to do anything to you."

I'd need more than A. J.'s assurances. Marcos's excuse for being missing around the time of the murder seemed sketchy. Could I trust that he wasn't the one who killed Nelson?

CHAPTER 10

I went home to change out of my "dress clothes," which meant I basically acted out Mr. Rogers' Neighborhood, switching out the boxy cardigan and blouse for a long-sleeved tee and my uncomfortable shoes for Keds. *Ahhh.*

The change in weather made me long for some soup, but not surprisingly, I was also in the mood for something cheesy. I decided on a riff of the classic combo of tomato soup and grilled cheese. While I heated up the canned soup, I cut a slice of crusty Italian bread. I lathered it with butter and stuck it under the broiler. I poured the tomato soup into my individual crock, rested the toasted Italian bread on the soup, and layered slices of cheddar cheese over the top like a blanket. I stuck it back into the broiler until it melted. Voila! The classic combo in a bowl. Why should French onion soup be the only one to get topped with a cheesy layer?

I took Loretta away from Ted Allen to the kitchen island to keep me company while I ate my cheesy tomato soup and told her about my day. I could always count on my fish to be a good listener. Unfortunately, revisiting it with her didn't give me any hints as to how to start my investigation. Mayor Trumbull seemed to believe one of the Harringtons was the culprit. The way I saw it, it had to be Summer. She was the one who invited Roman for a clandestine meeting at the garden shed. I could use more answers about that, but how was I going to talk to Summer? It wasn't like we ran in the same circles.

"You don't have any suggestions for me, Loretta?"

Loretta circled the bowl once, her vibrant red tailfin swishing behind her fluorescent blue body. Then she settled in behind her pineapple house. Too much TV made her tired. I clicked off *Chopped*. Maybe I'd see my friends at the hall, and they'd come up with an idea. I washed out my soup bowl, returned the fishbowl to the stool I called Loretta Island, and headed to Town Hall for the second time that day.

The Good Neighbor Committee varied the schedule between afternoon and evening times so all members could get a chance to decorate the hall. Since many businesses in town were closed on Mondays, the hall saw a good turn-out in doing it late afternoon. The F.U.N. dance was only four days away and there was still a lot to do.

I'd never been as ensconced in a community before as I was with Yarrow Glen. It was my first real home since Oregon, even though I'd lived in a dozen different places over the last ten years. When I was a teenager and couldn't wait to leave home, my mother would say, "*Your feet might leave home, but your heart never will.*" She was right about that, but it seemed I was finally making space in my heart for another place to call home.

When I arrived at the hall, I saw so many of my friends and neighbors chipping in to make the event special. Baz was hanging twinkle lights right above where his crush, Ginger, was painting. They often made excuses to be around each other over the last few months. I just hoped Baz didn't fall off the stepladder, since he seemed to be paying more attention to Ginger's backside than the lights.

It looked like Ginger was working on a wall mural with Sharice, who owned Read More Bookstore & Café, where Ginger worked at the café as a barista and provided a few vegan desserts. Deandra, from the *Gazette*, was also pitching in. I went over to say hi and get a closer look.

They'd taped craft paper to the wall and were painting almost-life-sized dancers. They'd created the winning harvest fair float last fall, so it was no surprise the mural looked great. Deandra was adding color to the background of hands clasped together.

The committee had decided "hand-in-hand" would be the dance's theme. Although there would be plenty of couples coming, the purpose of the event was for everyone to be included, especially those community members who didn't have a sweetheart, which was lucky for me. I had no idea where things stood with Roman. However, I knew I wasn't ready to write him off.

"That looks fantastic!" I said, appreciating the mural.

Sharice's round, makeup-free face looked up from her brush, her eyes indicating delight behind cat-eye glasses. Her hair was pulled away from her face, starting in cornrows and ending in an explosion of tightly coiled curls. I admired her fun tie-dye leggings, as I didn't have any that weren't black or gray. I never ventured farther than my deck in mine, even with a long shirt over them as she had.

"Thank you, Willa!" Sharice stepped back to get a wider perspective. "It *is* looking good. Pick up a brush and join us."

"My talents lie solely in cheese. I wouldn't want to ruin it," I said.

"You can't ruin it. It's a group effort. Isn't that what this committee is all about?"

"Careful, she's very persuasive," Deandra said. "I just came to take pictures for the *Gazette*, but she roped me in.

I haven't painted since making posters in high school."
Deandra had slipped off her Crocs, put on an apron, and
pushed the sleeves of her blouse and baggy sweater above
her elbows. She had a habit of wearing multiple layers of
clothing.

"You look all in now," I said to her.

"I forgot how much fun this is. I even decided to take
Sharice's painting class tonight."

"You're giving classes now?" I asked.

Sharice opened the used bookstore to supplement her
income as an illustration artist, which she was very talented at. Unfortunately, the arts rarely paid a living wage.

"Frank asked if I had any ideas to keep his group of
teens busy this week during their winter break. It's like
a Paint and Sip class but I'm calling it Paint and Snack.
You know how teenagers love to eat. You're welcome to
come. Even Baz signed up."

"Ginger signed me up," Baz clarified from atop the
stepladder.

"You don't want to go?" Ginger stopped painting mid-
brushstroke.

"No, no. I wanna go," Baz assured her, not sounding
very convincing.

"I thought you said it sounded fun when I told you I
was going," she said.

"Yeah, it sounded fun for *you*."

"So you don't want to go."

"No, I do. I absolutely do. Sharice said there's gonna
be Doritos."

"You want to go just because of the Doritos?" Ginger
fumed.

"No, that's not what I meant." Baz looked at me for
help, but I wasn't getting in the middle of this.

I let their little spat get me out of having to say no to

Sharice's invitation, since painting was not my thing. I slipped away to the other side of the room.

It looked like Lou came through with getting the produce—he was overseeing a whole table of high school kids, including Trace, in paring carrots and radishes to look like tulips. Archie was also in the group. It was hard for me to find something to do that didn't involve crafting. I was more useful during our initial meetings, contributing ideas and organizing. I went over to the table where Mrs. Schultz and Frank were sitting with the elderly Melon sisters, Daisy and Gemma. Between the two of them, they'd outlived three husbands. They were working on gluing together a paper chain of hands. *That* I could do.

"May I join you?" I asked.

Mrs. Schultz patted the chair between her and Daisy. The sisters weren't twins, but in their early eighties they looked so much alike that the easiest way to tell them apart was to look for some sort of daisy flower somewhere on Daisy. Today, she wore a daisy pin. She also had a large, appliqued silk daisy on the boxy yellow purse at her feet.

As I sat down, I took another quick scan of the room. I didn't expect to see Roman here, but I couldn't help but hope I would. Not surprisingly, Everett wasn't here either.

"Are you looking for Cyrus too?" Daisy asked me.

"Cyrus?" I was stumped for a moment. "Oh, you mean Lou's father?" I saw him periodically at the market.

"Yes. I was hoping he'd be here too," she said.

"I told her he's probably still at the market since Lou is here. He takes that market very seriously—even a heart attack couldn't keep him away," Gemma said.

"I don't know why I always go for the workaholics," Daisy lamented.

"You always go for the men with the heart conditions," Gemma corrected.

"Don't get all high and mighty. You only have one less deceased husband than I do, which only means I was married more times than you."

"But I was asked more," Gemma shot back.

I felt like I'd turned the clock forward fifty-five years and was listening to Chloe and Summer. Is this what having a sister was like?

"I think we need more glue on this one," Mrs. Schultz interjected, obviously trying to shift the focus. It worked.

"Are you doing okay after yesterday, Willa?" Frank asked.

Before I could answer, Daisy asked, "What happened yesterday?"

"Don't you remember? Lorna told us she found the mayor's nephew murdered," Gemma said.

"Of course I remember. But what does Lorna finding a dead body have to do with Willa?" Daisy asked.

"Lorna didn't find him, Willa found him."

"Then why did Lorna say *she* did?"

"She didn't!" Gemma shook her head in exasperation.

I hated to confuse the situation even more, but I had to ask, "Who's Lorna?"

"Polly's mother. Polly's the Harrington's housekeeper," Gemma answered, although I already knew that much. Then she returned to her sister, "Lorna told us Nelson was murdered right on the property and the cheese lady found him. And you said—"

"'She found another dead guy?' I remember now," Daisy replied, nodding her head.

All eyes were on me. "I'm doing okay," I said to Frank.

"Let's go measure this to see if it's the right length," Mrs. Schultz suggested, getting up from her chair.

She and Frank took the long chain of linked hands

and left the table, leaving me with a curious Daisy and Gemma. I decided to strike first.

"Did Lorna tell you anything else Polly said?" I asked.

Gemma started to regale me with the play-by-play of Nelson and Roman's altercation, which made my stomach twist in knots. If the Melon sisters knew about it, everyone in town would know the details very shortly.

I interrupted her colorful storytelling. "What about afterward? When Polly went back into the house."

Gemma slowly shook her head in thought. "She didn't say anything about that. By then the drama was over."

"Lou said Polly was afraid to talk about it," Daisy piped up.

"When did he tell you this?" I asked her.

"This morning at the market. We had to pick up a few things."

"No, we didn't. We were just there because Daisy wanted to see Cyrus, but he was in the back doing inventory, so we caught up with Lou," Gemma corrected.

Daisy rolled her eyes. "Anyhoo, we saw Polly and Lou chatting, but she left as soon as we walked up to them, which wasn't like her. She looked worried. Lou told us that she had to go to the police station for more questioning and she was nervous."

"What was she nervous about?" I asked.

"Saying something wrong, of course," Daisy answered.

"Polly's the third housekeeper they've had in the last year—they go through housekeepers faster than Daisy goes through men," Gemma answered.

Daisy patted her cotton candy–like hair, not miffed in the least.

I wondered if there was a more specific reason Polly was afraid to talk to the police. Did she know something about the Harringtons? Did she see something that afternoon?

"We need two more people to help us tack the chain to the ceiling," Frank called out to the room. He stood on a stepladder on one end of the hall holding the end of the paper chain while Mrs. Schultz stood beneath him with the rest of it.

"I can do the one in the middle," Mrs. Schultz said.

"You shouldn't stand on a ladder. You could fall," Frank replied.

To my utter surprise, Mrs. Schultz acquiesced.

Lou fumbled to stand up to help, but Baz was quicker to get there.

"Lou, I think you cut your hand," Trace said.

"It's nothing," Lou mumbled, taking a handkerchief from his pocket and sitting back down. "I told you kids these paring knives are sharp." He tried to make light of it as he knotted the handkerchief around his hand and picked up the small knife again.

It looked like they needed a third person to hold the chain on the far side of the room, so I excused myself and carefully took the final paper chain section from Baz to the third stepladder positioned at the hall's entrance. I climbed it and gently lifted the paper to the ceiling. My short stature was working against me. As I stepped up to the highest rung, the front of my shoe caught on it, causing me to slip. I felt myself topple to the side. I grabbed the ladder, but it had already shifted with my weight and began to go down with me. I braced for the fall but landed in someone's arms. I turned to see who my hero was.

Roman.

CHAPTER 11

"Roman." My legs dropped from his arms and I stood.

Archie came rushing over. "You okay, Willa?"

Baz, Mrs. Schultz, and Frank were there too.

"I'm fine. Roman got here in the nick of time. Thanks for saving me," I said.

"Anytime." Now that I was steady, his arm slipped from my waist.

"I guess you were right about falling," Mrs. Schultz said to Frank. Did she have something in her eye or was she batting her lashes at him?

"Uh-oh, the chain's ripped," Baz said, holding it now in two separate parts.

"Oh, I'm sorry," I said. I really *was* bad at crafts, even hanging them.

"It's only the end of it. We got this," Archie said. "I could use a break from the veggie bouquets anyway."

Archie, Mrs. Schultz, and Frank went back over to the table with the friendship chain. Baz quickly assessed the situation—Roman and I finally together—and returned to Ginger.

"I'm glad you're here," I said. "I mean, besides getting here just in time to save me." It was odd—the electric sparks I always felt when I was this close to Roman failed to ignite. For the first time, it felt awkward.

"I promised the committee I'd help with the twinkle lights," he said.

"I think Baz took care of that already. But can we talk for a minute?"

"Sure."

He followed me out to a quiet spot in the hallway.

"How are you?" I asked.

"I survived Detective Heath's grilling."

"Was it bad?"

"Not too bad, but I have a feeling I'll be seeing him again. How are you?"

I shrugged and stared at the tile pattern at my feet.

Roman tipped my chin up so I had nowhere else to look but in his eyes. "How are *we*?" he asked.

I stepped away from his touch. "I'm not sure. You tell me. You're the one who secretly met up with Summer when she was supposed to be at her wedding shower."

He sighed. "Let's go someplace more private."

We walked out of Town Hall and sat on a bench on the sidewalk where we wouldn't be overheard. Only a spattering of people were out on the sidewalks, as the clouds still threatened rain. The short bench forced us to sit knee to knee, closer than I would've liked.

"Listen, the connection I have with Summer and her family goes back generations," he explained. "Even breaking it off with her the way I did couldn't completely sever it."

So I guess that answered my question about how he felt about Summer. But I didn't want it to cloud the reality. "Don't you think you could be wrong about your connection?" The look on his face told me he didn't think so. I had to get through to him. "I'm afraid the Harringtons are going to frame you for Nelson's murder."

Roman almost always kept his cool and now was no exception. He didn't seem affected by my declaration. "They wouldn't do that."

"How can you be so sure? They're a powerful family." It was as close as I could get to telling him about the mayor's warning.

"There's history between the Harringtons and the Masseys," he began. "My grandparents were best friends with Summer's grandparents. They knew it was my grandparents' dream to have a vineyard and a winery. They'd already begun amassing their fortune, so they invested in Enora's for a small share of the winery. For the amount of money they put in, they could've had controlling share, but they didn't. They just wanted my family to have their dream. There's been a time or two over the years since her grandfather passed that my family had a rough season because of drought or wildfires nearby, and her grandmother helped get us through. That's what I know of the Harrington family."

"Is her grandmother still alive? She wasn't there for the shower. Is Summer's father in the picture?"

"Summer's grandmother lives farther north where my family lives and where our vineyard is. Summer told me she was diagnosed with Alzheimer's a few years ago. I can't imagine it—she was witty and sharp when I knew her. She was as much involved in all their investments as Summer's granddad was. She was the one in control of most of the family fortune when Summer and I were together. Summer's father travels all over the world for business, which I'm convinced is how he and Olivia have stayed married for this long. I'm sure both her grandmother and her father would've been here for the wedding."

"Okay, so your families are close, but do you think you can trust Olivia? She doesn't seem like your biggest fan."

"The Harringtons are good people. That's why I agreed when Chloe asked me to come back to the house with Summer. She told me there was a mix-up with the wine order, and since it was Enora's, I could figure out the problem quicker. I wasn't going to go, but she and Summer said their mother would appreciate that I was there to help. After the way our relationship ended, I thought it was the least I could do."

"Even after what happened at my shop Saturday night? It wasn't your fault, but . . ."

"I know, I know. I was being naïve. Wishful thinking, I guess."

I couldn't fault him for that. "I don't know if what she said about the wine was true, but I think Chloe knew Nelson was going to be there. She said she'd been looking for Summer all over, even in the stable. Nelson had to be there saddling the horse. She must've seen him."

"That's Chloe for you. She hasn't changed. She's always liked poking at her sister. I didn't think she'd do it at her wedding shower, though."

"What she did seems like a lot more than a poke."

"I suppose so."

"That explains why you were in the golf cart with Summer and Chloe, but why didn't you leave after it all went down when you walked back to your car?"

"I did leave. I needed to cool off, so I drove around for maybe . . . twenty minutes? Then I was on my way back to the meadery when Summer texted."

"Again?"

"She told me to meet her at the garden shed again. She

said that she got everything worked out with Nelson, but she needed to talk to me right away."

"You didn't find that strange?"

"I did, but when it comes to Summer . . ." His gaze left mine.

I nodded in understanding. He couldn't resist an invitation from her.

"So I drove back and waited near the shed," he continued. "I heard a car. I thought maybe she'd driven there, so I looked, but it was Baz's pickup truck driving away. Your car was still in the lot. It made me wonder what the heck I was doing sitting and waiting for Summer, no matter what she had to tell me. So I left."

"We thought you were at the stable, so we drove away as soon as we saw your car. Darn it, I wish we'd gotten out to look for you instead of driving away. This means you don't have an alibi."

"Afraid not."

"Oh, Roman."

"Hey, I didn't do it, so Heath will figure out who did."

"I'm going to help."

"You don't need to go sticking your neck out for me," he said.

"I'd do it for any friend. Don't you see they set you up? Summer and Chloe? Maybe this was their revenge for leaving her at the altar."

"They wouldn't do that to me."

"How can you be so sure? Do you really know these people? You didn't know if Chloe lied to you to get you to come to the shower. Maybe Summer lied to get you to the property in the first place. What was so important that she had to see *you* on the day of her wedding shower?"

Roman was silent. He wasn't going to share that with me. I was sorry I asked.

"Never mind," I said. "I have to get back to the hall. Don't trust them. That's all I have to say. Don't trust the Harringtons."

I left the bench and hurried back into the building. Roman returned to the hall a few minutes later, and we avoided each other like a carefully orchestrated dance, ironically. I decided to hide out in the adjoining kitchen, where I could busy myself unwrapping the paper goods for the potluck buffet and not have to put on a happy face for anyone. It hurt that all our conversations seemed to turn into arguments. As I sorted the plastic forks, knives, and spoons, I thought about how great this week would've been had we had that romantic dinner at Apricot Grille Saturday night. We'd be working together all week and going to the dance together. Then I reminded myself that Roman's secret would still be out there. Would I rather not know?

Back to the case, Willa. If I was going to think about Roman, I needed to stick to the murder investigation. Who else did I need to talk to? Lou. Maybe I could catch him alone to see if Polly gave him any information he hadn't shared with the Melon sisters.

When I finally left the kitchen, however, he and his vegetable centerpieces were gone. Roman had also gone.

Frank herded Trace and the seven others from the high school group toward the door as everyone began to amble out. Archie was cleaning up one of the tables. I went over to help just as Mrs. Schultz had the same idea. Baz joined us.

"Hey, Willa, do me a favor," Baz said.

"Sure, what do you need?" I began collecting discarded strips of construction paper.

"Take my place at that Paint and Snack class tonight."

I paused my cleanup. "I don't think Ginger's going to approve of that replacement."

"Yeah, but you can smooth things over for me. Everett just called and wants to meet with me tonight about some snafus at his bicycle shop, and I know Ginger's going to think I'm making an excuse not to go."

"I don't blame her. You sounded like you didn't really want to go."

"That's because I don't, but I would have. Everett really did call, and he wants to put the pedal to the metal on finishing up his shop. I don't want to put him off or he might find someone else."

"I'm surprised with his cousin just getting murdered that he'd be thinking about his shop," Mrs. Schultz said, helping Archie put the last of the scraps into a recycle bin.

"Maybe he wants the distraction? I don't know, but I do know that getting these bigger jobs every so often pads my bank account," Baz said.

"I don't know, Baz. Doritos aren't the incentive for me that they are for you." Ginger and I hadn't gotten off on the best foot last fall. Although we'd made up, we didn't have the easiest relationship. I doubted she'd be happy to see me.

"It could be fun, Willa. I'm going," Mrs. Schultz said.

"I just don't know if I'm in the mood." The conversation with Roman had left me cranky.

"Are you okay?" Mrs. Schultz asked. "Are you still feeling the effects of finding Nelson's body?"

"Maybe. I'm just not in the mood to be social. I talked to Roman earlier." I caught them up on what he said about the Harringtons.

"Maybe he's right about them and they didn't set him

up," Mrs. Schultz remarked. "He does know them better than you do."

Leave it to Mrs. Schultz to give it to me straight. I had to consider the possibility.

Baz looked around, making sure those who were still cleaning up weren't in earshot. "What did Mayor Trumbull want from you? Were you able to ask her where she and Everett were after they left the patio?"

"Not exactly." I filled them in on my meeting this morning with the mayor, entrusting them to keep the secret. "Roman doesn't have an alibi and he's counting on Detective Heath to clear him, but Mayor Trumbull thinks Olivia Harrington will keep the police from finding the truth."

"Does this mean we're investigating?" Archie asked, bouncing a little on the balls of his feet.

"I'd like to. I'm not sure how to go about it, though. It's not like I can knock on the Harringtons' door and ask them questions. The photographer at the shower, Marcos? He knows Chloe but he doesn't seem to like me much, so I don't think I can ask him for any help."

"Ginger knows Chloe," Baz said.

"She does?" My bad mood suddenly lifted. "Will you be okay if I ask Ginger about her?" Baz and I had gotten into our first and only argument the last time I'd tried to question Ginger.

"Yeah, as long as you don't accuse Ginger this time, why not? And I know just where you can talk to her." Baz had a glint in his eye.

"You win. I'll go to the Paint and Snack."

Hopefully Ginger would be able to paint me a better picture of who the Harringtons really are.

CHAPTER 12

Sharice's Paint and Snack was set up in the children's section of her used bookstore. The space was normally surrounded by books but open in the middle for tables, so kids could draw or write stories, which were showcased on the walls and on top of the bookshelves. Sharice was always supportive of children and the arts.

The tables were gone tonight and in their place were chairs with easels and paints. The only remaining table was pushed to the side and had baskets of snack-sized bags of chips, pretzels, and M&Ms along with beverages for those under twenty-one and bottles of Pinot Grigio for the rest of us. The wine was Roman's family's brand, Enora's.

This Paint and Snack was something Roman and I might've done together. Maybe my insistence that we take it slow over these past three months was the reason he didn't confide in me about his past. Maybe it was the reason he wasn't letting me in now. Or maybe he'd caught feelings for Summer again.

Tonight, I felt more like grumpy Lou, who'd walked in without a smile and taken a seat. His demeanor only got worse when the Melon sisters joined him.

I shook off my melancholy and left the wine where it was when I saw Ginger arrive. I grabbed a bag of Doritos to take to Baz later and nabbed the seat next to her so I could talk to her about Chloe.

"Oh, I'm saving this seat for Baz," she told me as soon as I sat down.

I cringed. Apparently, he'd left it up to me to tell her he wouldn't be coming. *Gee, thanks Baz.* I broke his absence to her nicely, but her annoyance was apparent. I pulled opened the snack bag—he wasn't getting Doritos tonight.

It was a good turnout, almost twenty-five of us, and about half were students from the high school. Trace was in the student group, but he sat quietly munching on popcorn while the others buzzed about. Sharice was offering the class free of charge so the teens could attend, but the rest of us voluntarily filled her Paint and Snack Funds jar. It was debatable which she'd spent more money on, paint supplies or the snacks that were quickly being scooped up three at a time by the teens.

Of course, Frank was here, making sure the teenagers didn't act up and checking that their cups were filled with juice and not wine. I couldn't help but notice that he and Mrs. Schultz took a seat next to each other. Mrs. Schultz was always outgoing, but I knew she still missed Mr. Schultz terribly. I didn't know much about Frank, but seeing how he made her act like a schoolgirl on occasion made me root for them. I hoped this was the spark of a new chapter for her.

Sharice turned down the music and asked everyone to take their seats, leaving the high schoolers scrambling to the snack table for another last-minute bag of chips. The painting we were going to try to replicate was at the front, next to her seat: two birds beak to beak, perched on a tree branch. She said it was titled Lovebirds for the approaching Valentine's Day. Like I needed the reminder.

Even with her assurances that it was expected for every painting to have its own "unique flare," I wasn't confident how close I could come to the original. Sharice was a professional illustrator, and the decorations I made for our harvest parade float last fall demonstrated without a doubt my lack of artistic ability.

Sharice began to show us each step of the painting. I was surprised to find it rather soothing, like listening to Bob Ross without the happy trees or the iconic perm. As we went along, I started to believe maybe my painting wouldn't be so bad after all.

"Will you save a dance for us on Friday night, Lou?" I heard one of the Melon sisters ask him.

"I might not be there," Lou responded.

"But you have to go," the other sister said. "You're on the committee."

"Maybe they should be called the Cougar sisters," Ginger whispered to me.

I chuckled. Nothing wrong with that. They were about thirty years older than Lou, but I thought they could loosen him up.

"Has Baz said anything to you about the dance?" Ginger said.

"Like what?" I asked, painting the birds like Sharice instructed.

"Like . . . if he's going to ask me to go with him?"

"He hasn't asked you yet?" I was genuinely surprised. She shook her head.

I thought after we'd talked about it on Sunday that he would've asked her. I didn't want to let Ginger know we'd been talking about her, so I replied, "Maybe he's wondering if you're over Chet?"

"I've been over Chet for a while now."

"I'll be sure to let him know. If you want me to, that is."

"Sure. Thanks." She smiled at me. After a minute, she said, "I wasn't sure if you'd want me and Baz to go together."

"Why wouldn't I?"

"I know you two spend a lot of time together." She kept her eyes on her painting.

"As friends only. Trust me, there's nothing more than friendship between us." I took my brush away from the blue and yellow birds I'd painted. How did I manage to make two birds look like one green bear?

"He said the same thing. He told me you and Roman are a couple."

"We were dating but we're not a couple. Especially not now," I added under my breath.

"I don't know everything that happened on Sunday, but Chloe told me he was the reason Summer showed up late for her own wedding shower."

"I wouldn't blame it all on Roman." I was relieved Ginger brought up Chloe, so I pushed aside my annoyance with Chloe's version of events. "How well do you know Chloe? Are you a family friend?"

"Oh no. I don't think Summer or her mother would deign to be friends with me. Summer hired me to teach a private vegan baking class for a gathering she had about a year ago. Everyone else treated me like the hired help I was, but Chloe and I hit it off. She hung out in the kitchen with me while I cleaned up after class. We realized we had a lot in common, so we started getting together. She's an excellent artist, much better than me. We do a lot of plein-air painting on her property. She does wonderful paintings of their horses."

"You must be pretty close if she talked to you about what happened on Sunday."

"I called to check on her. She seems remarkably okay, but I think it's just a front. In that family, I get the feeling you always have to buck up. She's upset that the police seem to be going after Roman, though. She always liked him."

"Did she tell you anything about what happened after the shower?"

"You mean about the murder?" she whispered.

I nodded.

"Are you looking into this one too?"

We were in a room full of people, and although there was music and chatter, I still didn't want to be overheard. I raised my eyebrows and lifted my shoulder in a "what do you think?" shrug.

"She didn't tell me anything about that," she said.

"Has she ever talked about Marcos?"

"You mean the hot photographer?"

"That's the one."

"I met him once. Yowza." Ginger shook her hand as if she'd touched something hot. "She told me they hook up every so often. When she's bored, mostly. She says he always bugs her to have a real relationship, but she refuses."

"Really?" That's interesting. Marcos outright lied about that. Did he provide that alibi of her being in her art studio at the time of the murder because he wanted to be her boyfriend?

"Can you imagine turning *him* down? But it's no wonder she's written off men. When your sister steals your boyfriend, you probably need time to recover," Ginger said.

My thoughts left Marcos. "Summer stole her boyfriend? Was Chloe dating Roman first?" *What else didn't I know about Roman?*

"Not Roman. Nelson."

I almost spilled my paint as I whipped around to face Ginger. That explained the tension between the sisters. "Nelson? That changes everything."

"What do you mean? You're not going to suspect Chloe now, are you? She's the only authentic person in that family."

I knew it wouldn't get me anywhere with Ginger to tell her that I suspected her friend of murder. "No, it's just . . . it's helpful to have the pieces to the puzzle. Summer stole him from her?"

"Well, according to Chloe, she was done with him. But even if I was done with a guy, would I want my sister dating him? And then marrying him?"

"I knew something was strange with their family dynamic."

"It doesn't even seem like Chloe ought to be a Harrington. If she didn't look just like Summer, I'd think maybe she wasn't. She's so down to earth compared to her mother and sister. That's why she and I are such good friends. She's like a regular person trapped in the Harrington mansion."

"I wouldn't mind being trapped by millions of dollars," I muttered, imagining what I could do to my shop with all that money.

"You wouldn't want Olivia for your mom, though. She's very controlling."

"The grass isn't always greener, huh? I got a good vibe from Chloe too, when they were at my shop doing the cheese tasting."

"She felt terrible about Nelson punching Roman. She's the only one who would still talk to Roman after he called off the wedding."

"I get the feeling her mother still holds a grudge. Do

you think Chloe would be open to talking to me some-time about what happened at the shower?"

"If it's to help Roman, I'm sure she would. And I would too. Roman's always been super nice to me. We got pretty close when Chet and I were dating. Do you want to paint with us the day after tomorrow? It's my day off so we're painting on her lawn in the afternoon if the weather co-operates. She insisted on still having me over."

"I'd love to. Thanks. You don't think she'll mind?"

"I'll ask her." Ginger glanced at my painting, which now looked like Yoda sitting on a tree branch. "On second thought, maybe we should get together for something besides painting."

I nodded in agreement.

CHAPTER 13

I was glad to get back to work on Tuesday. In the shop's kitchenette, I diced Gala apples and spicy Jack cheese and formed an assembly line with Mrs. Schultz and Archie to prepare our day's samples. We used toothpicks to spear a rolled slice of Coppa salami, one cube of apple, and one cube of spicy Jack on each toothpick. When we were done, we each tried one so we could discuss the flavor with our customers.

"Whoo! This will wake up their taste buds," Mrs. Schultz said after trying the peppery combination.

"That's why I'm taking out"—I went over to the re-frigerated case—"the Saint-André." I showed off the white wheel like a game show hostess.

"Ooh, that French cream cheese?" Archie's eyebrows shot up.

"Triple crème. It's the seventy-five percent butter fat that makes it so soft and buttery and rich. What kind of bread did you pick up from Rise and Shine this morning?" I asked him.

"You said it would be for a mild, soft cheese, so I chose raisin bread." He took the loaf out of the paper bag.

"Perfect." I was very familiar with Rise and Shine Bakery's flavorful raisin bread. "How's Hope doing?"

Archie sliced into the bread. The crunch of the hearty crust gave way to the dense and chewy inside, dotted with plump, sweet raisins. "Just as busy as ever. She was taking classes yesterday. That's why she hasn't been around to help us decorate the hall for the dance—she's been too busy with culinary school and the bakery. She feels bad about it."

"She shouldn't. She's doing what she has to for her business. Everyone understands that," I said. It was something she hadn't quite understood when her aunt ran the business.

"That's what I told her," Archie said.

Archie was a good friend, always supportive of Hope, whether it was about her dreams for the future or her significant sadness from her past. I empathized with his trepidation about transforming their friendship into a romantic relationship. If it didn't work out, it was difficult to return to a cherished close friendship. I could tell Archie was getting closer to making that decision, though.

He cut a slice of raisin bread in half, then half again, and I slathered on the impossibly creamy cheese. It practically melted in my mouth.

"As good as the bread is, I don't even need it. This cheese is ridiculous," Mrs. Schultz said, doing a little happy dance.

"I know what you mean," I said, rolling my tongue around my mouth so my taste buds would catch every last morsel.

We all washed our hands, then Archie cut the bread into small triangles for customers to sample with the cheese.

"I wonder if Lou knows how to make flower decorations from bread or cheese," he remarked.

"I was very impressed with him yesterday," Mrs. Schultz said, as she carefully moved the spicy appetizers onto a platter via their toothpicks.

"Those flower veggies were harder to do than they looked," Archie said.

"I don't just mean those. The way he was taking time with the high school kids. He seemed to have a good rapport with them."

"To be honest, it surprised me, but it was nice to see," I agreed. "I need to ask him more about Polly, the housekeeper. The Melon sisters had some interesting tidbits to share after they went to Lou's Market yesterday morning." I relayed what the elderly sisters had told me. "It confirmed we should be focusing on the Harrington women."

"Do you think it could be like *Murder on the Orient Express*? All of them in on it together?" Mrs. Schultz considered, referring to the famous Agatha Christie book.

"I suppose anything's possible, but I don't see a common motive."

Mrs. Schultz's eyes narrowed in thought as she put the clear cloche on the platter and brought it to the sampling counter at the front of the shop. She came back to the kitchenette with a theory. "How about this for a motive? None of them wanted him in the family anymore."

"That's a good thought. But since Summer and Nelson had just gotten into another fight, it would've been the perfect excuse to call off the wedding instead of killing him, don't you think?"

"True." When Mrs. Schultz was worried or deep in thought, she rubbed the tassels of whatever scarf she was wearing, like worry beads. Today's red and pink scarf had no tassels, which didn't stop her from rubbing the scarf itself. "So my Agatha Christie theory is out?" She pulled her lips down in an exaggerated frown.

"For now."

"Summer or Chloe could've killed him in self-defense," Archie suggested. He put the rest of the loaf back in the paper bag while I finished smearing the triple crème cheese on the triangles of raisin bread.

"That pitchfork looked like more than self-defense," I said, closing my eyes to the image of Nelson's body that flashed in my mind.

Mrs. Schultz was going to rub a hole in her scarf trying to come up with a plausible theory. "You might've been right the other night when you said maybe *he* was the one who wanted to call off the wedding."

"If I'm right about it, it would point to Summer as the killer, which aligns with her setting up Roman. He told me the reason he came back to the garden shed was because Summer texted him to meet her there, but she never showed."

"So then it's probably Summer," Archie said with a nod. He seemed satisfied to leave it there.

"I would be all in with that theory, except for something I found out last night from Ginger. Did you know that Nelson dated Chloe first?"

Their mouths hung open, a satisfyingly appropriate reaction to the news.

"That changes things," Mrs. Schultz said.

"It does. She was the only one who seemed happy that Roman showed up here on Saturday night, knowing it would cause a rift between Summer and Nelson. At the shower, when she went looking for Summer, I believe she saw Nelson at the stable getting ready to do his Prince Charming act. Maybe she tried one last-ditch effort to get him to call off the wedding, but he wouldn't. He was there to declare his love again for Summer. So when Chloe found out that Summer was with Roman, she was more than happy to make sure Nelson knew it."

"But her plan worked. Summer and Nelson fought. Why would Chloe kill him?" Archie said.

"It ruined the shower, but we don't know if it ruined the engagement. If she found out it didn't, she might've snapped."

Mrs. Schultz's fingers left her scarf. "That's a much better theory than mine."

"Ginger and Chloe are getting together tomorrow and Ginger's going to ask if I can tag along. I want to hear about Chloe's relationship with Nelson straight from her."

They put the Saint-André–covered raisin bread on a second platter while I cleaned up the kitchenette.

"So you think Chloe's still in love with Nelson?" Mrs. Schultz was still digesting the new theory.

"Could be. It would certainly give her motive."

"She could've easily gone to the stable. Nobody kept track of her," Archie said.

"Marcos said he saw her in the art room, and she told him to leave. He said he left right away and went to the driveway, remembered his car wasn't there anymore, and came back in, which was when I saw him. That means there was a half hour or so from the time she drove away in the golf cart until the time Marcos saw her—plenty of time for her to have gone to the stable, killed Nelson, and come back to the house."

"It could be either sister," Mrs. Schultz said. "Be careful tomorrow."

"Ginger will be with me and she's been invited. There's no reason they'd want to hurt us."

We brought the bread platter to the sampling counter and opened the door for business, sticking Guernsey outside by the door to welcome customers. We'd fitted our cow scarecrow mascot with a red outfit for Valentine's Day, which seemed like a fun idea before I soured on love. Our first customers of the day arrived shortly after, so we put our theories on hold.

The rest of the morning was a steady stream of customers, which was a nice bonus for a Tuesday. Perhaps the dreary weather was pushing people from their outdoor pursuits into our shops. Luckily, cheese is the perfect accompaniment for any weather.

I sent Mrs. Schultz to lunch once Archie returned from his lunch break. *Sweet Dreams Are Made of Cheese* sang from my apron pocket. I was surprised to see Heath was the caller. Did he want to ask me more questions about finding Nelson's body? I strode into the kitchenette, devoid of customers, and answered.

"Willa. It's Detective Heath. I'm sorry to bother you during your workday. Do you have some time today to see me? Maybe you have a lunch break coming up?"

Was he asking me to lunch? No, he wasn't asking me to lunch . . . was he? We'd never met up outside of an investigation before. My insides felt fluttery while I considered what it might mean to have lunch with Heath.

"Willa?"

"Oh, sorry. As soon as Mrs. Schultz comes back, I'll be free," I said, brushing my fingers through my hair.

"Great. Come down to the station. I won't take up much of your time."

Come down to the station? *Sigh*. Disappointment mingled with relief. Fine, I wasn't getting lunch, but maybe I could find out some new information about the case. "Okay. I'll be there soon." I ended the call and waited for Mrs. Schultz to return while questions percolated in my head for Heath.

CHAPTER 14

Mrs. Schultz returned from her lunch break with concern on her face.

"I'm sorry I took so long," she said after I'd finished with a customer. She retrieved her apron from under the checkout counter and replaced it with her purse.

"I didn't notice you had. Is everything okay?" I asked.

"I spent most of my lunch break at the police station."

"What happened?" Archie said, joining us.

"When I left for lunch, I reached into my purse for my lipstick and realized my wallet was missing," Mrs. Schultz explained.

"Someone stole your wallet?" It concerned me to think one of our customers might've swiped her wallet. I took my small purse from under the counter to check its contents. It only held a lip balm, an emergency adhesive bandage, and a coin purse with cash, a credit card, and my driver's license. I kept my apartment key with my shop keys in a bowl, also beneath the register. Everything was accounted for. "Do you think someone was able to get behind the counter this morning and steal it?"

"I doubt it. Someone would've had to have known my purse was there to be quick enough to unzip it and steal my wallet. It may have happened last night. I keep my keys in an outer pocket, so I didn't notice whether my wallet was missing last night when I went home or when I came in this morning. The last time I saw it was yesterday after we left the hall and I stopped for a cup of coffee. Luckily, Shep was the officer who took my statement. He's so nice and went through everything with me. He and I figured that it must have happened last night at Sharice's Paint and Snack."

"Do you want to call your credit card companies right now to put a hold on your cards?"

"I only have one card and I keep it at home unless I'm going to make a big purchase. I prefer to use cash."

"I hope you didn't lose too much."

Mrs. Schultz waved it off. "It wasn't that much. It's just unnerving that someone would do that. I've never thought of Yarrow Glen as a place you have to hold tight to your purse, especially not around neighbors."

"I'm so sorry, Mrs. Schultz," I said.

"Me too," Archie said.

We brought our attention to the door when we sensed a customer walk in, but it was Lou. He was carefully holding a small container with both hands.

"Hi, Lou. What's up?" I normally got a visit from Lou only when he wanted to complain about something. Had the teenagers doing a Good Neighbor Committee task accidentally left something on his sidewalk?

He placed the container on the sample counter and stepped back. We all stared at it. It looked to be mashed potatoes under the clear plastic lid. "It's my shepherd's pie." His voice croaked a little when he added, "I made them today to sell at the market."

"Oh! Lou, that's terrific! You've started cooking again!" I said, pleasantly surprised. Last year I'd discovered that Lou had gone to culinary school later in life to

pursue his love of cooking. Unfortunately, it ended with
a bad experience, and he gave it up once again. Maybe
taking up cooking again was why he seemed a little less
irritable lately.

"Smells good," Archie said when Lou removed the lid.

He looked to Mrs. Schultz, who had stayed silent.
"What's the matter? You think it's a bad idea?" Lou asked
her.

"I'm sorry, Lou. It's a wonderful idea. I'm just a little
preoccupied right now," she answered.

"She had her wallet stolen last night at the Paint and
Snack," I explained. I hoped her reaction wouldn't dampen
his enthusiasm. It wasn't often we got to see Lou's mood
elevated from grumpy.

"Do the police have any leads?" Archie asked Mrs.
Schultz.

"Not yet," she replied.

"You think one of those high school kids took it?" Lou
asked.

"I'd hate to think so, but I was sitting right in front of
them." Mrs. Schultz shook her head, as if shaking the
thought from it. "They were just a group of bored kids
when they took some of the harvest fair float decorations
last fall. Stealing wallets isn't in the same category. I
don't want to accuse any of them of this. Especially not
Trace. Frank's been taking so much time to mentor him."

Lou's face screwed up at the mention of Frank. "What's
that kid's deal anyway? It doesn't seem like he's even
friends with the others."

"He used to be, according to Frank. Trace got a guilty
conscience when Shep was asking around about the stolen float decorations. He was the one who tipped him off.
Of course, the other kids ended up finding out that he was
the snitch."

"That explains why he's usually on his own," I said.

"I don't think any of the students are responsible for stealing my wallet. I'm sure the police will get to the bottom of it," Mrs. Schultz finished.

"I'm sure they will. It's no fun spending your lunch break at the police station, though," I said as I was about to do the same thing.

"Here, have my shepherd's pie for lunch." Lou slid it toward Mrs. Schultz, a bit of his grin returning.

"That's kind of you, but I ended up having lunch with Frank," she answered.

"Frank." Lou's rare smile vanished instantly.

"He was with Trace at Everett's bicycle shop window when I realized my wallet was missing. He offered to go to the police station with me and then he took me to lunch."

I couldn't help but notice how crestfallen Lou looked. Was it possible he had a crush on Mrs. Schultz?

"Well, I'm digging in," Archie said, taking a spork from the basket under the counter and getting more than I thought a spork could hold. "That's good!" he said through a full mouth.

"Have at it," Lou said, dejectedly, and plodded out of the shop.

"I hope I didn't hurt his feelings about the shepherd's pie," Mrs. Schultz said, watching through the front window as he trudged back to the market.

"I don't think you did." I didn't want to tell her it wasn't about the pie.

Archie held out the container to me and Mrs. Schultz. I got us each a spork and we tried it too.

"That *is* good," I said. The buttery potatoes clung to the ground lamb that must've been marinated in the rich sauce that gave it a lot of flavor.

"It really is." Mrs. Schultz agreed. "I'll be sure to tell him when I see him again."

Archie hovered over the shepherd's pie.

"Go ahead, Archie. You can finish it. It's been what? A whole hour since you've had lunch?" I joked. Twenty-year-old guys were like newborns when it came to how often they needed to be fed. "I'm going to take my lunch break. I'll be making a trip to the police station too. Detective Heath wants to talk to me."

"About what?" Archie asked through a mouthful of shepherd's pie.

"I have no idea. Maybe he wants my thoughts on Mrs. Schultz's wallet theft, but he's never asked for my opinion before. I'll fill you in when I get back." I removed my apron and left Curds & Whey.

I saw Trace on his own at Everett's bicycle shop window.

"Hi, Trace," I said as I approached. His painted F.U.N. dance announcement was just about finished. I thought the stick figures he'd begun painting were supposed to be dancers, but his painting skills were only slightly above mine. I didn't see Frank around. "You're on your own?"

"I told Mr. Coogan I don't need a babysitter. He left after he had lunch with Mrs. Schultz."

I saw a discarded Lou's Market container on the ground. "Let me guess. Shepherd's pie?"

"How'd you know? Lou brought it to me for lunch. For free!"

"You and Lou seem to be really getting along." *Especially for Lou*, I wanted to add, but didn't.

"He doesn't try to be all fatherly like Mr. Coogan, always trying to make everything into a lesson. He lets me call him Lou and never says much, and he doesn't expect me to talk when I don't want to." He screwed up his face in thought. "Actually, I think he wishes I'd shut up sometimes." Trace laughed it off and flicked his bangs out of his eyes. They fell on his eyelashes again almost immediately.

"Did you happen to notice anything last night at the Paint and Snack? Mrs. Schultz had her wallet stolen."

"Really? That stinks. Nah, I didn't see anything. Sorry."

"Okay, well, thanks anyway. Great work here. Keep it up." I lifted a hand in a goodbye as I headed up the sidewalk toward Main Street and the police station. Maybe I needed to add "finding a thief" on my to-do list.

CHAPTER 15

I walked through the austere lobby upon arriving at the security complex. Deandra, wearing even more layers than
usual because of the cooler weather, was exiting when I
reached the police station's glass security partition.

"Are you scooping A. J.?" I said with a smile. We both
knew I was kidding. It wasn't a secret that A. J. kept the
big stories all to himself, which was perfectly fine with
Deandra. In her forties, she enjoyed her longtime job at
the *Gazette* reporting on small town life. I figured she was
getting the police's traffic notes that were included in the
midweek edition.

She didn't offer a smile in return, however. "I was filing a report. Someone stole my wallet."

"Oh no. You too?"

"What do you mean? Is that why you're here?"

"No. Mrs. Schultz had hers stolen from Sharice's Paint
and Snack last night."

"Mine must've happened yesterday at the hall. I wasn't
going to report it, but A. J. said I should. It was the only
place it could've happened. I put my bag in a corner
when I started painting the mural." Deandra carried an
oversized handbag. "Wasn't Sharice doing the Paint and
Snack for the high school kids?"

"Yes, but they weren't the only ones there." I didn't want the whole town to start jumping to conclusions.

"They *are* the troublemakers," Deandra replied.

Trace was the only one I'd really interacted with, but they all seemed like a pretty nice bunch of kids. Then again, they did vandalize the parade floats, even though they considered it a prank. In that group, good judgment might be in short supply.

"I hope they catch whoever it is, and you and Mrs. Schultz get your wallets back."

"Thanks. Me too." She trudged away, looking beleaguered.

I faced the guard behind the plexiglass. I'd taken to thinking of him as Bruce because of his bald pate and his *Die Hard* demeanor. "Hello."

Expressionless, he waited for me to make a formal request.

"Willa Bauer here to see Detective Heath. He's expecting me."

He used the phone to call Heath then buzzed me into the secured area. "Down that hallway, second door on your left."

On past occasions, I was escorted to one of the interview rooms, which were down the opposite hall past an open area for patrol officers who came in and out to fill out their paperwork or help citizens file complaints. Shep was the only one there now, on a computer at one of the shared desks. He must've been hard at work on the wallet thefts. This was my first time going to Heath's office. I didn't know whether I should be honored or worried.

I walked to the hallway as directed. The first office I passed belonged to the chief of police, according to the plaque on the door, which was closed. There was a large window from the hallway looking into the office, which at the moment only afforded a view of the closed blinds. If the size of the window was any indication, it was a big office. I'd only met Chief Jeffers at press conferences, where I noticed he liked to take credit for closing the cases. Even though the mayor wouldn't come right out and say it, she obviously didn't trust him to do his job. He was smart enough to hire Heath, but maybe he just wanted to ensure he could continue to take those long lunches I'd heard whispers about.

Heath's office was the next one I came upon. His door was open. It was bigger than my office but rivaled it for its lack of space in which to move. He at least had a nice window, even if it only faced the complex's parking lot. Most of the horizontal surfaces were covered with files, although there were four filing cabinets below the windowsill. A smaller pile had migrated to his desk, where he sat ignoring his desktop computer. I recognized the biodegradable Apricot Grille take-out container opened on his desk, an uneaten cheeseburger inside. He was hunched over the desk flipping through files, his broad shoulders more pronounced without his jacket on, which was resting on the back of his chair. To look at him outside of the office, you'd think he was a neat freak, impeccably dressed and never a strand out of place on his head of thick black hair. The one time I'd been to his home, it had been just as tidy. So I found myself pleasantly surprised at the mild chaos of his office.

He looked up when I tapped on his door. He closed the folder immediately. "Willa."

I swear, he must put on a work face along with his suit and tie every morning. A crinkle at his eyes and the slightest upturn of his mouth were the only social graces he made while on the job.

He rose and came over to shuffle me away from the

door so he could close it behind me. "Thanks for coming by."

"Did I have a choice?" I sat in the seat he'd indicated for me to take. My trained olfactory nerve immediately took note of the burger, detecting bleu as the cheese it was topped with.

He went back to his own seat behind the desk. "I could've come around to the shop."

"Exactly." As much as I liked running into him in town, a police detective on official business in my shop was something I preferred to avoid.

"I don't want to take up your whole lunch break, so I'll get right to it. I heard you were in Mayor Trumbull's office yesterday," he said.

I silently regrouped—this wasn't what I thought he wanted to see me about. "Yes, I was. Is there a problem?"

He leaned back and stared at me. Why did I get the feeling he could see right through me? Those nearly black eyes of his had magical powers.

"Were you trying to get information about the murder from her?" he asked.

"No, I wasn't," I said truthfully.

"What were you doing there?"

I weighed my options. I could decline to answer, but I didn't want to damage the relationship I'd built with Heath. Lying to him wasn't a great option either, but I'd also given my word to Mayor Trumbull. I tiptoed around his question. "She asked to see me."

He allowed surprise to show on his face, one of the few times I'd seen it. "Why?"

Here was the tricky part. "I assumed because I found Nelson's body." I felt antsy in the chair as he assessed my response. "I didn't have anything new to tell her." Another truth, as she did most of the talking.

He was still silent, a tactic he'd used on me before, and one that always worked to get me to spill my guts. But I didn't feel right about betraying the mayor's trust. I had no idea where Detective Heath's loyalty lay when it came to Chief Jeffers.

"Do you have any ideas about who might've stolen the wallets?" I said so he'd leave the subject of the mayor and me behind.

"Not yet. We've been working on it."

"*Been* working? Deandra and Mrs. Schultz's weren't the firsts?"

"There have been some reports of pickpocketing and wallets or purses stolen. The credit cards weren't used, so we haven't been able to track anything down that way. These are the first thefts that have happened back-to-back. Shep's on it. He's got a knack for overhearing important information."

"Speaking of, I do have a little something to add to my statement." Time for another pivot.

"Go ahead." He took out his pad.

"The housekeeper, Polly? She told Lou that she was nervous to give you her statement."

"She wouldn't be the first. Did she give him any particular reason?"

"Not that I know of. After talking to the Melon sisters, I got the feeling that she was afraid she'd get fired for whatever information she had, which tells me she knows something incriminating. She's been working in that house for months. She might hear a lot of things she's not supposed to."

He put his pad away. "Thanks for letting us know."

The condescending tone was as apparent as the taste of bleu cheese on a burger. I gave him a look to let him know it.

"Listen, I don't have time to chase town gossip," he said by way of explaining.

"That's what Shep does sometimes. You just said so yourself."

"He's a trained police officer. Willa, we've been through this before. You don't need to insert yourself in the investigation to help another friend. We'll get to the bottom of this. We always do."

"So Roman *is* being considered a person of interest?"

"I'm sure you know he doesn't have an alibi."

"Alibis aren't everything. You've said so yourself."

"I have to do this the right way," he reminded me. "Trust me, okay?"

I was frustrated he wouldn't give me anything, but I did trust him. "Do what you have to do."

His brows knit in confusion—I didn't normally give in so easily and it must've thrown him.

I left his office with a bad feeling in my stomach. Maybe I just needed some lunch. A burger with bleu cheese sounded pretty darn good.

I walked down the hallway and rounded the corner on my way to leave the police department's secured area. Maybe I should talk to Shep about Polly. He was more likely to take my hunch seriously.

I suddenly realized Bruce the security guard was staring at me. My contemplation had frozen me in front of the door.

"It's not locked from this side," he said. "You can go through."

"Oh, I know. I just realized I need to see Officer Shepherd about something." I turned and headed to the common area, but he was no longer at the desk. A female officer was getting coffee in the back.

"Can I help you?" she said.

"Did Shep leave?"

"No. He went to see Detective Heath. He'll probably be back in a minute."

"Is it okay if I wait here for him?"

"Sure." She took her coffee mug to one of the desks and concentrated on the computer screen in front of her.

I wondered if he was helping Heath look through any of those case files. I looked back at the officer to see if she was watching me. She was hidden behind her large computer screen. I stood next to the desk and casually glanced around. Uh-oh, there was a camera hanging in the corner by the ceiling. Bruce was probably watching me on his monitor at this very moment. Drats.

I went to sit in the chair beside the desk to wait like a good citizen when I noticed a pad plain as day on the desk. In messy but, thankfully, large handwriting, was written:

Has life insurance policy and inheritance!!

Shep found a motive I hadn't considered. Is that what he went to see Heath about? I left Shep's desk and strode down the hall toward Heath's office.

My pace slowed as I neared it. There was no way they'd share this information with me. I had to find a way to get it for myself. Shep's voice carried from inside Heath's office.

"So Nelson's inheritance goes to her?" Detective Heath was saying.

"Yes. And she also had a life insurance policy taken out on him," Shep said.

Who? I strained to hear a name.

"That puts a new person at the top of our suspect list, doesn't it?" Heath said.

"Yes, sir. Should we call her in for further questioning?"

Heath paused for a few moments. "Yes. Ask her to come in. Don't give anything away. I want to gauge her reaction when I tell her. We need to handle this carefully."

"You got it," Shep replied.

I sensed their conversation was over, so I skittered down the hall. I looked over my shoulder as I turned the corner and saw Shep exiting the office. I'd left just in time. I hurried past Bruce out of the secured area and continued out of the complex.

Who had inherited from Nelson? Had he already put Summer in his will? Why would that be a motive? The Harringtons had more money than Nelson Trumbull. Or did they? Roman told me how Olivia's mother-in-law helped the Masseys for only a small stake in the company when they could've taken control of it. Was it possible she had been too generous with their money? Had she made some bad financial decisions when Alzheimer's began to set in? Did buying *All Things Sonoma* put them in the red? Marcos said Olivia Harrington was always looking for men with money for her daughters. Maybe they needed this marriage. If Nelson *had* called off the wedding, they'd need to kill him quickly before he changed his will.

I wanted to stick around to see who came in for that interview with Heath, but I had to grab lunch and get back to the shop. I didn't have time for a stakeout, but I knew who might.

I walked up Main Street, past Ron's Old Fashioned Service Station, the post office, and the library to cross Pleasant Avenue. The aroma of grilled beef awoke my stomach as I hit Apricot Grille on the corner. It only worsened as I continued down the street where the Let's Talk Tacos truck was parked.

I was just about to cross the street to the *Gazette*

building when I heard someone shout my name. It was A. J., walking over from the taco truck in the parking lot. His satchel was slung crosswise over his Salvation Army jacket. I eyed the two street tacos nestled together in a paperboard food tray in his hands, spicy shredded meat overflowing the soft corn tortillas with guacamole and pico de gallo atop.

"I was just coming to find you," I said.

"You got something? What's up?" His eyes sparkled with anticipation.

I steered him across the street in front of the *Gazette* building to avoid the stream of customers walking to and from the taco truck. I told him what I'd overheard in Heath's office.

"What are you doing *here*? You should be watching the security complex to see who goes in!" He started down the sidewalk toward the station.

"If it's Summer, it'll take her a while to get here. I don't even know if she's going to come in today." I kept up with his quick strides. "What do you know about the Harringtons' finances?"

"I haven't looked into it, but I will now."

We reached the light where we had to wait to cross.

"I have to get back to the shop," I said.

"Fine, I'll go. I'll wait it out in the lobby." He shoved half a taco in his mouth.

"You won't have time to eat both before you get there. How about giving your *sidekick* one of those?"

He sighed and reluctantly handed one over. "Consider it payment for the information. I'll text you when I see who comes in."

The pedestrian signal gave us the okay to walk across the street and we parted at the corner. I was looking forward to proving to Mayor Trumbull that she was wrong about Detective Heath. He wasn't afraid to go after the Harringtons. If this was evidence against Summer, he was prepared to use it against her.

CHAPTER 16

I walked down the block back to Curds & Whey and happily ate my street taco—pork carnitas was the delicious mystery meat layered underneath the guac and pico. Baz's hulking pickup truck stood out in one of the diagonal spaces in front of Everett's bicycle shop. It looked like Trace had packed up and gone—his paints were no longer on the sidewalk. Lights were on in Everett's shop, the first time I'd seen signs of life there in weeks. Spotting Baz and Everett inside, I stopped in the threshold of the open doorway to say hello and was greeted by a friendly dog with a reddish-tan coat. His floppy ears perked up as he stuck his black muzzle against my thigh and looked at me with soulful eyes. I melted on the spot.

"Oh my gosh! Hello!" I said, petting his head.

"Hey, neighbor. I hope you don't mind George. He loves everybody," Everett said.

"Of course I don't mind George," I told him. I crouched to George's level, "I love you too, George. Yes, I do."

I scrunched his ears, and his nose burrowed in my hands, undoubtedly smelling the lingering aroma of carnitas. A couple of licks told him there was nothing there, so he left me and trotted between Everett and Baz, our bonding moment over just like that.

I stood. "Are you already his favorite, Baz?"

Baz gave George firm pats on his side. The last dog we temporarily took care of, Buttercup, fell in love with Baz quickly. Although Baz would deny it, it was obvious the feeling had been mutual. Like a proud uncle, he occasionally showed me photos of Buttercup, a.k.a. Bruiser, that his current owner texted him.

George did a three-sixty and slunk to the floor.

"What kind of dog is he?" I asked Everett. He had long fur, small, floppy ears, and a long snout.

"I got him at a rescue a few years ago, so I'm not certain. We think a mix of golden retriever and German shepherd, maybe something else in there. He loves to go hiking or run beside me when I'm cycling, but he's also up for vegging out in my apartment. He's going to love hanging out with me in the shop so much better than staying home by himself all day."

Hiking and biking. This is why I have a fish.

George seemed to understand what Everett said—he swished his long tail happily across the floor, sweeping away the light layer of construction dust underneath it.

"I'm happy for both of you." I surveyed the shop. I hadn't been inside since Everett had started the renovation. They'd made a lot of progress. I expected it to be more utilitarian, but he'd obviously spent a lot of time decorating to set an ambiance of nature. One wall was white-painted brick overlaid with a wood mural of the ridgeline of the Sonoma Valley mountains.

"Cool, huh?" Everett said.

"Very. I love it. You've managed to bring the feel of the outdoors in."

"Cycling and the outdoors go hand in hand, so I needed to replicate that in my shop. That's a custom wall, but it was worth what I paid the artist for it. I'll set up the bicycles in front of it."

"That accent wall is striking too," I said, referring to the opposite wall made up of horizontal strips of wood from floor to ceiling, which was higher than mine by about eight feet.

"That was Baz's idea. It's not just a pretty wall. Those are slats to hang our items from—wheels, helmets, bike locks, things like that."

I nodded, impressed. "Clever."

"I need Baz here to help me figure out the best way to suspend a platform from the ceiling so we can display some vintage bicycles." Everett became more animated as he spoke about his shop.

"Like Mrs. Schultz's. She'll be happy to hear it."

"That might be a tall order. It can get complicated," Baz said.

"I know, but I want to be more than your average bike shop," Everett said. "If it costs a little more, so be it."

"I'm here to help, but with these old buildings, there's a surprise around every corner," Baz said.

"Don't I know it. I've already run into some doozies," Everett lamented.

I could relate. "I remember all too well. I was so naïve, I thought I could do the whole renovation while I was still working in another state. If people think long-distance romances are hard, try to have a long-distance relationship with your contractor. I wish I knew Baz back then."

"I can't do it all, but I can troubleshoot," Baz said, humbly.

"Well, I'm glad we both kept going with our shops, despite the obstacles. It's worth it," I said to Everett.

George thumped his tail on the floor. He obviously agreed.

"We have to keep going, don't we? Nelson's death showed me we don't have as much time as we think we do," Everett replied.

"I'm really sorry about your cousin. You were set to be his best man. You two must've been close."

Everett stuck his hands in his jeans pockets and let out a big sigh before answering. "The socially acceptable answer would be yes, right? But in reality, we weren't. My mom and uncle weren't close, so I only saw Nelson maybe once or twice growing up. It wasn't until after his parents died that mom wanted to be a better aunt to him. He leaned on us at first, but with all that money he inherited, we were in different brackets, had different responsibilities. I couldn't keep up with the stuff he was doing. I was working five days a week while he was playing every day. He picked me as his best man because I'm the only relative who fit the bill. I think my mom pushed him into it."

"You were a good best man—you helped him plan that surprise for Summer."

"He planned it on his own, but he wanted me to help him execute it. I thought it was a good idea after the way he acted at your shop. That's what he was like, though. He liked the drama of the big gesture."

"What about afterward? Was he still upset with Summer? Did he want to call off the wedding?"

He crouched next to George and focused on stroking his silky fur. "I wouldn't know. I didn't go after him."

"But Chloe may have. Right?"

He stood. "How would I know?"

"She was the one who left in the golf cart," Baz said. Everett's discomfort was obvious. Like his mother,

Mayor Trumbull, he must've known better than to publicly point the finger at any of the Harringtons, even in conjecture. I resisted asking any more questions about Chloe or Summer, but there was a false alibi he could shed light on—his own. I knew he was supposedly in the driveway to intercept the guests, but neither Baz nor I saw him there.

I couldn't come right out and ask him where he was at the time of his cousin's murder, so I disguised my question. "Maybe there were more people on the property at the time of the murder than we thought. Did you turn any of the guests away after the shower was called off?"

"My mother found the guest list, so we were in the study making phone calls. She thought it was better to head them off that way."

Well, he didn't lie about being in the driveway when he wasn't. That was a checkmark in his favor. If A. J. could confirm that Summer inherited Nelson's fortune, it was looking like my initial instinct was right and Summer was the culprit.

George lifted his chin from his paws and scrambled to get his feet underneath him to hurry to the door, where Ginger had just appeared.

"Mind if I come in?" she asked. She wore a Read More Bookstore long-sleeved tee knotted at the waist above her skinny jeans, and carried a drink in a clear plastic cup.

"Course not," Everett replied with a wide grin. "You're always welcome. That's George."

She greeted the furry welcomer with pats until the dog was sufficiently sated. He returned to his post and plopped down on Everett's steel-toed boots.

Ginger's gaze swept the room. "This is amazing."

It hadn't seemed possible, but Everett's smile grew even wider. "You think so?"

"I'm so jealous. Having this space, knowing it's all yours . . ." Ginger had her sights set on opening her own vegan café someday.

"You'll get there too. Your cakes and smoothies deserve their own place," he told her.

"Thanks, Everett." She touched his arm, which seemed to light him up.

Baz must've noticed too. "Did you get my text?" he asked her.

"I did. Thanks for apologizing for being a no-show last night."

"I think that was my fault," Everett interjected. "Baz was helping me out in here."

Guys always stuck together, even when they liked the same girl.

"I spotted Baz's truck, so I brought one of my new turmeric smoothies for him." She gestured to the drink in her hand, a thick mustard-colored one. "I should've thought to bring enough for everyone."

"Don't feel bad," Baz said quickly. "I'll give up mine today. Let Everett try it."

"Are you sure?" she asked.

"It's not fair that I get to try them all. Go ahead, Everett," Baz said.

I pressed my lips together to keep from laughing. I knew Baz disliked Ginger's healthy drinks but didn't have the heart to say so.

"Well then . . . here you go." She tentatively handed the drink to Everett.

"Thanks," Everett replied. Unlike Baz, he appeared genuinely pleased about trying her new smoothie.

"I better get back to the café. Oh, Willa, since you're here—Chloe was excited to have you join us tomorrow, but I told her painting might not be your thing."

"Thanks. I appreciate that."

"So she wants to do horseback riding instead. Have you ever ridden?"

Horseback riding? "Uh, yeah, once."

"Oh good."

Not so good. It was during my days working at a cheese shop near the coast of Washington. My blind date must've watched too many episodes of *The Bachelor*, because he thought it would be a fun first date to go horseback riding on the beach. I didn't want to be a party pooper, so I agreed to it. The horse I'd gotten was feeling stubborn and decided to go his own way, which looked like it was going to be straight into the ocean. I got off as fast as possible, which was a bad idea. I ended up on my backside in the sand. My date tried to help me up when a wave washed over us. It was not a *From Here to Eternity* moment. The only time I heard from him again was when he sent me half the bill for having had the wet sand cleaned out of his car.

"So let's plan for two o'clock?" Ginger said, pulling me out of the embarrassing memory.

I considered nixing the invitation, but it would give me an excuse to go into the stable again, which might allow me to peek around. I'd been in too much shock to take in anything important I might've seen the last time I was there.

"Sure. Two o'clock tomorrow," I answered. "And thanks, Ginger."

"You bet."

Everett thanked Ginger again for the drink and Baz walked her out. I heard him start to apologize again for missing last night's Paint and Snack as they exited the shop.

My phone dinged a notification. I'd turned the volume

all the way up after talking with A. J. so I wouldn't miss it if he had info to share. Sure enough, it was a text from him. I tapped it.

She just came in, he wrote cryptically.

That was just like A. J. to text me like he's crafting one of his stories, complete with suspense.

Who is it?? Summer? I texted back impatiently.

The dots seemed to gallop forever indicating he was typing until they suddenly transformed into letters for his reply: *Mayor Trumbull.*

CHAPTER 17

I immediately pressed the phone to my chest, even though Everett wasn't near enough to it to see his mother's name. My face got hot, as if *I* were the one guilty of something.

"Is everything okay?" Everett asked. I guess I wasn't good at hiding my feelings.

"Yeah, yeah. I just need to get back to the shop." I turned to leave when Baz came back in. "When you get a chance, I'll need your help with that uh, that thing at the shop," I said to him.

"What thing?" he asked. His thoughts must've still been in *Gingerland*. He didn't pick up on my cue.

"You know, that *thing*." I widened my eyes at him and stared him down.

"Ohh. You mean the toilet thing," he played along. "Sure. I think we were just about finished here anyway." Baz looked to Everett for confirmation.

"Yeah, we know where we're at with this. I'll see you here tomorrow," Everett said.

"Glad you're almost up and running, Everett," I said, as Baz and I headed toward the door.

"You mean up and biking?" Everett replied.

"What?"

"It was a joke. Biking, not running? It's a bike shop . . ."

"Ohh." I laughed too loudly.

George waylaid us before we could get out the door, seeing us off in a friendly fashion.

We hurriedly left the bicycle shop and crossed the alley to Curds & Whey.

"What's up?" Baz said.

I didn't want to chance being overheard by shoppers strolling the sidewalk. "Let's wait until we get into the shop."

There were several customers in Curds & Whey when we got there, so Baz stuck around and helped himself to the remaining fresh raisin bread and triple créme cheese Mrs. Schultz had recently replenished. A. J. and I agreed via text to meet up tomorrow. I knew he'd be following this lead like a bloodhound who'd just been given a smelly shoe.

It was almost a half hour before the shop cleared of customers and we gathered around the sampling counter so I could share what had transpired.

"Wow. Just when we had it narrowed down to one of the Harrington sisters, it looks like Mayor Trumbull's our prime suspect now," Archie said after hearing the news.

"If she needed the money," Mrs. Schultz said, not completely convinced.

"A fortune's a fortune, whether you need it or not," Archie said.

"How much are we talking about?" Baz asked.

"I don't know any details yet," I replied, as my brain filled with questions.

"Do you think that's why she asked you to investigate? So that you might lead Detective Heath to suspect the Harringtons?" Mrs. Schultz was back to rubbing her scarf. It was a good question.

"She did say to give Detective Heath whatever information I came across," I recalled.

"She could've been hedging her bets that he'd listen to you since you solved the last two murders. This puts you in a tough spot," Baz said.

"I can only imagine how Heath feels. He had to interrogate Mayor Trumbull!" I felt second-hand anxiousness for him. "I'm not sure what to do now. How am I supposed to double-cross the mayor?"

Mrs. Schultz patted my arm. "Don't get ahead of yourself. It could be a coincidence. It's possible the mayor was just being kept apprised of the investigation."

"That's a valid point." Okay, I didn't feel quite so panicky. "How will we know? Heath's not going to tell me."

"What about A. J. and all his supposed sources?" Baz said.

"I'm sure he's making phone calls as we speak. I don't know how much he'll share with me, though. He's usually only chatty when he wants something from me in return. He comes through sometimes, but I don't like relying on him."

"Why don't we do it ourselves?" Archie suggested.

"Yeah, but how?" My panic was starting to rise again.

"That little thing called the World Wide Web?" Baz said sarcastically.

I wished I had a comeback, but he was right. I'd looked up some articles on the Harringtons, but I didn't even think to research Mayor Trumbull's background.

"That's what we should do. Tonight!" Archie proclaimed.

"You guys must have better things to do after work," I said.

"Not me," Archie was quick to respond.

"Me neither," Mrs. Schultz added. "We'd like to help."

"I'm in too! On one condition, though," Baz said.

"What's that?" I asked.

"F-O-O-D."

I laughed. "You got it. I'll whip us up something," I promised.

"Can you make it bigger than bite-sized? My fingers are too big for this sample stuff you got here."

"It appears your fingers did just fine today," I ribbed, plainly staring at the empty sampling platter.

With assurances he'd be fed well, Baz left to make one more house call.

I mentally sifted through the catalogue of easy cheesy meals in my memory and came up with one everyone would be sure to love. It called for a quick trip to the market, which was a convenient excuse to speak to Lou about Polly, the Harringtons' housekeeper. If she'd said something to him that he hadn't relayed to the Melon sisters, I wanted to know about it. Maybe he could shed some more light on the Harringtons. I had to admit to myself that I wasn't being objective. I wanted to discover something that would return suspicion to them and not Mayor Trumbull.

Customers began to trickle in again, so it wasn't until later that afternoon that I stopped into Lou's Market two doors down. Before going in search of Lou, I put macaroni and a pint of cream in my basket for tonight's dinner. Salad fixings were the final items on the list. I found Lou's dad, Cyrus, hunched over the lettuce with a young male employee, both sporting green market aprons.

"Hello, Cyrus," I said.

Cyrus turned to me with a smile already on his weathered face. The employee turned too. To my surprise, it was Trace.

"Trace! You're working here?" I asked.

"Lou just hired me this afternoon part-time." Trace sounded pleased about it.

"That's great. And I see you have the top dog as a mentor." I gestured to Cyrus.

"Who knew lettuce had all these different names?" Trace said, scanning the greens.

Cyrus clapped a wrinkled hand on Trace's shoulder. "We'll get you there, son."

I imagined Lou as a young man, like Trace, being taught the ropes by Cyrus. I'd witnessed Cyrus being consistently patient and kind to his staff and to his customers, which had garnered him a loyal clientele forty-five years on, even amid grocery superstore competitors. His heart attack may have slowed him down physically, but it hadn't slackened his enthusiasm for his market. Lou had inherited the same commitment to the market, but not his dad's charming manner—he was polite but all business. Perhaps having his future planned out for him at thirteen years old by his dad was the reason he never had that same spark.

"What can I help you with, Willa?" Cyrus asked.

I was about to say *lettuce* but now I reconsidered. "How about a spring mix?"

"We just bagged some fresh this afternoon." He waited for Trace to find the correct bunch.

Trace looked them over several times before finally picking the bag of spring mix. "This one?"

"Quick learner," Cyrus boasted.

Trace placed it in my basket with a proud smile.

"Thanks. I was also looking for Lou," I said.

"Look no further," Cyrus replied.

"You can go home now, Trace. It'll be dark soon," Lou said from behind me.

"Okay. Thanks again for the job," Trace said to Lou.

"Don't make me come to regret it," Lou replied in his usual gruff manner.

"You won't." Trace pointed to each of the lettuces in the refrigerated case. "Romaine, endive, iceberg, green leaf."

"Good man," Cyrus said.

He and Trace fist-bumped. Trace pivoted to Lou, fist still in the air, but Lou left him hanging. Trace opened his palm. "High five?"

Still no reaction from Lou.

It didn't seem to bother Trace. "All right. See you to-morrow." He left with a smile, untying his apron as he went.

A flirty voice called, "Good afternoon, Cyrus." It was Daisy Melon, wearing a pink track suit with a porcelain daisy pin on the lapel. The short straps of her daisy-embellished yellow purse hung from her forearm as she used both hands to carry a market basket in front of her. Her sister Gemma, in an identical track suit—hers peach and sans daisy pin—shuffled beside Daisy.

"If it isn't the prettiest sisters in Yarrow Glen," Cyrus replied.

"Do you mind holding my basket, Cyrus? It's getting a little heavy for me," Daisy inquired sweetly.

"For heaven's sake, Daisy, it's got two yogurts in it." Gemma grabbed the basket's handles from her sister's outstretched hand.

Daisy's smile faltered. "I plan to get some bacon," she told her sister.

"Let me accompany you, just in case," Cyrus said.

Daisy preened and shot Gemma a look. Gemma rolled her eyes and followed them to the other side of the market.

"Daisy's got game," I said to Lou.

"It's a lost cause with Dad. It's been almost twenty years since Mom's been gone and he hasn't been with anybody else."

"Well, maybe it's time," I replied gently.

"Even when he was with her, she'd always say the market was his mistress."

I shifted the conversation from Cyrus's personal life to why I wanted to see Lou. "Last time I saw the Melon sisters, they said you'd spoken with Polly and that she was scared to talk to the police?"

"Yeah. So?"

"Was there a particular reason why? Does she know something about the Harringtons that could be incriminating?"

"I don't know. All she said was she was nervous. She's afraid to get fired. I told her it was natural to be nervous and that she'd have nothing to worry about if she didn't talk too much."

"You told her not to say anything to the police?"

"No, I didn't tell her not to say anything, I told her not to say too much."

This was par for the course for Lou. He hadn't learned his lesson from the other times he'd kept information from the police. "Not saying too much could still mean Detective Heath doesn't get the information he needs from her. Are you sure she didn't tell you anything?"

He shook his head. "Nope."

"Would you tell me if she had?"

He laughed, and for a split second I saw the resemblance to his father. He laughed again and walked off without answering my question. I guess I wasn't getting anything from Lou but my dinner ingredients.

CHAPTER 18

Later that evening, with the Closed sign on the door and the front shop lights dimmed, Archie, Mrs. Schultz, Baz, and I retreated to Curds & Whey's kitchenette.

I tasked Mrs. Schultz with bringing me Monterey Jack, Gruyère, cheddar, and parmesan for the easy cheesy dinner I planned. Archie went to my office to retrieve my laptop. I kept Baz busy assembling the salad so he wouldn't see that the macaroni and cheese cups I was making had more than just cheddar in them.

"We ought to have a name," Archie proclaimed when he returned with my laptop.

"It's in big letters above the door, dude," Baz said, laughing.

"Ha, ha," Archie said, not impressed with Baz's joke. "I mean a name for us when we're doing this, being a detective team."

Mrs. Schultz clapped her hands excitedly. "I think it's a great idea! Every investigative team needs a name. It *is* our third case. We might as well make it official."

"I thought you said we were the Scooby Gang. I was just about to trade in my pickup for my own Mystery Machine," Baz said.

"Basil." Mrs. Schultz's teacher stare hadn't lost its bite in retirement.

"Ruh roh." Baz handed off the salad bowl to Mrs. Schultz and shrank down on the bench next to Archie, who was highly amused.

"Does anyone have a name in mind?" I asked.

They looked at one another, each one waiting for someone else to come up with a suggestion.

"It can't be too obvious in case someone overhears. We want to keep ourselves undercover," Archie said.

While we thought about it, I retrieved the rest of the Saint-André triple créme we'd used that morning. "How about Team Cheese?" I suggested.

"Team Cheese! I love it," Mrs. Schultz declared.

"That's perfect," Archie said.

"I'm actually into that," Baz said, nodding.

I refused any more help so I could keep my mind occupied preparing dinner. Mrs. Schultz remained standing at the island while Archie and Baz started their search for information about Mayor Trumbull's finances.

I had a hard time shaking the dread that crept in with this latest discovery. The thought that Mayor Trumbull might be the culprit left me feeling like I was walking too close to a steep cliff. I was excited to have my friends' help tonight, but I was afraid what we might find could mean there was no way out but down.

As the macaroni was boiling, I grated my three cheeses. After making a roux, I stirred in milk, sour cream, dried mustard, and my Saint-André. Then I added my grated cheeses, watching them melt and meld with the sauce, creating a creamy wonderland with a gentle kick from the addition of the dried mustard.

"Find anything?" I asked.

"If you look up any of their names, what happened at the shower is the top story," Baz said as Archie continued to search the internet.

"Olivia Harrington's not going to like that. Anything we don't already know?"

"Nope. Surprisingly detailed, though. Somebody at the shower blabbed," Baz answered.

Archie looked up from the laptop. "There's nothing specific about Nelson's inheritance. A couple of articles estimated his dad's net worth at around twelve million."

"Wow. Making bird sculptures? Cheese is never going to make me that much," I lamented.

"How about cheese sculpting? It could be a niche field," Mrs. Schultz said.

"Very niche." I drained the al dente pasta, returned it to the pot, and poured the creamy cheese sauce over it. My final secret: I grabbed a container of cheddar cheese curds and mixed them in.

"That's twelve million dollars' worth of motive depending on how much Nelson blew through. He'd been living off it for years, right?" Baz said.

I nodded. Almost ten years, by my estimation. I scooped the cheesy mixture into ramekins and topped each with a mix of panko breadcrumbs and aged parmesan. I stuck them in the oven to bake.

Archie continued to sift through more news articles. "Did you know Mayor Trumbull is divorced?"

Mrs. Schultz was rewrapping the unused portions of cheese. "I remember reading about it at the time. It happened during her last reelection campaign."

"Ooh, bad timing," I said.

"Her opponent tried to make something of it, if I recall."

I couldn't deny that shadows of a motive were starting

to form. "Was there a scandal involved? If she divorced because of an affair or something, she could've paid off a blackmailer, which would leave her needing money," I shared.

"Let's find out," Archie said, tapping at the keyboard again.

They researched while I checked the mac 'n cheese cups. Almost done. I switched the oven to *broil*. "Dinner's almost ready."

Mrs. Schultz dressed the salad with a light vinaigrette and placed it on the table.

"Anything?" I asked.

"Here's something from a blogger," Archie called out.

My focus left the oven. "What does it say?"

Archie summarized: "According to the blogger, it was her husband, Oscar Strathmore, who had the affair. It says a quickie divorce ensued."

"That doesn't align with a motive for needing money."

"And a 'quickie divorce' means she didn't spend all her money on attorneys either," Mrs. Schultz added.

"Then those photos we saw before don't make sense," Baz said.

Archie nodded.

"What photos?" I asked, confused.

Baz pulled the laptop in front of him, tapped a few keys, and turned it to face me. I sat down at the table and peered at the screen.

There was a real estate photo of a substantial home with thumbnail pictures of multiple rooms and a swimming pool. It was listed for more than three million dollars.

"What am I looking at?" I asked.

"This is the house Mayor Trumbull and her husband sold when they got divorced," Baz answered.

"She's got plenty of money by the looks of it then, huh?" I said, kind of relieved.

"She *had* plenty of money. *This* is her house now." Baz clicked another window.

A ranch house cottage came on screen. Decidedly cute, but exceedingly less grand than the last house.

"If he's the one who had an affair, why does it look like she came out of the divorce without a dime?" Baz said.

"That's if that lone blogger is to be believed," Mrs. Schultz added.

"Even if there's no affair, why the vast difference in financial circumstances?" I wondered.

"A prenup?" Baz threw out.

"The mayor came from humble circumstances. I remember that about her, because it was one of the reasons I voted for her. She didn't have anything handed to her," Mrs. Schultz said.

"I remember that too," Baz agreed.

"She mentioned to me that she had a baby in college and raised him on her own, so maybe she and her ex Oscar Strathmore weren't married for that long. Or he's just a bad guy," I said.

Archie started sniffing emphatically. "I smell—"

"A rat?" Baz finished.

"My mac 'n cheese!" I cried, racing to the oven. I pulled the ramekins out just in the nick of time. A few more seconds and the breadcrumbs would've burned. I was relieved to see a warm brown, crunchy layer atop the creamy, cheesy macaroni.

Baz came over to the counter, concerned. "Did you save dinner?"

"Yes."

With potholders, I put each ramekin on a plate and warned everybody not to touch them while eating.

"Did you make them individual like this so I wouldn't eat your portion?" Baz asked while he brought the plates to the table.

I laughed. "No, it sets up faster in the oven. I made two for everybody."

"You can have mine too, Basil. I think I'll stick with the salad tonight." Mrs. Schultz passed her plate to Baz.

"Oh, I'm sorry, Mrs. Schultz. I should've asked if everyone wanted mac 'n cheese." Now that everyone was served, I joined them at the table.

"No, no. I'm sure it's delicious. I'm just watching my figure."

She got up to get a bowl for her salad while Baz, Archie, and I looked at one another, eyebrows raised and smiles playing on our lips. Could this have anything to do with Frank?

I cracked open my mac 'n cheese with my fork to let the steam escape. Things were worse than ever with me and Roman, so I planned to eat my entire two ramekins' worth.

Archie tapped at the keyboard while his cooled. He read the screen. "This old *Gazette* article says they were only married thirteen years." He pushed the screen so Mrs. Schultz and I could see it and tucked into his dinner.

"Lucky thirteen," Baz said. He pulled up a forkful from his own ramekin. Cheese clung to the macaroni, stringing like a zipline from ramekin to fork. "Ooh, cheesy!" He blew on it.

"That's thanks to the curds." I happily gave up my secret as I studied the computer screen.

Mrs. Schultz summarized the article aloud. "Just like you said, Willa, she had a baby her junior year of college. That would be Everett." She continued to scan the article.

"She never married the father and raised Everett on her own. And she finished college on time."

Archie looked shell-shocked. "She was my age with a baby? I can't imagine."

"It happens. It's impressive, all that she's done as a single mother," Mrs. Schultz remarked.

"Oscar Strathmore must've come into the marriage with money and a prenup," I said. "That explains her circumstances."

"And it could mean she had a motive if she was the one who inherited from Nelson," Baz reminded me.

"Killing her nephew for his money?" Mrs. Schultz shook her head. "I don't know. It doesn't seem to fit with Mayor Trumbull's character. Her son is in his thirties and making his own way too, from the looks of it. After getting this far, why would she succumb to greed?"

"It could've been a coincidence that she showed up at the police station when she did." I was still holding tight to my theory that Summer was the murderer. "What do you guys think? Baz?"

"You could be right. There are plenty of rich people like the Harringtons who'd kill to stay rich," Baz said.

Archie filled his fork with macaroni. "Does that mean our first official Team Cheese meeting is a bust?"

"No way. These mac 'n cheese cups are the bomb," Baz kidded, going in for his second ramekin. "Are you sure you don't want yours, Mrs. Schultz?"

"Dig in, Basil." Mrs. Schultz said, scraping the bottom of the salad bowl for her third helping.

"I wouldn't say it was a bust, Archie. We know more than we did before. Eventually all the information will come together and lead us to our answers," I told him.

"You're going into the bear's den tomorrow, aren't you? That should yield something," Baz said.

I chuckled. "Yes, I'm going to the Harringtons. I don't know if I'll find out anything more about Summer, but I've got some questions for Chloe too. Everyone saw her take the golf cart around the back of the house. I want to find out once and for all if she went after Nelson."

"You think she'll tell you the truth?" Mrs. Schultz asked.

"Probably not, but maybe I can bluff my way to learning the truth."

"How are you going to do that?" Archie asked.

"Very carefully."

If Mayor Trumbull was to be believed, I didn't want to get on the bad side of the Harringtons.

CHAPTER 19

The next day at work passed quickly. I gave Archie and Mrs. Schultz extra time on their lunch breaks to allay my guilt for playing hooky in the middle of the afternoon to go to Chloe's. They assured me they were eager for me to go and further Team Cheese's investigation. I felt comfortable leaving them in charge of the shop, since they were both incredible cheesemonger students.

Before I knew it, Ginger's car had pulled into one of the spaces out front.

"I'll have my phone with me, so text or call whenever you need to," I told them. I scanned the shop one last time to ensure I'd done everything I could to lighten their load while I was gone.

"Yes, Mom," Archie replied with a glimmer in his eye.

"Yeah, yeah, okay. Thanks again, you two. I hope to be back to help you close."

I hurriedly dispensed with my apron and left. I waved to Ginger and hopped in her car. Her hair was pulled back in a ponytail and she was dressed in boots over her jeans, a long-sleeved shirt, and a cute vest jacket. She looked casual and chic. Once again, I was reminded of how maybe I should look in the mirror occasionally. My horseback riding wardrobe—switching from khakis to jeans—wasn't on par. I told myself I'd be able to look like that if I'd had the day off too, but who was I kidding? I ran my fingers through my hair, as if that would make up for the difference.

"Thanks again for letting me tag along," I said as we pulled out of the parking spot.

"Anything to help. Are you sure you're okay riding a horse in tennis shoes?" She glanced at me skeptically.

"The last time I rode, I was barefoot on a beach, so this is a step up, right?" It wasn't like I had a riding outfit hanging in my closet waiting for just such an occasion.

I tried to think of something to talk to Ginger about while we drove to Chloe's. Baz was the friend we had in common, but neither of us brought him up. I got the feeling she still wasn't completely comfortable with my friendship with him. Unfortunately, after yesterday's discovery that Mayor Trumbull might be a suspect, I forgot to ask him about taking Ginger to the dance. We made small talk about the weather, then fell into more silence.

"Oh, I love this song," I said, unable to hear it, but hoping she'd turn up the radio to give us something to do besides talk.

It worked like a charm. She turned the radio up, only to have it be an insurance jingle.

"It's catchy," I said, trying to save face.

A series of songs came on directly afterward, putting us out of our awkward misery for the rest of the car ride.

It was an odd feeling pulling up to the Harrington mansion as a guest rather than as the cheese lady. I doubted I'd be welcomed with open arms by Olivia. Luckily it was Chloe who answered the door. She looked older with her hair pulled back and her ponytail tucked under itself. The way she and Summer acted and the fact that they still lived at home made me sometimes forget they were almost thirty, only a handful of years younger than me. She greeted me like an old friend and not the person who found her sister's fiancé's body in their horse stable three days prior. I was glad for it, and that it wasn't Officer Lurch leading me through the foyer again.

We passed the grand staircase and a room I hadn't noticed before with a beautiful view of the side garden. When we reached the living room where we'd all sat waiting to be interviewed by the police, I considered that the house had more rooms than I'd realized. It made me rethink my suspicions when I didn't see anyone in the house during the time of Nelson's murder. The study was beyond the curved staircase that spanned the living room. Its door was closed. I hadn't even noticed the room until Heath used it to conduct interviews. If Everett and Mayor Trumbull had been in there making phone calls like Everett said, it was very possible I wouldn't have heard them. It was also plausible that Summer and Olivia had been upstairs without being seen. I couldn't rule out anyone's alibi.

"Are you ready to go riding?" Chloe asked. "We'll take the cart to the stable."

I belatedly noticed she was also dressed in riding boots identical to Ginger's. I hadn't even brought a jacket. Maybe this would work in my favor.

"It doesn't look like I'm dressed right for horseback riding. I guess I can just hang out at the stable while you two go riding." I didn't let on that I wouldn't mind an excuse to poke around.

"No way. I can lend you boots and a jacket. Come up to my room," Chloe insisted.

Drats.

Before we ascended the stairs, I caught sight of Olivia standing at the wrought-iron railing in the upstairs balcony hall, looking judgmentally down upon us. My mind couldn't help but harken back to my numerous viewings of *Rebecca*—Olivia was giving off diabolical Mrs. Danvers vibes.

The goosebumps at the nape of my neck tingled at full force by the time we reached the top of the stairway. As I'd suspected, Olivia looked displeased to see me in her house. Summer came from one of the bedrooms, startled by my presence.

"I'm going riding with my friends," Chloe told them, prompted by her mother's disapproving glare. She turned without further conversation and sauntered down the hall. Ginger timidly smiled then hurriedly followed. Olivia descended the stairs without a word to any of us, leaving Summer and I the only ones left at the top of the staircase.

I felt I had to say something to Summer. I couldn't just pretend we didn't know each other . . . even though we *didn't* really know each other. I had so many questions for her, but none that I could come right out and ask. I didn't know whether she was hoping to get back together with Roman or setting him up to take the fall for murder.

"How are you doing, Summer?" I said, heeding my mother's adage, *When in doubt, lead with kindness.*

"I'm getting through."

Summer peered over the railing and watched her mother leave the living room before she whispered, "How's Roman? I know he's not the one who killed Nelson."

"Of course he's not. Who do *you* think did it?"

"I have no idea. It must've been some stranger who came onto the grounds."

Blame it on a stranger and no one will ever get caught. It sounded like the reasoning of someone who might be the murderer herself.

"It's a scary thought that a murderer is still out there. It doesn't sound like the police have any evidence. That's why I'm worried for Roman," she continued.

I was unmoved by her large Disney-princess eyes glassing over as she summoned tears.

"Motive might lead them to the truth," I said.

"Roman didn't have motive. If he wanted to be with me, he wouldn't have had to kill Nelson to do it."

"I wasn't talking about *Roman's* motive."

Any tears that were about to bubble over quickly evaporated. Her eyebrows stitched together in confusion or annoyance—I couldn't tell which.

"Willa! You coming?" Chloe called from her bedroom.

Now Summer's face read definite annoyance—she was still mad at Chloe. Was it because Chloe had instigated the fight between Roman and Nelson or did Summer suspect her sister was involved in her fiancé's murder?

Summer brushed past me and made her exit down the stairs.

I went in the direction where Chloe and Ginger had disappeared minutes earlier and came upon Chloe's bedroom. It was a large room, much more vibrant than the rest of the house. Colorful rows of hanging beads separated the bedroom from a sitting nook. It gave off a free-spirited Peace & Love vibe. It was not what I'd expected, although Chloe was rarely what I expected.

"Why is she still stuck on Roman?" Chloe said with a roll of her eyes as soon as I entered. They'd obviously been listening in on our conversation.

"You think she is?" Was there something more Chloe knew about her sister and Roman?

"Obviously. And he must feel the same way about her. Why else would he have been here that day? If they've changed their minds about being together, I wish they'd just get on with it already. It would save Mother from having to cancel all the wedding arrangements."

I pretended to be interested in all the art on the walls so I wouldn't have to face Chloe or Ginger. I was never good at hiding my feelings, and the thought that Summer and Roman might've rekindled their romance brought up a lot of feelings. With effort, I swallowed them down. Just a minute ago, Summer all but said she would've left Nelson for him. Had Roman wanted her to?

"Aren't these paintings spectacular?" Ginger said from behind me. "Chloe painted them all."

I focused on the art that I'd been staring blankly at. Layered paint in various bright colors rendered abstract horse portraits, zoomed in tight to their heads. As Ginger had said, they were spectacular.

With effort, I tamped down my heartache, so I could face the women again. "You're very talented," I said to Chloe.

"Mother thinks it's just another useless hobby of mine," Chloe responded with a wave of her hand, but she looked at the paintings with affection.

"Your mother didn't seem the biggest fan of Roman's. I'm surprised you think she'd be okay with him and Summer getting back together."

"She'd come around. It would be preferable to two engagements and no wedding, that's for sure. Grandmother still held out hope for them, but then again, she remembers more about what happened ten years ago than yesterday, so . . ."

"Alzheimer's is awful," Ginger said.

"I hate it. The only saving grace is that she doesn't even remember Summer was engaged to Nelson." Chloe sighed. "Come. Let's see what I've got for you to wear, Willa."

On my way to her walk-in closet, I glanced through French doors that led out to the shared terrace I'd seen when Baz and I inadvertently took the scenic route to the garden. Her room had a beautiful view of the back of the property, including the paddock and stable where Nelson was murdered while the three Harrington women were supposedly in the house. Nobody saw anything?

I kept my questions to myself for now and followed Chloe and Ginger to Chloe's closet—a connected room about the size of my bedroom. It had multiple cubbies for handbags and shoes, even though most of them were piled on the floor. Upper and lower racks were packed tightly with clothes, reminding me of the clearance section of a store. Chloe stuck her arm into the abyss of upper racks.

"Check over there for riding boots. You need a short heel for the stirrup." She indicated where the boots were with only a glance back, as she was using her arms to try to separate the jackets to get a look at them.

Ginger and I scanned the closet. In the corner was a stack of boot boxes. I knelt and lifted the lid off the top one. It was empty. I began unstacking, waiting to feel a box with some heft that let me know there were boots inside.

"What's this?" Ginger slid out an unframed canvas resting against the wall hiding behind the boxes. I only saw the back of it from where I was kneeling. "Did you paint this?" she asked Chloe, staring at it.

Chloe's back was still to us. "Got it!" she said in triumph, managing to pull out a blazer-type jacket from the rack. "What did you say?" She turned and saw Ginger holding the canvas. Her triumphant smile disappeared. "The boots are over there." Chloe pointed to a mound of discarded shoes at the back of the room. She strode over and took the painting from Ginger. We sensed she wasn't pleased we'd found it.

"It's really good," Ginger said, shooting me a look that said *oops*.

I still hadn't gotten a look at it.

Chloe ignored Ginger's comment. "Try this." She handed me the jacket.

Ginger and I snuck a glance at each other, feeling bad that we'd overstepped our bounds. Chloe stuck the painting behind the boxes again without a word about it and went over to the pile of shoes.

I slipped the jacket over my blouse. To my relief, it fit. Luckily, I remembered to wear jeans. There was no way her petite pants would fit me. While she and Ginger were rummaging through the boots, I snuck a peek at the painting that now faced outward. Ginger was right, it was good—I immediately recognized the portrait as Nelson.

CHAPTER 20

"Nelson sat for the portrait as a gift for Summer," Chloe said.

I guess staring at the painting, slack-jawed, wasn't very stealth. I couldn't help it—Nelson was Chloe's boyfriend first and she might've been the one who went after him that day. I wondered if the portrait really was for Summer or just an excuse for Chloe and Nelson to be together.

I hoped she'd forgive me for being nosey. "I'm sure everyone's sending condolences to Summer, but Nelson's death has to be hard on you too," I said.

Chloe shrugged, but the sadness in her eyes told a different story. "I'm used to everyone paying more attention to Summer."

Ginger put an arm around her.

"Not Marcos. He sure seemed to like taking pictures of you at the shower," I said.

Chloe smiled. "He's like a puppy. It's cute when he follows me around, but then it gets annoying. I think that's my problem with any guy who really likes me. After a while, I want them to go away, but come back when I tell them to. Is that too much to ask?" She laughed and Ginger joined in. "Try these. She handed me a pair of boots that fit snugly. "There! You almost look like a proper equestrian. We ready to go?" She grabbed a jacket similar to mine, and the three of us left the room to head downstairs.

We exited the house through the mudroom side door where the golf cart was parked right outside. It occurred to me again that anybody who'd been in the house could've made their way to this little hallway and slipped outside. The stable had to be about a five-minute walk from here. By cart, the ride would be less than a minute.

We bounced along on the dirt path. "It's convenient to have this," I said, holding on from the back seat, thinking of how easy it would've been for her to have gone to the stable, murdered Nelson, and gotten back to the house without anyone having known she was ever there.

"Isn't it, though? I keep trying to get my mother to buy another. She says there's no point since she'll be the only one using it soon."

"Are you moving out?" Ginger asked.

"No. Mother likes to threaten us with it, though, whenever she's mad at us. Dad insists we move out by the time we turn thirty. Ha! What would Mother do without us? Dad's never home. He'd hardly know if we lived here or not." Chloe's laughter followed the breeze as we zoomed the rest of the way to the stable.

The police must've finished processing the crime scene—the yellow Do Not Cross tape was down. Or maybe the Harringtons decided the police were done with it. According to Mayor Trumbull, they had that kind of power.

We walked into the stable, where I couldn't help being drawn to look down the stretch of stalls to the one I'd seen Nelson's boots sticking out of. The shock that was imprinted in me resurfaced, and for a moment all I registered was a buzzing in my ears.

"Willa?" Chloe's voice snapped me back to the present. She and Ginger were staring at me.

"I'm sorry," I said, slightly embarrassed. "What did you say?"

"That's right, you're the one who found him," Chloe said. She ambled over to the stall. She stopped in front of it and stared in. "The police say this is where it happened."

I took a few steps toward her. I couldn't make myself go all the way. "It must be hard for you to be in here too, it being the last place you saw him."

"Who told you that?"

Ginger's eyes bugged out. She apparently didn't realize what she was getting into when she offered to let me come to Chloe's with her to investigate.

"I saw you drive to the stable from the yard," I bluffed.

Chloe's expression hardened. "I knew it! Mother said nobody could see. Since it wasn't all over the internet like the rest of what happened that day, I thought maybe she was right." She looked to the ceiling in annoyance.

Ginger and I glanced at each other, our mouths hanging open at the confession. I shut mine quickly—I was supposed to already know this information.

I shook off the surprise. "It might help Roman if we could figure out what went on before Nelson's murder," I coaxed. "What happened here that day?"

She strolled over to a horse in its stall and stroked his neck. The horse nuzzled her. "When I got here, Nelson was still furious about Roman showing up with Summer. That's how he was—explosive temper, but he always calmed down in no time. He threatened to call off the wedding. I told him not to be stupid. He was all bark, no bite. I reminded him that he'd regret it by the time he got home." She paused, finally looking at us. "That was it. I left."

"Did you tell Detective Heath?"

"Mother didn't want me to, but I had to. It would've looked worse if Everett had told him first."

"Everett saw you at the stable?" *Why wouldn't Mayor Trumbull have told me this?*

"Yeah. I figured he'd help cool Nelson off and take him home, so I left after he got there."

"You're telling me Everett was with Nelson alone at the stable." *Now I see why.*

"Don't tell anybody I told you either of us was there. You swear?"

Ginger and I readily nodded.

"Mother's already angry enough at me. Once that behemoth of a police officer left our house, our mothers made us promise not to tell anyone outside of what we'd already told the police. They don't want the public judging us or worse by assuming one of us killed Nelson."

"Nobody who knows you could think you killed Nelson. Besides, the police haven't arrested you or anything, so they must know you didn't do it," Ginger said naïvely.

"That's what I think. The police don't seem to be concerned, so why should anyone else be? But my mother is hypersensitive to scandal. Me? I don't like keeping secrets. People can think what they want." She walked away from the horse. "Where's Rick? I wonder why Sunrise isn't saddled up yet. Rick?" she called, leaving the stable.

Ginger moved closer to me, eyes still wide. She whispered, "That's good information, huh?"

I nodded.

"And now we know she didn't do it," she added.

I wouldn't go that far, but it did give me a whole new perspective. This was why Mayor Trumbull was so determined to steer the investigation toward the Harringtons, and she was using me to do it. She had just as much power over the police—maybe more—as she claimed the Harringtons did. The APB Heath put on Roman was after Olivia's interview but before Chloe's. Mayor Trumbull worked me up into thinking Roman was Heath's prime suspect when she must've known all along it could be Everett. But what would Everett's motive be? Then I remembered. "The money."

"What about money?" Ginger asked.

I hadn't realized I'd said it aloud. "I was just working things out in my head. We should probably find Chloe."

CHAPTER 21

Ginger and I left the stable. We found Chloe with an older man near the paddock. His weathered face and tanned skin made it clear he'd worked outdoors all his life. Two horses frolicked in the paddock.

He and Ginger said hello to each other. She must've met him before. I said hi and Chloe introduced me. "Willa, this is Rick, our stable hand."

He put his fingers to the brim of his baseball cap in hello.

"Rick says Sunrise isn't herself today so we're not going to be able to ride her. Poor thing. She's such a gentle soul. She's probably still traumatized from charging Roman and seeing what happened to Nelson," Chloe said, looking worried.

"I called Dr. Canton. He'll be by a little later to check on her," Rick told her.

"I hope she's okay," Ginger said.

Rick tsked, chastising himself. "I wish I'd still been here, so I could've made sure she was saddled up properly and taken care of afterward."

"It's not your fault, Rick. Nobody was supposed to be riding that afternoon," Chloe said.

"Thunder and Dash are ready to ride today." Rick

looked out to the horses in the paddock, playfully shaking their manes at each other.

"If there are only two horses, I'll just stay back today," I readily offered. I'd already gotten a good piece of information about the case. And I'd rather not ride any horse named Thunder or Dash.

"No way. You're my guests. You two will ride first, then one of us will switch off," Chloe said. She took two riding helmets from Rick.

I tried protesting again, but Chloe wouldn't hear of it. We followed Rick into the paddock.

"Who's the better rider?" he asked.

I pointed to Ginger.

"You take Thunder," he said to her.

Ginger easily mounted the horse.

That left me with Dash. With Chloe's jacket and boots, at least I looked the part. Maybe I could fool myself into believing I could ride well. Unfortunately, the horse was no fool. As soon as I approached, he sensed my unease. I stroked him on his strong shoulder until we both felt more comfortable.

I needed the mounting block and some extra help from Rick to pull myself up and sling my leg over the wide animal. I wiggled myself properly into the saddle. I was reminded yet again why cheese was my hobby. It required no equipment, special outfit, or risk taking—if you didn't include eating a funkier piece of cheese than you bargained for as a risk. And, most important, you got to keep both feet on the ground.

"Don't worry, Willa. We'll start slow," Ginger said.

My horse followed Ginger's in a circle around the paddock a few times. I began to relax a little. Maybe I *had* been psyching myself out. This was actually kind of fun.

"How are you doing?" Ginger called to me.

"I'm good. This is nice," I said.

Leaning on the paddock fence where she was watching, Chloe gave me a thumbs-up as I passed her again. I returned the signal as confidently as I could. At the next pass, Chloe was opening the paddock gate and Ginger's horse was leading mine through it.

"Follow the trail. It's much more fun than going in circles," Chloe said.

"I don't mind going in circles," I replied, but nobody paid attention.

"It'll loop back around in about two miles. We'll switch off then," she called.

Okay, I just have to stay on this horse for four miles.

The dirt trail steered us toward the garden shed, turning into a wooded area surrounded by brush. It eventually opened again to grasslands and a spectacular view of perfect rows of grape vines leading to swooping hills and rising to mountains.

Ginger held back and let my horse fall in beside hers. "Too bad Chloe's not riding with us. This isn't exactly conducive to getting information out of someone, is it?" she said.

"Not unless Dash or Thunder have something to tell me."

"I'll switch out with her if you want. This way you two can chat while you're riding."

"Oh no, that's okay." I was mildly enjoying the ride, but still looking forward to my own two feet being on terra firma. "Finding out that she and Everett were at the stable was good information. Inviting me along has already helped."

"Good." She nodded, satisfied. "I might trot for a bit. You okay with me going a little ahead?"

"Umm, will my horse start trotting too?"

"Not unless you tell him to."

"I only know how to stop him. I think."

"Then you'll be fine. I won't get too far ahead, I promise."

Ginger brought her horse to a trot, her lead quickly growing wider. To my relief, Dash continued walking.

"You're a good boy. You're doing fine," I told the horse and myself.

What Chloe had told me confirmed that I couldn't count on Heath for information—he'd kept this huge piece of the puzzle to himself. Everett was at the scene of the crime and his mother may have inherited Nelson's money. Just like this horse trail, the path led only one way—straight to Everett.

It was hard to think of Everett as a killer. He seemed so sweet. I'd been looking forward to having him and his bicycle shop as my neighbor. And what about his dog, George? What would become of him if Everett went to prison?

I could no longer see Ginger on the winding trail, but I wasn't so focused on getting to the two-mile mark anymore. I felt my body loosen with the rhythm of the horse's gait and the gentle sound of his hooves on the dirt trail. It wasn't as relaxing as cozying up with a hunk of apple cinnamon cheddar, but it wasn't as bad as I'd thought.

I allowed my gaze to stray from the path directly in front of me to the changing view. To one side was a meadow dotted with scrub brush and a smattering of trees in the distance. To the other was a backdrop of old-growth oak trees. My eye caught a piece of color on one of the majestic trunks. I peered closer. There was something small and red attached. It also looked like someone had carved something into the trunk, although I couldn't make it out as I passed.

The quiet was suddenly pierced when a shot rang out, scaring the bejeezus out of me and the horse. He whinnied and took off. As Dash lived up to his name, I flattened myself against him and hung onto the saddle horn for dear life. The view I'd just been admiring flew past me. I fixed my gaze ahead, but the trail bounced before me, the horse's long neck bobbing up and down with each gallop, his mane blowing in the breeze.

Ginger's horse was suddenly by my side, running in stride with mine. Our speed gradually decreased until we were at a trot and then a walk. I echoed her "Whoa, whoa." The horses finally came to a halt. I immediately threw one leg over the side and clumsily slid down off the horse, but my boot caught in the stirrup. I landed hard on my shoulder.

"Are you okay?" Ginger asked.

I sat up. A shooting pain seared through my left arm from shoulder to elbow. "I think I'll be okay," I said stubbornly.

I used my good arm to get myself off the ground. Ginger was off her horse and had ahold of both their reins.

"What the heck happened? What was that noise?" Ginger said. She stroked Dash on the neck to relax him.

The golf cart whirred into view and stopped behind us. Rick and Chloe hopped out.

"Are you okay?" Rick asked us.

"I don't know what happened," I said. Now the pain traveled up my neck, ending in a dull throb of a headache. "There was a loud noise, like a pop."

"It spooked the horses. I got ahold of mine, but Willa had quite a ride before I could catch up to her," Ginger said.

"We both heard it. It sounded like a gunshot," Chloe said.

"Maybe your mother or Summer were doing some skeet shooting," Rick speculated.

"They knew we were going riding." Chloe dismissed the suggestion.

"Did you fall off?" Rick noticed I was cradling my arm at the elbow.

"I got off a little too fast," I said.

"I'll take the horses back. You ladies get in the cart and go back to the house." He took the reins from Ginger.

"Thanks, Rick." Chloe patted Dash's neck before getting back in the cart.

We echoed her thanks, and I gingerly got in the passenger seat of the cart, hoping Chloe would drive more slowly back to the house. I didn't know if my bruised body could take another bumpy ride.

To my relief, she went slowly. "How hard did you fall?" she asked.

"I was partway off before I fell. I landed on my shoulder."

"So what happened to your helmet then?" She took her gaze off the trail to eye my helmet.

I unfastened the strap under my chin and removed it to have a look. My fingers traced the crack that ran through it.

"Did someone shoot at you?" Chloe said, wide-eyed.

"Oh my gosh. We should call the police," Ginger said from the back seat. She patted her thighs. "I don't have my phone with me."

"Let's get out of here." I suddenly felt very vulnerable.

I braced myself as Chloe's foot pressed the golf cart's pedal and we took off. I peered across the field as we left the horse trail, trying to discern any figures hiding among the brush.

CHAPTER 22

My finger traced the jagged crack in the helmet. It wouldn't stop a bullet, would it? I didn't remember feeling anything hit my head. Even though the bumping of the golf cart activated the pain in my shoulder, I was glad for Chloe's haste. I was in a hurry to get out of there.

Chloe and Ginger kindly offered to help me walk from the cart into the house, but there was nothing they could do to ease the pain in my shoulder. Ginger and I sat on the couch in the living room. Chloe took my helmet from me. She held it up to her face and stared closely at it.

"That could've been your skull," she said, wide-eyed.

Thanks for the reminder.

She put the helmet on the coffee table. "I'm calling that Detective Heath. Where did I put his card?" she asked herself.

"I have his number," I said, clumsily taking out my phone and showing her the number. I was happy to let her make the call to give Heath some time to cool off before I had to deal with him. He would be upset that I was here, even more so that I might've been somebody's target. Maybe it was nothing. Maybe I hit my head when I fell off the horse. Maybe the sound was a car backfiring or someone skeet shooting.

Chloe called Heath from her phone and put it on speaker. I heard it go to voicemail, so she tapped the number that transferred the call to the police dispatcher. She told her who she was, and before she could even fully explain what happened, the dispatcher said she was sending an officer over. It must be nice to be a Harrington. She ended the call.

She handed me my phone. "They're sending someone over. Well, I guess you heard that."

I nodded. We sat together in the pristine living room. I noticed bits of dirt had shed from the bottoms of my boots. Come to think of it, I was probably covered in dust. I moved to the edge. "I probably shouldn't be sitting on your couch. Shouldn't we at least take off our boots in the mudroom?"

"Don't worry about it. Polly will clean it up tomorrow. She gets half days on Wednesdays or else she'd be here today. Too bad—she's much better at making drinks than I am."

"If you can show me where your spices are, Chloe, I can whip up an herbal remedy to help the pain in Willa's shoulder," Ginger offered.

"That's not exactly the kind of drink I had in mind, but you're welcome to scour the kitchen. I have no idea where the spices are kept," Chloe said.

"Just some ibuprofen would be fine," I said, wary of one of her drink concoctions.

"I don't mind. It'll make me feel useful," Ginger said, heading to the kitchen.

"I'm going to feel royally stupid if the police come and someone didn't try to shoot you," Chloe said. I *think* she was kidding.

I had to consider that it might've been an attempt on my life, which meant I needed to collect as much information as I could, and I needed to do it now. "Chloe, do you know if Nelson had a will?"

"Yeah, that was another one of his grand gestures to prove his love to Summer after one of their fights."

"You mean *she* was the beneficiary?" *Was it Summer, not the Trumbulls, who stood to gain?*

"He said he left her everything, but who knows?"

"You don't believe it?"

"Oh, I believe it. It's on par with how their relationship worked. Something would happen—usually it was jealousy—they'd have a blow-out fight, he'd buy her something ridiculously expensive or make some big, romantic gesture, and they'd make up. I have to admit, that Prince Charming thing was pretty creative."

"Do you think she would try to get him jealous?" I asked. *Did she use Roman as a pawn?*

"Both of them were too jealous. You might not know this, but he and I dated first before he was with Summer."

I knew, but I wasn't going to rat out Ginger. I pretended to be surprised. "Were there still feelings between you two?"

She rolled her eyes at the idea. "No. He liked to use me against her sometimes, which is why Summer and I aren't close anymore. I told her it was stupid to believe him, but she was always a little insecure about it. I think he started dating her to get back at me after I broke up with him, but then he really started liking her. It didn't bother me at all—if she could handle all that drama, she was welcome to him."

The bong of the doorbell resounded through the house. Chloe rose to answer the door. Ginger came in with a chartreuse-colored, opaque drink for me.

"This should make your aches feel better," she said, sitting on the couch next to me.

"Thanks, Ginger. That's really nice of you." It *was* really nice of her, and I was determined to drink it no matter what.

Olivia Harrington came downstairs just as Chloe returned with Detective Heath, Shep, and Officer Melman.

"What are the police doing here?" Olivia said. She looked even more perturbed than the last time I saw her.

Uh-oh.

Summer walked in from the back of the house. "Did I hear you say the police are here? Have you found out something about Nelson's murder, Detective Heath?"

"No, I was told there was another incident," Heath said.

"What incident?" Olivia looked questioningly at Chloe.

"Someone shot at Willa," Chloe announced.

Heath's head jerked in my direction.

"Possibly. We don't know for sure." I gulped. Which was worse, being shot at or Heath knowing I was shot at?

"We heard what sounded like a gunshot," Ginger said. "We were on horseback, and it spooked the horses. Willa fell off."

"I *got* off," I corrected. "But I still kind of fell when I was getting off," I mumbled.

"For goodness' sake, Chloe, why didn't you tell me first?" her mother scolded. "You're wasting Detective Heath's time. I heard it from the terrace. It sounded like a motor backfiring. It was probably one of the landscapers on that old tractor."

Another lame excuse like Summer had for Nelson's murder. It must run in the family.

"Look. Here's Willa's helmet." Chloe picked up my helmet and handed it to Heath, pointing out the crack.

Olivia stretched her neck to have a look. "That helmet's not going to stop a bullet. Tell her, Detective Heath."

"Olivia's right. This would be shattered, not cracked," Heath said.

I let myself breathe and put my hand on my heart, but the motion sparked another bolt of pain up my arm.

"Maybe it grazed it," Chloe said.

"Didn't you just say she fell off the horse?" Olivia continued to counter.

"She probably hit her head on the ground," Summer said, studying the helmet too. "You really ought to go to the hospital in case you have a concussion."

"I'm fine. It's my shoulder that hurts." I took a swig of Ginger's drink with my good arm, choking it down.

"Did you hear it too, Summer?" Detective Heath asked.

"Yes. It sounded like a motor backfiring."

Chloe rolled her eyes. "Of course she'd say that. She says everything Mother says."

Ginger spoke up. "Rick heard it too—the stable hand. He came out to the trail to help."

"Where is he?" Heath asked.

"He was putting the horses back in the stable," Chloe answered. "He's probably gone home by now."

"Wasn't he expecting the vet?" Ginger reminded Chloe.

"Oh, you're right. I forgot." She threw a pinched smile Ginger's way.

"Do you have any firearms on your property, Mrs. Harrington?" Heath asked Olivia.

"You think one of us is responsible for this?" She looked at him incredulously.

Heath didn't reply.

"We have skeet guns," Summer offered. "They're secured in a cabinet in the study."

Olivia's glare went from the detective to her daughter.

"We might as well let them see that we haven't done anything wrong, Mother. I'm sure they're all accounted for."

"I'm sure they are. Come with me," Olivia said through gritted teeth. She strode off and Heath followed. They returned within minutes with Olivia looking satisfied.

"Were all three of you on horseback?" Heath asked us.

"No, just Ginger and Willa," Chloe answered. "Our other horse wasn't feeling well, so I stayed back at the paddock with Rick and the two of them took the trail."

"Would you be able to show me where you were when you heard the noise?" he asked me and Ginger.

"I'm not quite sure," Ginger said.

"I think I'd be able to. I'd just passed a tree that looked like it had some writing carved in the trunk and there was something red attached to it." I was glad to finally be able to offer something useful.

"I know which tree she's talking about. I can show you where it is, Detective," Chloe said. "We can take the cart."

Heath turned to Shep and Melman. "Go to the stable and talk to Rick. Keep him there. I'll come as soon as I can."

"I can't believe this," Olivia said, throwing her arm in the air and allowing it to slap her thigh on the way down. "I thought you said a bullet wouldn't cause this, Detective."

"She wasn't hit by a bullet, but that doesn't rule out

that someone may have shot at her. It's worth investigating," Heath said. He nodded at the officers to follow his orders.

Shep and Melman left the house.

Olivia turned to her elder daughter. Her jaw tightly set, she spoke through her teeth: "Haven't we had enough scandal, Chloe?"

"Haven't we had enough murders, Mother? If someone tried to shoot Willa, we need to know. We're going." Chloe stared at me and Ginger until we stood up from the couch. I tried not to wince in front of Heath.

Another painfully bumpy ride in the golf cart led us to the horse trail. I looked at the trees, trying to recall where I'd been, but Chloe was driving faster than I'd been riding. Another bump made me knock my elbow into the side. *Ouch.*

Finally, we slowed down and came to a stop.

We climbed out of the cart.

"Is that the tree you saw, Willa?" Chloe asked me.

It had the markings I'd noticed on my ride and the red trinket.

"That's the one," I said. "What's the red thing?"

"Nelson and I carved our initials into that tree three years ago and nailed that red metal heart to it. Mother was so angry. She said we'd killed the tree. Obviously, it's still standing."

We walked closer to it. It was carved with *N.T. + C.H.*, the initials for Nelson Trumbull and Chloe Harrington. The red heart was there too. I was shocked that Chloe would admit to Heath that she and Nelson used to be a couple. She was either naïvely sure that her innocence would prevail or she was a murderer with too much confidence. As a wealthy woman with a family name that carried a lot of weight, perhaps she couldn't fathom life not going her way.

Heath told us to stay back on the trail as he poked around among the trees. When he emerged, he ordered us back into the cart. He took out his phone and made a call, looking out at the field while he spoke.

In a few minutes, Shep and Melman had joined us, shining flashlights on the path in front of them. Dusk was settling in. Melman carried the dreaded police tape. Heath went back into the woods with them. I strained to hear what he was saying but couldn't make it out. They emerged, and Shep and Melman began to cordon off a wide swath of the trail and woods. Heath returned to the cart.

"Did you find something? Are they looking for a bullet?" I asked.

He ignored my questions. "Let's get out of their way. I have to talk to your stable hand," he said to Chloe.

We took the cart back to the stable, where Rick was waiting. Heath got out and put his rigid arm out like a barrier to stop us from exiting. "You three go straight back to the house and wait for me there."

Drats. I wouldn't be able to hear his interview with Rick. Chloe turned the cart around and we returned to the house.

"We need a drink," she said as we reentered the living room. She disappeared into the kitchen.

I did a quick scan of the rooms I could see before Ginger and I sat down and was relieved there was no sign of Olivia or Summer.

"Do you think you were really shot at? I'm so sorry, Willa. I didn't know it would be dangerous for you to be here," Ginger said.

"I'm sorry too. You could've been in danger, as well. I wish Heath would tell us what he found."

I looked at the floor, dotted again with dirt. "We should probably take off our boots."

In the mudroom area, I turned on the weak light and we sat on the bench. Ginger quickly removed her boots, but with one arm, mine were taking a bit longer.

"You need help?" she said.

"That's okay. I got it." I bent over to grab it from the heel with my good arm.

"Are you going to tell me what happened?" Summer demanded from the end of the hallway.

Startled, I sat up.

"Oh, sorry. I thought you were Chloe."

"She's in the kitchen," I said.

Summer turned and left.

I allowed Ginger to help me off with my boots. We returned to the living room, where we heard tense voices coming from the kitchen. Unfortunately, whatever heated discussion was happening between Summer and Chloe wasn't loud enough for me to hear it properly.

Ginger went back to the couch, but I tiptoed closer to the kitchen in my stocking feet, cocking an ear toward their voices. Chloe suddenly appeared from the kitchen with a bottle of wine and three glasses, and I straightened my creeping stance.

"I, uh, I wanted to make sure it was okay to get my shoes from upstairs," I said, thinking on my feet.

"Sure. You know where my room is," Chloe replied.

I left her and Ginger in the living room opening the wine as I headed upstairs. In Chloe's closet, I struggled out of her jacket with my bum arm and put it back on its abandon wooden hanger. I couldn't fit it in between her ocean of clothes on the rack, so I left it lying on the ottoman. It could use a cleaning anyway. I sat down to put my Keds on, and once again spotted Nelson's portrait propped against the wall on the floor. This time his painted face was slashed from top to bottom. The tiny hairs on the back of my neck stiffened. Was this Summer's doing?

CHAPTER 23

I didn't know what to make of the slashed painting and I didn't want to be caught contemplating it, so I hurriedly left the closet and went back downstairs.

When Heath returned, Summer and Olivia appeared too.

"What did you find?" I asked Heath, hoping he'd tell me this time.

"Nothing yet," he replied curtly. He turned to Olivia. "My officers are setting up a barrier on the property by the trail."

"What possibly for?" Olivia demanded. "You just said you've found no evidence of any gunshot."

"There was an indication that one of the trees may have been grazed."

"Oh, come on, Detective. What is it, a piece of missing bark? And you're going to assume it's from a gunshot?"

"I'm not assuming anything, which is why my men are out there," Heath responded calmly. "I'd like to speak privately with you, Chloe."

Olivia huffed as he and Chloe walked off into the study together. Ginger and I sat on the couch in silence while Olivia paced and Summer stared lasers at the study door. After a few minutes, Heath and Chloe returned. For the first time, she seemed agitated instead of her cool, collected self.

"No one is to penetrate the tape on the property. Officers Shepherd and Melman will return tomorrow morning in the light of day to search the area for shotgun casings, bullets, or pellets with the aid of a metal detector. If we find anything, we can lead it back to the gun and possibly the shooter," Heath said. "I'd also like your permission to take the skeet guns."

Olivia balked. "You'll have to get a warrant, Detective."

Heath accepted her answer with a nod.

I'd never before heard him elucidate on how they'd be proceeding. Was it because we were at Olivia Harrington's that he felt the need to explain?

The clarification didn't seem to placate Olivia. If Mayor Trumbull was telling the truth when she said Olivia held sway over the police, a phone call to Chief Jeffers would be forthcoming.

"Excuse me," Ginger spoke up timidly. "Can we go now?"

"Yes, you can leave. I'll bring Willa to the hospital for her shoulder," Heath said.

"I don't need to go to the hospital," I said.

Hospitals. You ended up sitting in a waiting room for two hours only to see a doctor who tells you to go home and rest.

"Fine, I'll take you home, then," Heath replied.

I figured he wanted to talk to me privately, so I didn't protest.

Once outside, my muscles tensed at the chilly temperature now that daylight was waning. The pain in my left shoulder flared, mocking my earlier declaration about the hospital. I didn't change my stance. I just needed to get home and rest, as a doctor would surely order. I'd be fine tomorrow.

As soon as we got in the car, I asked, "Do you really think a bullet grazed one of the trees?"

"No. I wanted to make them think there might be evidence out there. Shep and Melman are staking it out tonight to see if any of them go looking for shotgun casings or anything they may have left if they used one of those skeet guns."

"That's why you gave that explanation." I was relieved that it wasn't because he was intimidated by Olivia. "What if nobody shows?"

"There's nothing more we can do. We'll look to see if any other guns are registered to them, but we have a murder investigation taking up our resources. I'm sorry."

He sounded like he really meant it.

"I understand."

Heath started the car. "You can do your part and stay away from the people involved with the case."

I knew he wouldn't be able to resist.

"I was invited," I said. I didn't look at him, but I could sense the eye roll.

He sighed. "What did you find out?"

I was taken aback. This response wasn't the norm. "You're not going to lecture me?"

"I've learned that *stubborn* is your middle name, so I won't waste our time. I'd rather find out what you learned about them while you were there. Start with Chloe."

"Oh." I took a moment to regroup, but I was all in with this new and improved version of Detective Heath. "Well, I found a painting Chloe did of Nelson that he sat for. She claimed it was going to be a gift for Summer, but I'm not sure if I believe it. Either way, that tells me they spent a lot of private time together. Seeing as how they used to date, I'm starting to think Chloe still had a thing for Nelson."

"She was pretty open about their relationship in my first interview with her. It's possible she wanted to look like she was cooperating by telling us information that we'd easily find out soon enough."

"That's not all. When I happened to see it again after the whole shooting thing, it was slashed."

"Slashed?"

"Yup. Crosswise, top to bottom. It had to be Summer, right? Why would she do that?" I answered my own question. "Because she knew Chloe and Nelson were still in love."

"Go on," he said without offering any counter-theory.

I continued, "Remember I told you Roman showed up at my shop the night before the shower? Chloe seemed pretty pleased about it, like she knew what was going to go down. And at the shower, I told her Roman was with Summer at the garden shed, because I thought she'd make sure he left before anyone found out. Instead, she brought him front and center."

"How would she have known Nelson would be there? Everett said it was a surprise—he and Nelson were the only ones who knew."

"When Chloe was looking for Summer, she told me she looked everywhere, even in the stable, but didn't find her. She could've seen Nelson in his Prince Charming costume, saddling up the horse. If she was still in love with Nelson, it would explain why she tried to sabotage his marriage to Summer at the shower and it would've given her motive to kill him if she discovered it didn't work."

Heath nodded. His angular features were highlighted by the shadows made by the passing cars' headlights. "That all makes sense."

"But if the person who killed Nelson also shot at me tonight, it couldn't be Chloe. She was at the paddock with Rick."

"Not according to Rick. He was alone in the stable and came out when he heard the noise. He also thought it sounded like a gunshot. Chloe and her golf cart were nowhere to be found. She only caught up with him on the trail as he was running out to make sure you were okay."

"Where was she?"

"She says she went back to the house to use the bathroom, but she didn't provide me with that information until I asked her a second time. The first time, she led me to believe she was still at the paddock with Rick. It's suspicious when people aren't forthcoming."

"Do you think she set the whole thing up so I'd be on the horse and she'd be free to shoot at me?"

"That's one theory."

It scared me to think I was with her the entire time after the shooting and hadn't even suspected her. "Do you know anything about Rick? He says he wasn't around on Sunday afternoon."

"We looked into all the staff. He was working his second job that day and he has no connection to Nelson. We always keep all options on the table, but we don't believe he had any part in Nelson's murder."

"What about Olivia or Summer? Do you know where they were at the time Nelson was murdered?"

Heath glanced at me then studied the road ahead of him again noncommittally.

I pressed on. "If my theory about Chloe and Nelson is right, Summer or Olivia could've found out about them.

Or maybe Summer was tired of Nelson's temper and still in love with Roman. She could've decided killing off Nelson would be the only way to get rid of him. Maybe she didn't want to disappoint her mother with another failed wedding. And given that she was going to inherit all of Nelson's money . . ."

This time Heath more than glanced at me. "What are you talking about?"

It was time to fess up. "I overheard Shep tell you that someone took out a life insurance policy on Nelson and they were set to inherit his millions. I've been trying to guess who it is, but it would be easier if you'd tell me."

"So you're guessing that it's Summer. You know I can't confirm or deny," Heath said.

I knew it, but it didn't mean I had to like it. There was no point in asking him about Chloe and Everett being at the stable either.

"I'll have to escort you out of the station next time," he said, figuring out how I overheard about the inheritance.

"It doesn't matter. It's not a guess—I found out on my own. At first, I thought it was Mayor Trumbull, but Chloe told me that during one of Nelson's grand gestures, he said he put Summer as his sole beneficiary in his will."

Heath seemed interested again. "Did she tell you if Summer has a copy of that?"

"Chloe said he never produced any proof, but I wonder if it matters. If that's what Summer believed, then she could've killed him for it."

"If she and Roman rekindled their romance, that also keeps him as a suspect right beside her."

"Maybe it wasn't rekindled. Maybe Summer set him up like I said all along. Did you look at the text she sent him to meet her again at the garden shed after the shower? Did it reveal anything?" I asked.

"There was no text on her phone."

"Of course there wasn't. She'd have to delete it if she was going to set him up, but it would still be on *his* phone."

"There's nothing on his phone either. He claims he deleted it too."

"Why would he go and do that?" I was ticked off. Roman sure wasn't making this easy.

My frustration was pushed aside when I saw that Heath was pulling into the parking lot of the Glen District Hospital.

"I said I didn't want to go to the hospital," I told him.

"It's my duty to get you checked over and make sure you're okay," he said.

I softened. "You know a thing or two about stubbornness too."

For once, he didn't disagree.

CHAPTER 24

Heath escorted me into the one-story building that serviced Yarrow Glen and three surrounding small towns. It had emergency equipment and employed hospital hours but looked more like a medical center with maybe fifty beds. I'd read up on it when choosing a new primary care doctor, but I'd luckily never had the displeasure to step foot inside. We used the urgent care entrance.

He stayed in the waiting area as I gave the desk receptionist what seemed like my entire life history before she'd even address what my symptoms were. Finally, I took a seat next to Heath, where five other individuals were seated strategically apart from us and one another. None of them looked in dire need, thank goodness.

"This is going to take too long," I lamented.

"There aren't too many people waiting."

"It doesn't matter. Hospitals always take forever. You don't need to wait with me. I'll catch an Uber home."

Heath stood without saying goodbye, but he didn't head for the exit. Instead, he went to the reception desk and spoke with the clerk in a hushed tone. He returned to the seat next to me within moments.

I appreciated that he must've tried to use his influence, but I was bound to be here at least for the next hour.

The receptionist handed a file to a nurse and whispered in her ear, then pointed to Heath. The nurse walked over to us. "Detective Heath? Do you want to escort Ms. Bauer to her room now?"

I turned to Heath in surprise. "Thanks."

He came with me as the nurse led us out of the waiting area, down a hall, around the circular desk, and finally to a room. Heath didn't follow the nurse and me inside.

"I'll see you later," he said to me from the doorway.

"You're not going to stay?" the nurse asked.

"She'll be fine," he told her. He disappeared from the doorway before I could thank him.

The nurse took my vitals. I sensed she was nervous, which made me nervous. Did she see something wrong with my numbers? The doctor who eventually came into the room checked me for a concussion by shining a light into my eyes. He asked me to lift my arm over my head. My arm was stiff and sporting a bruise where it had met the ground. Lucky me, I needed two different procedures to determine the severity of my injuries: a CAT scan for my head and an MRI for my shoulder.

For once, being hard-headed worked in my favor. The CAT scan result showed no concussion.

"Just a shoulder contusion," the doctor proclaimed after the MRI. "You're lucky. There doesn't seem to be any torn tendons or ligaments."

I did feel lucky. My job relied on two good arms and one hard head.

Almost three hours and one sling later, I was a free bird with a throbbing ache around my shoulder that the doctor assured me would go away in a day or two if I iced it tonight and kept it immobile.

As I looked for the Exit arrows that would lead me

out of the hospital, I saw Heath once again sitting in a waiting-room chair.

"You're still here," I said, surprised.

He stood. He had a cardboard container in his hand. "You need a ride home."

"I do, but you didn't have to wait."

He nodded at my arm in a blue sling. "Looks like you hurt your arm."

"Okay, Detective Smug. You were right. It really is going to be fine, though. Just a bruised shoulder."

"I figured you'd be hungry too. Here." He handed me the container.

As soon as the warm box was in my hand, I smelled its aroma. "Truffle fries."

"From Apricot Grille. It was the only thing I knew for sure you like."

I clumsily tried to open the top, which was closed like an envelope.

"Here, let me." He pulled open the flaps and held it for me. "They're probably not hot anymore."

I used my good hand to pluck one out. "I prefer them soggy." Just like the time I had them at The Cellar with Heath when I first discovered there was something more underneath that serious detective persona. "Thank you."

He continued to hold them so I could eat them from the box as we made our way to his car. He opened my door and put the box of fries on my lap after I settled into the seat. We drove to my apartment not saying much, but this time it was a comfortable silence. Heath even tried a couple of soggy fries.

He parked next to my CR-V in the lot behind my apartment. He was out of the car and at my side, ready to help, as soon as I'd opened the passenger door.

"Leave it," he said when I went back for the discarded fry box on the seat.

"Thanks for the ride. And for getting me in to see a doctor so quickly. It must be one of the perks of being a police detective, getting first dibs in line," I said, as we walked toward my building.

"I'm not sure how far that would get me," he replied.

"What do you mean? Isn't that why I was seen so quickly?"

"Not exactly. I told them you were connected to a crime and I needed to get you back to the station."

"WHAT?"

Heath broke into laughter. His face lit up as it was overtaken by his pearly whites.

"Police humor. I get it," I said, chuckling to myself. I wasn't going to give him the satisfaction of laughing aloud at his joke, but he did catch me smiling. No wonder the nurse seemed nervous.

The sensor light clicked on as we approached the steps that led up to my apartment above my shop. Like a gentleman, he allowed me to go first. I was hyperaware that he was behind me. Should I invite him in? Our relationship was so unconventional. It was hard to pinpoint what we were because there was no label. I'd been to his home once before, but it wasn't *exactly* at his invitation. We weren't colleagues, much to my disappointment. We butted heads often enough, but we weren't adversaries. If I had to categorize it, I suppose we were . . . friends. So why was I nervous about asking him in?

When we reached the deck landing, I couldn't locate my key in my purse, which solved the problem. Heath clumsily tried to help, but his big hands were no match for my tiny purse. The thin purse strap somehow twisted around both of our wrists, until we began laughing at the absurdity of trying to get ahold of one little key. I finally managed to extract it and handed it to Heath to unlock my door.

"Willa!" a voice called from below.

It was Roman, climbing up the steps.

CHAPTER 25

When Roman joined us at my doorstep, his attention was focused on my sling. "What happened?"

"I fell off a horse. Long story."

He looked back and forth between me and Heath. "I wanted to talk to you. Is this a bad time?" he said to me.

"My chauffeuring duties are done," Heath answered, handing me my key. "Follow doctor's orders. And stay safe."

"Will do. Thanks again, Heath." As he headed down the stairs, a longing I hadn't let myself feel before followed him. Heath was comfort. Roman was . . . a knot in my stomach. "Come on in," I said.

I left my purse on the counter and invited Roman to take a seat in the living room. I continued into the kitchen to take a look in my freezer. *Aha! Peas!* I grabbed the bag and wrapped it in a dish towel.

He watched me walk in with the cold bag pressed against my bum shoulder. "Is your arm all right? What did you do to it?"

I didn't want to sit next to him, so I took the chair. "I had a little horseback riding accident. It's just sore." I stuck the wrapped frozen veggie bag between my shoulder and the chair's back cushion.

"I didn't know you rode horses."

"I don't. I fall off them."

He allowed himself a brief grin, but the moment of levity quickly vanished. He was here to finally talk, I hoped, but our last two attempts didn't go so well. I fussed with my makeshift ice pack out of nervousness.

"You want me to help you with that?" he asked, starting to get up.

"No, no. It's fine." I left it alone. There was nothing else to do but face the uncomfortable conversation.

He leaned forward in his seat, elbows on his knees, fiddling with the leather cord bracelet on his wrist. He looked at me with sad eyes. There was more to that look than him feeling bad about my shoulder. I was already emotionally spent by what I'd been through this afternoon. Was I ready to hear what I was afraid he was going to tell me about Summer?

"What brings you here?" I asked, ready or not.

He took a few moments to answer. "I know you said last time that you didn't care about my wedding to Summer."

"I care, I just wanted you to know that it didn't matter as far as wanting to defend you in Nelson's murder."

"I appreciate that, but it's about time I told you about it."

Past time. "I'm listening."

"I told you how the Harringtons and Masseys have been family friends for generations."

I nodded. "Did it make you feel pressure to be with Summer?"

"No. Well, I felt pressure to *stay* with her." He sat up and focused on me. "We were friends as kids. She's five years younger than I am, so I never thought about her in that way until she came home from college, and I saw her again all grown up." He paused, obviously recalling the vision of beautiful, twenty-one-year-old Summer Harrington. The knot in my stomach twisted tighter. "She told me she'd always had a crush on me, and I began to think of her in a different way. We started dating, but I was twenty-six. I wasn't ready to be forever with anybody."

"So why did you propose to her?"

"Our families were so happy we were together. Our grandparents had been wanting this all along. Marrying Summer was a perfect solution for the families to stay connected forever. I did love her, and I know she loved me, so I convinced myself that getting engaged was the next step." He shook his head and cringed before saying, "As soon as I proposed, I knew I'd made a mistake. Then the wedding plans started. The bigger the wedding got, the colder my feet got. But Summer was happy and in love, so I told myself to make it work.

"I even talked to her about it once. I hoped she was feeling the same pressure and we could just agree to call it off, but she wasn't feeling the same way. She wanted the whole thing—the wedding, marriage, kids." He leaned back on the love seat and twiddled with the rope band on his wrist again. "That killed me because I really cared about her. I didn't want to hurt her, so I decided I was going to go through with the wedding. But when the moment came . . ." He shook his head slowly. "I was standing up there on our wedding day, in front of our families and our friends, and hundreds of other people I didn't know, and the reverend asked if I'd love her forever. I couldn't tell the biggest lie of my life. I just couldn't. I know I was a coward for not doing it sooner and I hurt her a million times more by doing it in that moment than if I'd just told her it was a mistake earlier, but I knew the marriage wouldn't last. I didn't want the breakup to happen after we had a life together and a couple of kids."

I could see his pain in reliving the story etched around his eyes. I had no doubt he was being truthful with me.

"I'm sorry you both went through that," I said.

He nodded silently.

"Is that when you broke away from working at your family's winery?"

"Not too long after. My family didn't disown me or anything, but they weren't happy with me, that's for sure. It took a long time for the Masseys and the Harringtons to come together again. It was best I stayed away. I'd been wanting to strike out on my own and sell my mead for a long time. It was the push I needed."

So that was it. That was the story. Did it change anything about where we were now?

"Can I ask you something?" I asked tentatively.

"Anything."

"Is that why you haven't gotten serious with anybody you've dated since?"

"Huh. I never thought about it. But yeah, I guess it does still affect me. When I'm unsure of a relationship, I'd rather cut and run sooner than later." He finally met my eyes. "I'm sure that doesn't make you feel better about me."

He wasn't wrong about that. "I appreciate your honesty."

He didn't offer up anything else, like, *But it's different with you* or *I'm not unsure about you.* He was going to make me ask, wasn't he? Fine. I'd ask. "Have you fallen back in love with Summer?"

He looked genuinely surprised by the question. "No. I have a soft spot for her, but I'm not in love with her. I don't regret not marrying her, if that's what you're thinking. I just regret the way I did it."

My stomach knot loosened a bit.

"I regret not telling you," he added. "I knew you had a similar experience, so I thought if I told you, it would blow my chances with you. Can you honestly say it wouldn't have made a difference?"

I thought about it. "I don't know how I would've reacted. I guess we'll never know."

I rolled my neck, but it didn't help the pulsating pain creeping up from my shoulder. "I have to take some ibuprofen." I got up from the chair.

Roman stood too. "I'm going to let you rest."

I had no desire to stop him from leaving. There was a lot to digest. "Okay. Thanks for coming by. I appreciate you telling me everything."

At the door, he turned back and looked at me. It was a long few seconds before he said, "Feel better," but I had a feeling that wasn't what he really wanted to say.

I wasn't in the right headspace to think about it, so I let him leave.

I had to get rid of this headache. It took me a few frustrating tries before getting the right leverage on the medicine bottle cap to pry it open. I took three pills and then walked over to Loretta Island to feed Loretta. "You never have to worry that I'll replace you for a horse, Loretta." I sprinkled some fish flakes into her bowl. "Or a man, for that matter."

There was a knock at the door. Did Roman decide there was more to say after all?

I opened it to see Baz, not Roman. I was surprised at my relief.

"I came by to ask you how it went today." He pointed

to my sling as I let him in my apartment. "Looks like you've got a story to tell."

"I do, but I just realized I'm starving. You hungry?" I asked.

"Is that a real question?"

"My apologies." I locked up and we headed to The Cellar.

CHAPTER 26

I decided the two-block walk would be easier than climbing in and out of Baz's truck. And the cool air would make my head feel better. With my left arm cushioned in the sling and three ibuprofens in my system, my shoulder pain seemed to have lessened. Maybe it had just been overtaken by my appetite. On the way, I filled Baz in on my harrowing afternoon.

When I finished, he said, "Holy huckleberry, Wil. Maybe you should leave this thing alone."

"Believe me, I'm staying away from the Harringtons from now on. The worst part is, we might not find out what really happened. Do you think Heath's plan will work?"

"It's worth a shot." He laughed at his own pun. "Too soon?"

I couldn't help but laugh too.

We came upon the historic Inn at Yarrow Glen, a white boxy two-story building with matching wraparound porches on the upper and lower floors. The only adornments were the urns of pink snapdragons and yellow pansies on either side of the door.

The unassuming exterior did not extend to the quaint lobby, which consisted of a cozy seating area of early twentieth-century furniture nestled before an arched

fireplace. At the rear of the lobby past the spindle staircase was Constance Yi, who greeted guests with a chip-
per welcome and an encyclopedic knowledge of Yarrow
Glen. She noticed us right away even though she was helping a couple check in. Constance had eyes and ears on
everything, which was an even greater feat given how
much she enjoyed chatting. We waved and she waved
back, but then made a concerned face and pointed to
my sling. I gave her a thumbs-up to indicate it was no big
deal. I was glad she had guests so I wouldn't have to explain my sling. It would be impossible to keep what happened from eventually meandering its way around town,
but giving Constance the details would ensure it went the
direct route—do not pass go, do not collect two hundred
dollars.

We took the hallway off the lobby to the unmarked red
door, which led downstairs to the pub known as The Cellar. Luckily it wasn't as crowded as a weekend night—my
arm couldn't take being jostled. We even scored my favorite U-shaped booth tucked into one of the nooks.

"I'm gonna order at the bar. Do you know what you
want?" Baz said.

"I feel like I should have something good for my body,"
I replied, unnecessarily perusing the table menu I knew
by heart. The winter specials caught my eye. I remembered one I enjoyed last week. "I'm going to have the
Brussels sprouts grilled-cheese sandwich."

"I don't understand what you're saying."

"The grilled cheese with Brussels sprouts," I repeated.

"You want Brussels sprouts instead of French fries?"

"No. The sandwich has Brussels sprouts in it." I pointed
to the menu item.

"That's a good way to ruin a sandwich."

"It'll be good. You'll see," I told him.

He rolled his eyes. "You sound like Ginger."

"It could be our next favorite seasonal sandwich like the Raclette Reuben was. I bet next time we'll be sharing it."

"You're on your own with this one. Do you want something strong to drink for that arm?"

"Just water, thanks."

He and his conventional tastebuds walked off to the bar to order.

Only after he was gone did the deep ache in my shoulder register again. I was glad I was out with him to take my mind off it and especially to get my mind off Roman. I wasn't much of a drinker, but I was second-guessing the water order I gave to Baz.

When he returned to the booth with our drinks, A. J. appeared with his own drink in hand and his satchel over his shoulder. As usual, he must've been lurking nearby.

"What happened to you?" he said to me.

"Is that actual concern I hear in your voice or are you just interested in a story?" I asked.

"It's actual concern. Unless you're fine, then I want to know the story."

I laughed. At least he was honest.

"It's a lot to tell, but I'm fine," I said to close the topic. I was tired of talking about it.

"Well, *I've* got some stuff to tell. Move in." A. J. swatted Baz's arm with the back of his hand to get him to move over. Baz reluctantly obliged and A. J. scooted in. "I looked into Mayor Trumbull's finances."

"We read up on her too," Baz said.

"Her financial situation seemed to change drastically after her divorce," I added.

A. J. took out a pad of notes from his satchel. "Public tax records show she has no income other than her salary as a mayor, which means she's not getting any alimony.

She also doesn't have that many assets, so it looks like she didn't come away from the divorce with much. No big lump sum."

"That was our guess," Baz stated, sipping on his soda.

It still didn't make sense to me. "Why would she walk away with nothing? Archie found a blogger that said it was her husband's affair that ended the marriage."

"Then you have your answer. *His* affair is *her* scandal. My guess is, she didn't want a drawn-out, contentious divorce interfering with her reelection campaign. Olivia Harrington might not have liked that," A. J. said.

"What does Olivia have to do with it?"

"She was her biggest donor that year."

"That's weird," I said.

"Why do you say that?" A. J. asked.

"I got the feeling her relationship with Mayor Trumbull was . . . strained," I said by way of an explanation.

I was relieved that Baz was smart enough to stay quiet. Sharing my questions with A. J. would break Mayor Trumbull's confidence, so I wrestled with this new information on my own. Why would Mayor Trumbull be so adamant about pointing the finger at the Harringtons if Olivia had helped her get reelected? Mayor Trumbull alluded to how powerful they were. Maybe she had a personal experience with Olivia wielding that power if Olivia expected favors in return for her large donation. Or maybe it *was* only because Mayor Trumbull wanted me to focus on the Harringtons and not on her son, who Heath knew had been at the scene of the crime. I hated that this put suspicion back on the mayor and Everett.

A. J. brought me out of my rumination with another piece of information. "Well, you're right, it *is* weird because Olivia Harrington contributed to her opponent's campaign the election prior."

"What years are we talking about?" I asked.

"I know what you're thinking. She didn't switch her allegiance to Mayor Trumbull's campaign because of Summer—Nelson and Summer weren't dating yet," A. J. answered.

"But *Chloe* may have been dating him. Did you know she had first dibs?"

A. J.'s eyebrows shot up. "Didn't Marcos say that Olivia was always on the lookout for wealthy bachelors to pair her daughters up with?"

"Olivia might've had her sights set on Nelson, regardless of which daughter he ended up with. Maybe she thought it would help to cozy up to Mayor Trumbull by donating to her campaign."

Baz played devil's advocate. "She could've just liked what she saw in Mayor Trumbull's first term in office. She's a popular mayor."

Liz, one of The Cellar's regular servers, came with our sandwiches and A. J.'s change from his bill, which he told her to keep. My face must've not hidden my surprise at his generous tip.

"Servers hear things, and they're more likely to tell you about it if they like you," he explained without my asking after she left.

I knew there had to be something behind it. A. J. was a give-and-take kind of guy.

I carefully lifted my sandwich from the plate and ignored Baz's look of disgust. He was discriminating against the Brussels sprouts, but I could hardly blame him. My childhood experience with boiled Brussels sprouts wasn't much better. It was only when I first had them roasted that I changed my tune.

"Don't worry, I'm not going to make you try it," I said. I took my first bite. The crunch of the grilled multigrain bread and the roasted, shredded Brussels sprouts were a delicious contrast to the melty Havarti. The drizzled balsamic glaze gave it a nice kick. "You're missing out," I told Baz, enjoying my choice.

"You're still not selling me on it." Baz had already bitten into his own bacon barbeque cheeseburger, which I had to admit, looked darn good too.

"If the Harringtons are contributing to campaigns, their finances must be fairly solid. Did you find any red flags there?" Baz asked A. J.

"No, although they're not in public office so their finances aren't as open as Mayor Trumbull's. I did find it interesting that Olivia is named as CEO of *All Things Sonoma* magazine. She's not listed on any of their other businesses. They're all in her husband's name, some just changed over from his mother a couple years ago." A. J. took a bread plate and squirted ketchup on it. He proceeded to steal a handful of my fries.

I gave him a look but ignored it otherwise. He gave me his taco yesterday—fair's fair. I went back to the matter at hand. "That doesn't seem that suspicious to me. Her husband travels all the time, so maybe she wanted something to do, something of her own. What about Chloe and Summer? They both live at home. Do they even have jobs?"

"Doesn't look like they need them," Baz remarked.

"They're in their twenties, they ought to do something. It's not like they're Paris Hilton. Marcos said Chloe did some modeling a while back, but she gave it up," I told Baz.

"I looked them up. Summer's official title is 'influencer,'" A. J. said.

"She and half the girls I know," Baz threw in.

"Chloe did say their father wants to kick them out of the house when they turn thirty. She didn't seem worried about it, but it's possible she and Summer are going to be cut off financially pretty soon. That's only a couple years away," I said.

"It happens. Some parents do that so their kids will have an incentive to make something of themselves." Baz reached for his second napkin, and I took one too. The sandwich was delicious, but messy. "My dad didn't give any of us a break. If you work for him, you have to pull your weight. If you don't, you have to make your own way." Baz made his own way after working with his brother and three sisters at his father's custom home building business for a few years. Being a handyman fit his sociable personality better, which strained the family ties. I couldn't imagine having a fraught relationship with Baz, who was such an easy-going guy and had quickly become like a brother to me.

"The question is, if Summer inherits, was it an incentive for her to kill Nelson?" I posed.

"I thought we'd decided it was Mayor Trumbull who inherited," A. J. said.

I filled him in on Nelson's stated gesture to leave all his money to Summer.

"We're going on a lot of assumptions here. I need to talk to one of the Harrington sisters myself. Maybe Marcos can get me an interview." A. J. put his notes away.

"I wouldn't do that," Baz said. "Not unless you want to get yourself shot at like Willa."

A. J. choked on a French fry. "Excuse me?" he sputtered when he recovered.

I gave him a summary of my Wild West moment at Chloe's this afternoon. I honored Chloe's request to not repeat that she and Everett were at the stable with Nelson. Members of Team Cheese were the only people I relayed everything to.

"Talk about burying the lede." He reached in his satchel again and brought out his voice recorder and notepad. "What was I thinking? Tell me everything again. In detail."

"Put it away. If you want to write about it, you'll have to talk to Heath and get his official statement on it. I'm only telling you as part of our mutual investigation, not for tomorrow's story."

"The next issue doesn't come out until this weekend."

"You know what I mean."

"I'll expect to hear from you later for my *Case Closed* feature when this is all wrapped up," he said.

Running a small-town paper like the *Glen Gazette*, A. J. couldn't chance printing sensational headlines about Yarrow Glen's citizens being possible murder suspects. However, the *Case Closed* feature articles he ran after a culprit was caught detailing all aspects of the case were popular among the residents and fed his appetite for investigative journalism.

"For now, I'll talk to Detective Heath," he continued. "You know, Willa, we're asking questions about two powerful families—the Harringtons and the Trumbulls. You better be careful."

I planned to, but the only way I was going to feel completely safe was to find out who killed Nelson.

CHAPTER 27

The next day, following doctor's orders meant that I spent too much time trying to convince Mrs. Schultz and Archie I was still capable of doing my job with my arm in a sling. They didn't realize that watching them work from a stool behind the counter was more painful than my shoulder. I think they were mostly shaken up that I might've been targeted, so I finally acquiesced to their pampering.

It made it worse to watch each minute tick by, waiting for the phone call from Heath to find out if Shep and Melman caught anybody creeping around the Harringtons' property in search of something incriminating.

Mrs. Schultz brought one of our cheese boards to the counter to make today's sampling tray. "Let's do something fun with the cheese today," I said, wanting to take my mind off the impending phone call.

We discussed compiling dessert cheeses. Before I spent a college semester in France, the only cheese I ever ate as a dessert was in the form of cheesecake. I wanted to help introduce Americans to the custom of serving cheese after a meal.

We made a game of it and each looked for one independently then met back at the sampling counter after we'd made our choices. They sampled my pick first, which was one they hadn't yet tried—Fenacho cheese from Oregon, a semihard goat's milk cheese dotted with fenugreek seeds. The seeds added hints of maple-syrup-like flavor.

Mrs. Schultz chose the popular Norwegian Brabander Gouda, aged ten months using a higher temperature and humidity that gave it a fudge-like texture. Its decadent flavors of vanilla, cinnamon, and candied pecans in deep cream made it a perfect dessert cheese.

I wasn't too surprised to see Archie come back with the Brillat-Savarin, another triple crème like the Saint-André. This one from France also had a buttery and mild flavor and was especially delicious paired with berries.

After our tasting, Archie and Mrs. Schultz banished me back to my stool while they cut samples for the cheese board.

"If you were going to make me sit here, you could've at least gotten me a throne. 'Let them eat cheese!'" I declared in my most regal voice.

I watched them proudly as they prepared the arrangement on the board. In less than a year, they'd absorbed an impressive knowledge of cheeses.

"Are you going to feel up to going to the F.U.N. dance tomorrow night?" Mrs. Schultz asked me.

"I should be fine by then. My arm's feeling much better today, but people seem to keep yelling at me for not heeding advice, so I decided to follow doctor's orders and keep the sling on. I still plan to help finish decorating the hall tonight."

"Do you think Roman will be going to the dance?" she asked, trying to be nonchalant but failing.

"You mean are Roman and I going together? No." I didn't tell them about our conversation when Roman came to my apartment last night.

"Well, it's not a sweetheart's dance, anyway, it's for friends and neighbors," Mrs. Schultz said, obviously trying to make me feel better about it.

"Has anybody special asked you?" I countered.

Mrs. Schultz pressed her lips together and rearranged cheese that she'd already had just right. She'd said once that she was too mature to blush, and it must've been true. Still, I knew something was up.

"Frank did ask me," she finally said.

Archie, who seemed to only be half listening to our conversation, snapped his head up, eyes wide. "Mrs. Schultz, you have a date?"

He and I shared matching grins.

"No, no. It's not a date. I'm"—she cleared her throat and said more quietly—"I'm not quite ready to date. It's only been four years without Mr. Schultz."

We quelled our excitement. I squeezed Mrs. Schultz's arm. "It's understandable. It's perfectly all right to take your time."

"Mr. Schultz made me promise to have adventures and find someone to have those adventures with, but I never meant to keep the second part of that promise." She sighed.

"But you know he wanted you to, right?" Archie said.

"You're right, Archie, but somehow it doesn't make it any easier."

"You can take it as slowly as you want to. Just enjoy Frank's company for now," I said gently.

"That's what I intend to do. We've agreed to meet at the dance. Besides, what do I know about dating?" She chuckled.

"I don't know if this makes it better or worse, but you know as much as those of us who have been in the dating pool for a long time, I'm afraid." *I* sure didn't know much. My dating life was in shambles.

She put her hand on mine and squeezed back.

I turned the spotlight away from myself and Mrs. Schultz. "What about you, Archie? Have you asked Hope?"

"Who, me?" he said.

"I think you're the only Archie in the room," Mrs. Schultz replied.

"I-I don't know. I'm kinda nervous about it. Should I ask her as a friend or as a, you know, a date?"

"What would you like it to be? You two have been seeing a little more of each other lately, haven't you?" I said.

"She's gotten in the groove of classes and she's comfortable letting her new manager take care of more of the bakery responsibilities. It's given her some more time."

"Which she's been choosing to spend with you," Mrs. Schultz pointed out.

"I guess you're right. I would like it to be a date," he admitted.

"Then go for it!" I said, wincing a little, as I expected a lightning bolt of hypocrisy to strike me in that moment. I was even more cautious than Archie these days. Then again, I wasn't twenty years old experiencing my first real crush.

"It's just that, well, she owns her own business and she's going to culinary school and all that and I'm still living at home with my mom."

"She inherited the bakery from her mother. You're making your way just as she is. Have you been looking for apartments?" I asked.

"Yeah, but they're farther from town, so I think Baz was right when he said I should get a bike. I was thinking of seeing if Everett was in his shop today to ask him how much I could get one for."

"Why don't you do it now? Nothing's going on here."

Archie's face lit up. That was one thing about Archie— he never stayed down long. He took his apron off and left the shop with a skip in his step.

"Hope will be lucky to have him," Mrs. Schultz said after Archie left.

"It's always the good ones who don't know how good they are," I agreed.

I checked my phone to make sure I hadn't missed a call from Heath.

"No call from the police yet?" Mrs. Schultz asked, reading my mind.

"Nope. Have you heard from them about your stolen wallet?"

"Shep told me he's working on it, so I don't doubt it'll be wrapped up soon. I just wish it would happen before the dance. I don't like the gossip I've been hearing about it." Mrs. Schultz put the clear cloche over the cheese board.

"What have you been hearing?"

"People think it's one of the teenagers who've been volunteering. They were at the hall when Deandra's wallet was stolen and at the Paint and Snack when mine was taken. I don't want the dance to be ruined by anybody accusing them."

"Archie said he ran with a different crowd in high school, so he wasn't friends with any of them. He's closer in age to them than we are, so maybe they'd let him in on it if they've heard anything."

"Maybe he could speak with them at the hall," Mrs. Schultz said. She was now rewrapping the cheese wedges they'd cut the samples from. "Will Detective Heath make an appearance at the dance?"

"I wouldn't know." I shrugged, which I immediately regretted—it was the first zap of pain I'd felt in my shoulder since getting dressed this morning.

"Didn't he drive you to the hospital and then back home?" Mrs. Schultz probed.

"It never came up." Why was my voice suddenly higher? I cleared my throat before adding, "We mostly talked about the case."

I was happy when two women entered the shop—they were potential customers and they got me out of talking about Heath. Our dessert cheese samples won them over. We were wrapping up their purchases when my phone rang. I fumbled with it in my apron pocket as I pulled it out to see Heath in large letters on the screen. I finally managed to answer it.

"How's your arm feeling?" Heath asked after our hellos.

I walked to the unoccupied kitchenette area. "It's feeling better. Mrs. Schultz and Archie are taking very good care of me. What's the word on last night?"

"They had a lot of animal visitors, but no one else in the woods or field all night. I'm sorry."

I was disappointed but also relieved. "Don't be. Maybe it means I wasn't shot at."

"You should still be careful."

"I'll keep my distance from the Harringtons. Tell Shep and Officer Melman I'm sorry they had to spend the night outside." I felt especially bad because it had drizzled overnight.

"Don't feel bad. It's their job."

I ended the call just in time to offer goodbyes to the women happily taking home their cheeses. Once they were outside the shop, I relayed Heath's news to Mrs. Schultz.

"It means either none of the Harringtons were nervous

about possible evidence, or I wasn't shot at after all," I told her.

"To play it safe, I say we should still go on the assumption that you were a target yesterday," she said.

"Then it's a toss-up between Summer and Chloe. One of them had to have done it. They both had opportunity."

"What about Olivia? She was at the house too."

"You're right. I know she didn't want me there. So we have three suspects. I wish I could figure out how that slashed portrait of Nelson plays into this. I know it must mean something."

Mrs. Schultz's fingers played with the fringe of her scarf, which had tiny anchors on it, adding a sailor theme to her navy striped dress. "After you and Ginger saw the portrait, Chloe might've decided she'd scare you both into keeping quiet, so she shot at you."

"But why destroy the portrait *after* we saw it?" I shook my head. All the pieces didn't fit.

"Let's go back to the inheritance as a motive." The scarf seemed to be helping Mrs. Schultz puzzle it out. "Everett might not know that Nelson promised his money to Summer. If Everett thought his mother was inheriting, he could've decided to take the opportunity of the public argument to kill Nelson. Didn't Chloe say she left Nelson at the stable with Everett before Nelson was murdered? Everett had opportunity and motive." Mrs. Schultz wore a triumphant look, which vanished just as suddenly. "But he couldn't have shot at you. He didn't know you were horseback riding at Chloe's."

"That's right," I said, about to make another argument for Summer being the culprit. "Oh, wait a second. That's *not* right. I was at Everett's bicycle shop when Chloe and I made the plans. He was standing right there, listening. Time, place, horseback riding . . . everything." I didn't like how this was shaping up. "And he's making all his renovations top notch, no expense spared. And Archie's over there right now."

Mrs. Schultz and I instinctively went to the door and looked down the sidewalk toward Everett's shop.

"He wouldn't have any reason to hurt Archie," she said.

"Unless Archie decides to put on his Team Cheese detective hat and start asking questions." I didn't bother taking off my apron. I needed to get Archie out of there before he made himself Everett's next target.

CHAPTER 28

I hurried up the sidewalk to Everett's bike shop. If Everett was the murderer and did shoot at me, I didn't want him to view Archie as a threat too.

The lights were on, so I pushed open the door. There in the middle of the shop, I saw Archie splayed on the floor, facedown.

"Archie!" I ran over to him.

He rolled onto his back, startling me. "Willa! What's the matter?"

George, Everett's dog, trotted over with a ball in his mouth and dropped it beside Archie.

"Good boy!" Archie said, scratching the dog on the head. He rolled the ball across the room. George went after it. Archie stood and wiped the dust off his shorts. "What's up? Do you need me at the store?" he asked, not realizing my heart was just now starting to slow to a proper rate.

"No. Everything's fine."

Everett came in from the back room then, pushing an electric bike. George joined us once again with the ball. "Hey, neighbor," Everett said when he saw me. Then to Archie, "This is the bike I was talking about. I'm just starting to get my inventory in, but this gives you an idea."

"It's definitely an upgrade from my skateboard."

"What happened to your arm?" Everett asked me as Archie looked the bike over.

"Bruised shoulder. Horseback riding at Chloe's didn't work out so well," I said, gauging his reaction. Did his eyes read guilty?

"Bummer. Did you ice it? I wiped out on my bike once and dislocated my shoulder. I popped it back in place and it was good as new in a couple of days."

"Ouch!" Archie said, rubbing his own shoulder. "Are you sure you should be telling that story to a potential customer?"

"You're probably right." Everett chuckled. "This type of bike isn't meant for mountain biking, anyway, but it goes at a pretty good clip."

"I'll take something like this if I can't find an apartment near town. Otherwise, a regular bike will do."

"Come back in when you find a place and I'll hook you up with something just right for you," Everett replied. "I should be open for business very soon and I'll give you a great price, seeing as how you're my first customer."

While they talked, George had been picking up the ball and dropping it at our feet, hoping to get someone's attention. Everett rubbed the dog's head and he finally laid down, flopping his chin on his front paws in disappointment. "It must be time for his W-A-L-K. He gets as stir-crazy about going outside as I do. I can't wait to lead some bike tours once the shop gets up and running."

"That'll be great," I said. This once again confirmed why I chose cheese as my career choice and not bikes—you have to practice what you preach. "You're a real out-doorsman. Hiking, biking . . . hunting?"

Archie's focus went from George to me. He knew I was up to something.

Everett answered, "No, that's not for me. I couldn't kill an animal. I spent three weeks rehabilitating a squirrel last fall. He and George hit it off."

"Chloe wanted me to go skeet shooting yesterday, but I've never handled a gun," I said. The skeet shooting part was a lie.

"It might've been safer than the horse," Everett joked.

I forced myself to laugh with him when Archie asked him, "Have you ever done that?"

"Skeet shooting? I went a handful of times at my stepfather's estate when my mom lived there. I prefer to do things that are more active, but it was challenging. It's not so easy hitting a moving target."

Lucky for me.

"Speaking of the Harringtons," he continued, "Olivia insisted on having everyone at their home after the memorial tomorrow evening. The service is private, but you're invited to come afterward to pay your respects. I know it overlaps with the dance, so my mother and I understand if you don't come."

"I'll try to make it. Thank you for letting me know." I could hardly ask him any more questions about yesterday or the murder now. "We'll let you go so George can get his walk."

George's head lifted and he looked up at Everett. His eyes widened in anticipation.

Everett chuckled. "Yes, George. Let's go for a walk."

George scrambled onto all fours. Archie and I gave him one last pat and left Everett's shop.

Mrs. Schultz stood at the door of Curds & Whey, working her scarf with nervous fingers. She looked relieved to see Archie safe and sound and asked him about their conversation.

"We didn't talk about anything but the bikes. I thought

after what happened last night, the Harringtons were our prime suspects."

I filled him in on my realization that Everett knew I'd be on horseback yesterday.

"And we just found out he knows how to shoot," Archie said, wide-eyed.

"And Heath said that none of the Harringtons took the bait and went in search of anything last night. So that means either I wasn't shot at or Everett was the shooter."

"Are you going to the memorial reception tomorrow to find out more?" Archie asked me.

I was conflicted. I'd just told Heath on the phone that I'd stay away from the Harringtons. Archie and Mrs. Schultz sensed my indecision.

"Where else are you going to have all the suspects in one room?" Archie coaxed.

"It'll be like an Agatha Christie novel," Mrs. Schultz remarked excitedly.

"I'm hardly Poirot. Besides, I can't be investigating for Mayor Trumbull anymore in good conscience when so many signs point to her son being the murderer. Maybe I should lie low for now."

My phone dinged a text. I slipped it out of my apron and showed the others. It was from Mayor Trumbull, requesting to meet with me in her office that afternoon.

It looked like lying low was not going to be an option.

CHAPTER 29

It was still drizzling when I left for Town Hall, so I took an umbrella, which was easier to manage than taking my sling on and off to put on a raincoat. The short walk would give me some time to think about what I was going to say to Mayor Trumbull. I had to tell her I would no longer be investigating the case for her without telling her the real reason, that she and her son were now added to my suspect list. I supposed it would be easy enough—I may have just been shot at. The tricky part was going to be how to discover if either of them were involved in Nelson's murder.

This time the mayor's administrative assistant, a guy in his thirties, neat in appearance, was behind the desk of Mayor Trumbull's outer office. In a librarian's hushed voice, he told me the mayor was expecting me.

Her door was open, so I stepped through, belatedly realizing I still had my drippy umbrella.

Mayor Trumbull left her desk and solicitously welcomed me into her office.

"Sorry about the umbrella," I said.

"You can put it right in the stand," she said, pointing to an umbrella stand by the door. As I did, I noticed the bronze eagle sculpture again—its wings outstretched, head pushed forward, sharp-eyed, hunting for prey. Was there a reason the sculpture her brother gave her was an eagle on the hunt? Did he know her better than most?

She stuck her head out of the office door. "Collin, coffee?" She then pushed the door almost all the way shut behind me. "How are you? I heard what happened." She showed me to the more comfortable chair in the seating area this time and sat across from me on the sofa.

"It's just a bruised shoulder. I'll be fine, thanks. How did you hear?" Curiosity overtook my imprudence.

"Well, I *am* the mayor."

That was a nonanswer, but one she probably got away with often. I couldn't very well ask if her son told her after he'd shot at me.

Collin padded in discreetly with two coffees. He set the cups and saucers on the low table between us, smiled at our thanks, and left promptly, closing the door behind him.

"I feel horrible that you got hurt," Mayor Trumbull continued. "Especially because I'm sure you were over there for . . . a reason. Did you find out anything?"

That explained the coffee and the cushy chair—she wanted information.

"I'm afraid my accident cut the day short," I answered, being purposely obtuse.

"You think it was an accident? Detective Heath implied otherwise."

"So it was Detective Heath who told you about it?"

She picked up her coffee and took her time sipping it before responding. "I've asked him to keep me informed of any developments."

"You *are* the mayor."

We smiled at each other. She wasn't going give me anything on her own. I'd have to be more direct.

"There were a few things I did find out before then."
As soon as the words left my lips, a nervous flutter in my
gut told me I should've kept my mouth shut.

"Oh?"

No, Willa, don't do it!

"What do you know about Nelson's inheritance?"

There, I said it.

Mayor Trumbull was taken aback. "Obviously, I've
spoken with our family attorney, but I don't see how that
has any relevance to this."

"Some might consider it motive."

I was all in now. There'd be no going back. I might've
just blown my amicable relationship with the mayor.

She took a leisurely sip of coffee and carefully placed
the cup back on its saucer. She ran her palms along her
lap, needlessly straightening her pencil skirt.

A childhood memory flared—the time my brother
almost stumped me at hide-and-seek by hiding in the
creamery on our dairy farm. It was only after I'd given
in to worry that I bothered to look there. We both knew it
was strictly off-limits for playing. But right after I made
my discovery, so did my father—finding both me and
my brother in the creamery with our barn boots on. I recalled how our dad decided to polish one of the stain-
less steel tanks while we stood frozen, waiting for him to
speak. He was either biding time while he figured out how
to handle us or he wanted to prolong our agony in not
knowing. This moment felt similar.

Mayor Trumbull looked up at me, apparently resolv-
ing something in her mind. "It's obvious you're aware Detective Heath questioned me about the inheritance."

"I didn't hear it from him directly." I didn't want to
get Heath in trouble, and it was the truth. I hadn't known

for certain until just now that Mayor Trumbull was the beneficiary.

"I had no inkling Nelson would leave anything to me, much less everything. I'd assumed he'd already made a will leaving it all to Summer. In fact, I took out a life insurance policy on him after his parents died. I had no idea where his money was going and just in case something happened to him, I wanted to be able to give him a proper funeral. I didn't expect to get anything from him, and I certainly would never kill him for it."

"I-I wasn't suggesting—"

"Of course you were. It's not possible you helped solve those other cases without suspecting everyone who might've had motive. But I don't want you to waste your time looking at me, so I have to disclose something to you now that Detective Heath knows."

I leaned in.

"I'd made a pact with Olivia that we wouldn't tell anyone outside of the police. As I told you last time, I don't want to be the one to point the finger at any of the Harringtons."

Yet, once again, you are.

"However, it's time you have all the facts. Everett overheard Nelson and Chloe." Mayor Trumbull took a breath. "Let me start from the beginning. After Nelson charged Roman with the horse and galloped off to the stable, Everett and I went into the house. My idea was that he'd go out front and keep the guests away. But I was able to get the guest list from Polly, and since we had some time before their arrival, I decided texting and making phone calls to keep them from coming was a better system. I told Everett to get Nelson, instead, and make sure he left." Mayor Trumbull closed her eyes for a moment, as if to fortify herself for what she was about to say. "Everett went to the stable, like I asked. But when he got there, Chloe was there and he overheard them talking."

I didn't let on that I already knew this much. "What did they say?"

"Nelson said that Chloe was right all along and that *she* should've been the Harrington daughter that he married."

I had wondered if their breakup had been as easy on her as she said it was, but I had no idea he still had feelings for her.

Mayor Trumbull paused, making sure I was listening raptly before she said, "They kissed."

"They kissed?" That, I didn't know.

"Yes. Then Everett said they had an exchange that was hard to hear because they were entwined with each other. It was quick, and immediately after, Chloe pushed Nelson away and Everett heard her say something like, 'You'd better make up your mind.' That was when they spotted Everett. Nelson told him to leave. After what he'd just overheard, he did. He didn't want to be involved in that."

If this was true, Chloe left out a lot in her version. And it contradicted Chloe's story that she left Nelson with Everett. Everett could be lying, but what if he wasn't?

Aloud, I worked out what was in my mind. "So maybe after Everett walked away, Nelson did choose Summer. Chloe could've been tired of playing second fiddle and killed him."

"Yes."

"Or Everett wasn't the only one to catch them together. Summer could've overheard them too." This gave me a lot to think about. "Why did you keep this from me if you wanted me to help solve the case?"

"This puts my son at the scene of the crime. I didn't want you wasting your time suspecting him."

"You could've at least told me Chloe went to the stable."

"We all agreed that no one outside of the police would know. If Olivia could've gotten to any of us before we spoke to Detective Heath that night, she would've kept us from telling even him."

"How would she have done that?"

"Olivia Harrington gets her way. That's what I've been trying to tell you. Why do you think Chloe's not arrested yet? Detective Heath had all of this information the very first night. The police won't chance arresting a Harrington without every piece of evidence in place." Her hands were pressed together, almost in prayer. "Olivia and I made a pact that we would protect our children. We wanted to keep them from public scrutiny. I asked you to investigate, but I had to keep my promise to Olivia. I need you to not be swayed by the Harringtons. If the police have to decide between Chloe and Everett, Everett will lose. Olivia will make sure of that."

I was more conflicted than ever before. I needed time to think. "I have to get back to the shop," I told her and stood to leave. She followed me to the door.

"I hope you're coming to the reception after Nelson's service tomorrow. I'd planned to be at the dance, but this can't be helped," she said.

"Everett mentioned it to me."

"I'm glad he did. We'll see you there."

I didn't respond. I couldn't tell Mayor Trumbull now that I wouldn't investigate any further for her. She needed me to believe in her son. But did I?

CHAPTER 30

My head was spinning as I left the mayor's office. How much of her story could I believe?

I thought about what Everett supposedly overhead between Chloe and Nelson. Everyone knew Nelson dated Chloe first. Did Everett use that information to make up a story about what happened between them at the stable? Or did Chloe murder Nelson because she was still in love with him, and he ultimately wouldn't choose her? There was also the possibility that Summer somehow discovered Chloe and Nelson, just as Everett had. It could've been Summer who killed Nelson in anger.

As the three possible culprits—Summer, Chloe, and Everett—bounced around in my brain like lottery-number balls in a spinning cage, A. J. was suddenly in front of me. I would never get used to the way he always seemed to appear out of nowhere.

"Are you stalking me?" I said.

"No, I'm stalking the mayor," he whispered. "How is it that you keep having meetings with her?"

"I told you, I'm the F.U.N. dance liaison."

We walked outside and stood on the wide steps of Town Hall. The rain had stopped.

"You don't look like you were discussing a dance. You look shook."

I hadn't shared anything with A. J. about Chloe and Everett even being at the stable, so I had no intention of sharing this revelation. Considering how much Mayor Trumbull feared the Harringtons' backlash, keeping her confidence seemed more important than ever. I came up with an excuse. "I heard from Heath. They didn't find anything to prove a shooting took place."

"I know. Shep just gave me a statement. That should make you feel better, right? Maybe nobody shot at you?"

"Maybe. I was hoping they'd discover something definitive, and the case would end there. I feel like I'm getting half-truths and half the story from everyone."

"I know how to ask the right questions to get information out of people, but it's nearly impossible to get access to the Harringtons. Nobody in their circle is willing to say anything. You think we should put the heat on Everett?"

"Why Everett?" I knew why, but what did A. J. know?

"He could be an indirect beneficiary of the inheritance if the money went to Mayor Trumbull. He's starting a new business. He might need the cash influx. He's got motive and his mother's his only alibi."

I didn't want A. J. suddenly questioning Everett. Mayor Trumbull might think I'd told him her secret. What I needed to find out is which one of them was telling the truth about what happened at the stable—Everett or Chloe. A. J. knew Chloe and Nelson used to have a relationship, so he could help me follow that path, even if he didn't know about their tête-à-tête just before Nelson was murdered.

"The missing link is whether Chloe was still in love

with Nelson. I think we should find out more about their past relationship," I said.

"We can get help from Marcos. He's known Chloe the longest," A. J. decided.

"Can we count on him to tell us the truth? Chloe said he's been after her for a relationship, even though she's not interested. That was a different story than he told us."

"Who likes to admit they've been turned down?"

"Okay, but he also disappeared at the time of Nelson's murder."

"He told us he was making a phone call," A. J. said, unbothered.

"You can walk a few steps away to make a phone call. He was gone for at least a half hour. I'm not saying he killed Nelson, but I think he's lying about something. I just don't know if we can trust him."

A. J. pursed his lips and threw a glance skyward. "A 'phone call' in paparazzi-speak means he was giving someone the inside scoop on what happened. He couldn't supply the photos, but he could make some cash by delivering the story."

"So that's how the story got all over the internet. He's not afraid Olivia will find out?"

"That's the favor he was paying me back for, why he agreed to show me the photos of the shower. He called me that afternoon right after it happened, and I called our guys in the media. If somehow word got out, the trail would lead back to me."

"But you weren't there."

"But I'm the editor of the *Glen Gazette*. Ostensibly, I could've gotten anyone who worked the party to tell me about it and sold the story to the outlets myself. Marcos would have plausible deniability."

"That all makes sense." I couldn't fault A. J. for keeping Marcos's secret since I had some secrets I was keeping too. "Can you contact him now and set up a time to meet?"

A. J. pulled out his phone and began texting. I was suddenly chilled and envied his dependable Salvation Army jacket. I only noticed it had started to drizzle again when a drip fell from one of his black curls. The closed umbrella I was holding wasn't doing me much good. I popped it open and sheltered both of us with it using my working arm.

A. J. read the return text. "He's finishing up a photo shoot for the magazine at the inn. We can meet him there now."

I nodded. I was tensed from shivering.

"You cold? Do you, uh . . . want my jacket?" he asked tentatively.

I could tell he was asking because it was the right thing to do, not because he wanted to do it, but I was touched by the offer. I knew that jacket was a part of his identity—a near-permanent fixture on him. I wouldn't ask to borrow his beloved jacket. Besides, who knew when it was washed last? It could probably walk over to me on its own.

I was about to decline, but he was already taking it off.

"It's okay," I said.

"Here." He clumsily draped it over my shoulders.

"Thanks," I answered awkwardly. I did feel warmer. "Let's get to the inn."

I collapsed my umbrella when we arrived on the inn's porch, shaking off the droplets of rain before going inside. I was happy to enter the warm and welcoming lobby, and was surprised to see Constance there in the afternoon. She usually worked the reception desk in the evenings. She was away from the desk now, chatting to Marcos and another guy, likely an assistant, who were packing up lights and camera equipment by the seating area. She tended to keep talking until something interrupted her. As soon as she saw us, she skittered over, looking perky in her black slacks that skimmed her petite frame and a sunny yellow silk blouse that played off her dark blunt-cut hair and equally dark eyes.

"Willa! A. J.! *All Things Sonoma* is doing a feature article on the inn—a proper one, not like when the Lippingers ran the magazine. And guess who'll be in the pictures?"

"Ummm, you?" I guessed.

"Yes! Well, the Stewarts, of course, they're the owners, but the photographer said he got some great shots of me, as one of the faces of the inn. Apparently, I was so helpful during the interview last week, they said I just *had* to be behind the reception desk for the photo shoot."

"That doesn't surprise me. You know everything about everything around here. I'm sure you were a wealth of information for them."

She leaned in and whispered, "Spending an hour with him wasn't a hardship, I'll tell you that much. Have you ever seen anyone look so hot in ripped jeans?" She fanned herself with her hand as she peeked at Marcos. "I hope you're okay? I heard you fell off a horse." She tried to look under A. J.'s jacket to see my bum arm.

"Thanks. It was just a silly accident," I said, downplaying it.

"Glad you're all right. Oops, I'd better get back." She scurried to the reception desk as a couple walked in with luggage.

I couldn't wait to get near the blaze in the fireplace and warm up. Marcos had been hunched over his equipment and noticed us as we walked over.

He stood. "Hey, guys."

I hated to admit it, but Constance was right—hot. You just knew he was hiding a six-pack under that T-shirt.

His assistant, a burly guy with sagging jeans, was done collecting the equipment. "Are we all set?" he said to Marcos, hitching up his pants.

"Yeah, good job today. Keith, this is my old pal A. J. Stringer. We knew each other back in our L.A. days."

"Paparazzi too?" the assistant asked.

"Writer," A. J. said.

They shook hands.

"He's the editor for the *Glen Gazette* now. And this is . . ." He snapped his fingers, his brown eyes crinkling at the edges as he searched his memory for my name.

"Willa," I reminded him. He was getting less attractive by the minute.

"Right. Willa."

The assistant threw me a polite smile.

"Do you mind sticking around a few minutes more? I said I'd have a quick chat with them," Marcos said to Keith.

"No problem. I wouldn't mind grabbing a drink downstairs now that we're done," Keith replied.

"Meet you down there," Marcos said.

Keith went down the hallway to The Cellar.

Now that we were alone, I had to think fast. I led with small talk. "The magazine's doing a story on the inn?"

"We've got one planned for Apricot Grille too," Marcos replied, smiling.

That's good news for Mayor Trumbull.

"Do you mind if we sit next to the fireplace?" I was

already on my way to the Chesterfield sofa nearest the arched fireplace. The furniture had been moved around a little for the photo shoot, so Marcos pushed a wing chair in to make a snug seating arrangement for the three of us to talk privately. A. J. sat beside me on the sofa.

"What's up?" Marcos asked.

The couple of minutes that it took to walk from Town Hall to the inn was the only time A. J. and I took to prepare what to say. I looked at A. J. *Your turn.*

He picked up the metaphorical baton. "I have a few questions for my *Cased Closed* story. I wanted to get some more background on the players involved." He took his mini voice recorder from his satchel.

"Okayyy." Marcos sounded guarded. "What's the rush? Why's the cheese lady here again?"

A. J. and I looked at each other, both searching for a good answer. It didn't feel like the sidekick excuse was going to work again.

"Oh, I get it," Marcos said, eyeing A. J.'s jacket still draped over my shoulders. "You two are an item."

A. J. guffawed. "Her?" he said incredulously.

Marcos interrupted his denial. "It's cool, man. She's cute. Ya know, for *you.*"

I wasn't sure which one of them I was more offended by, but I kept the bigger picture in mind. "I'm his silent partner." I leaned closer to A. J. to bring home Marcos's assumption and to also annoy A. J. as a bonus.

"So what do you want to know?" Marcos asked.

A. J. turned on the recorder.

"We heard Nelson and Chloe were an item before he started dating Summer."

"Yeah. So? It wasn't serious."

"Are you sure?" Those carved initials in the tree trunk told me something different.

"Chloe's up for romance and fun and adventure. She's never been serious about anybody, not long-term anyway. She falls madly in love at the drop of a hat and then three months later, she moves on to the next guy. She's done it plenty. Carpe diem."

From Chloe's description, she might've done it to Marcos too. If he was right, then Everett must be lying about what he overheard at the stable. Then a new thought occurred to me—a whole new perspective on it. What if Everett *did* overhear some playful banter between Nelson and Chloe and it made him angry?

"Could she have done it to Everett? Did she ever date him?"

"Not Everett. Even for Chloe, that would've been too weird."

"Because he's Nelson's cousin?"

"No, because he was Oscar Strathmore's stepson."

"I don't get it. Working class, stepdad's got money . . . . He seems to fit her MO."

Marcos reached over and turned off the recorder. "This doesn't go into any story anytime, anywhere. Got it?" he said to A. J.

"Come on, you're killing me," A. J. said.

I elbowed him so he'd make the promise.

A. J. sighed. "Fine. Just for you, Marcos, it'll stay off the record."

"Chloe doesn't care who knows, but her mother apparently does." Marcos paused again. "Maybe it would be better for Chloe if she didn't have to keep the secret anymore."

A. J. and I leaned in to hear what this secret was.

"A few years ago, Chloe had an affair with Oscar Strathmore," Marcos said.

"Mayor Trumbull's husband?" I sputtered.

"Ex now, thanks to the affair. And Everett's stepfather, which is why she'd never hook up with him."

"Does Everett know?" I asked. Now I *really* had a change in perspective.

"I can't be sure, but I don't think so. Chloe said Mayor Trumbull caught them and kicked him out."

"If he's the one who had the affair, how did Oscar Strathmore keep all his money and the mayor ended up with nothing?" A. J. asked.

"Mayor Trumbull was the one who wanted to keep it a secret, so he had the leverage. He didn't care at that point. Chloe told me he even wanted to keep it going with her, but once her mother found out, that was it. She said she was bored with him by then anyway. Then she moved on to Nelson."

Marcos's assistant Keith was back. He slapped Marcos on the shoulder. "The grande dame has been trying to reach you."

"Olivia?" Marcos confirmed.

"She's in the office today and is expecting us."

Marcos reached for his phone in his bag and saw the missed call. "Not good. Gotta run, guys."

He and Keith loaded their arms with their equipment and briskly headed out the door.

A. J. and I sat for another minute. I was too stunned to move, although the fire felt too warm for me now.

"I can't believe I didn't find this out when I did that piece on her after she was reelected," A. J. said, staring straight ahead.

"You were doing a nice story on her for the *Gazette*. You weren't trying to uncover anything salacious."

"I did look into her finances, though. I knew something was off. I should've dug deeper. What kind of a journalist am I? The *Gazette*'s made me soft."

"Well, we managed to find out now, didn't we?"

"And I have to keep it to myself. This is torture."

"It would only hurt Mayor Trumbull and she's done nothing wrong, at least as far as her marriage is concerned."

"You're right. I wouldn't print it anyway, even if he let me. Mayor Trumbull's done good things for this town." He noticed me staring at him. "What? What's that look for?"

"I think you try to portray that tough L.A. journalist on the outside, but on the inside you're really a softie. Maybe the *Glen Gazette* is the right place for you."

"You're reading too much into it. But I do love keeping one hand in the grittier side of things with my *Case Closed* features. I, uh, I appreciate you working with me."

I could tell his uncommon display of vulnerability was uncomfortable for him. "Are you thanking your sidekick?" I kidded.

"You're not going to let me live that *sidekick* comment down, are you?"

"Nope."

"You want to get some lunch while we're here?" he asked, changing the subject.

"I've got to get back to the shop. Thanks for setting this up with Marcos. Oh, and here's your jacket. Thanks for that too, you old softie."

I'd managed to annoy him again, which brought our relationship back in balance. He headed to The Cellar while I left the inn. I started the damp walk back to Curds & Whey determining if and how this bombshell that just landed on my lap would help me solve this case.

CHAPTER 31

A honking horn caught my attention. A white pickup, Baz's truck, pulled to the curb beside me. With army left arm hurt, it took all my core muscles to climb up into the cab.

"Sorry. That was probably more effort than it was worth. I shoulda let you walk, huh?" he said when I was finally in.

"I have so much to tell you," I answered.

"Spill it."

"Let's go back to the shop, so I can fill in Mrs. Schultz and Archie too."

The early drizzle had suddenly picked up to a full-fledged rain. All the diagonal parking spots in front of the shop were available, so Baz pulled in to the one closest to the door and we hustled inside to a shop vacant of customers. I closed the door behind us to keep out the blowing rain.

Although Curds & Whey relied heavily upon strolling sidewalk shoppers, today I almost didn't mind their absence. I needed the collective smarts of my friends to help me figure out this case. It was too bad for the shoppers, though. The dreary weather outside made Curds & Whey even more inviting, in my eyes. Amid the darker skies, the mellow lights of the sconces on the antique raised-panel accent wall were more noticeable against the warm oak. It felt as if we were in a library of cheese.

Plenty of customers told us how much they enjoyed spending time lingering at Curds & Whey. It had made me begin to dream about rearranging the kitchenette area to add some bistro tables and chairs for in-house snacking. We could start serving the cheesy dishes and cheese boards Archie and Mrs. Schultz loved creating. Adding a new revenue stream would mean a lot more work than just putting in some tables, but the thought of customers spending even more time enjoying my shop was exciting.

I deposited my umbrella and Baz's slicker in the stockroom. The four of us collected in the kitchenette as I rounded up a quick snack, since I never did get any lunch during my lunch break. I pilfered from our fruit bowl and rinsed and sliced a couple of Bosc pears for sharing. Nothing was easier to grab when you're hungry than cheese. I decided on a trio of Manchego, Parmigiano-Reggiano, and some aged cheddar, in case Baz wanted to partake.

Gathered around the farm table, I told them everything that had transpired with Mayor Trumbull and Marcos. Their shocked faces mirrored my feelings.

"So the mayor found out about the affair and got a no-fuss, no-muss divorce faster than you can say huckleberry to keep out any scandal before her reelection," Baz said, summarizing the news aptly.

"It explains why Olivia Harrington donated to the mayor's campaign. She wanted to ensure everything was kept quiet," Mrs. Schultz added.

The wheels in my brain turned as I finished chewing the Parmigiano-Reggiano and pear combo I'd popped in my mouth, savoring the pronounced flavor of the dry cheese with the sweet-tart pear. "I wonder if Mayor Trumbull regrets taking that money. You'd think she'd applaud the fact that Olivia was able to keep it under wraps even amid the reelection scrutiny. Instead, she seems to resent her."

"Did Mayor Trumbull really want them to be one, big happy family when Nelson and Summer got engaged?" Baz said.

That felt odd to me too. "Maybe that's why she's been nudging me in Chloe's direction. She wants me to suspect her. When she came to the shop on Saturday night while the Harringtons were here, I picked up on some tension, but it didn't occur to me that it was directed Chloe's way," I said. "And she kept saying how happy she was about the match because of how the magazine would benefit the town. Has Mayor Trumbull been lying about everything?"

"We're assuming Marcos knows everything about Chloe and told you the truth," Baz said, eating only the cheddar, as I'd suspected.

"I think he's telling the truth, but he might not know everything about what happened. We could be missing something important."

"I could talk to Everett," Baz said.

"You can't. I was told everything in confidence. And I don't know if Everett knows about his former stepfather's affair. I sure don't want us to be the ones to break it to him."

"You're right."

I put the cheese down. "I feel like this new information opens a whole new bag of possible puzzle pieces, I just don't know how to put them into place. This whole time Mayor Trumbull's been making it seem as though she's scared of Olivia's power, but the mayor's got just as much on her, if not more. It's Chloe's reputation on the line."

"Mayor Trumbull obviously has some sway with her. Olivia agreed to use Curds and Whey and Rise and Shine Bakery for Summer's shower because Mayor Trumbull asked her to," Mrs. Schultz pointed out.

"Did she ask her to or *tell* her to?" Archie said, drumming his fingers on the table.

"That's a good question, Archie. All this time, I've been worried about Olivia based on what Mayor Trumbull's been feeding me."

"Well, Olivia Harrington *is* kind of scary," Baz said.

Archie bobbed his head in agreement.

"Unfriendly, but not particularly scary. Not without the mayor's innuendos about her. I wonder if we've been focusing on the wrong family." I picked up another piece of cheese as I pondered that.

The front door swung open, and a group of customers blew in. Archie and Mrs. Schultz went to the front to help. I wrapped the leftover cheese and kept it in the kitchenette.

Baz retrieved his slicker from the back. He put it on and said quietly, "Look, Wil. Now that you suspect Everett and Mayor Trumbull, there's no reason to keep investigating for her."

"You're right. Except if someone did try to kill me, I wouldn't mind knowing who it was."

"Yeah, except for that."

"Mayor Trumbull did invite me to the memorial. All the suspects in one place is very tempting." I couldn't help but consider going.

"What are you going to say to them? 'Sorry for your loss, and by the way, did you kill him?'"

"I guess you're right. I'm going to give Heath this

new information about Chloe and Mayor Trumbull's ex-husband. I'll let him sort it out."

"Good." He looked toward the front windows, still being lashed with rain. "I hate to go out in this, but I've got a couple more jobs to do." He pulled his hood over his head. "I think it's a smart move, you bowing out of the investigation. Like A. J. said, these are powerful people."

As I watched him leave, I couldn't help but wonder which powerful family might get away with murder.

CHAPTER 32

I showered after work, popped a couple of ibuprofens, and changed my clothes. My shoulder was feeling tender but significantly better, so I left my sling off. No sense in going to the hall to help if no one would let me because of a hurt arm. By the time I left the apartment, I realized the security complex would be closed. I'd have to call Heath later to update him on what I'd learned.

Things were already abuzz at the hall when I arrived. My determination to put the murder out of my mind went by the wayside as soon as I saw Everett. He and Baz had their heads together over something on a laptop. I caught sight of Shep, standing on his own out of uniform, his back to the wall and his gaze sweeping the room. The police knew Everett was at the stable long before I did. Was Shep keeping an eye on him? Did Heath ask him to look out for me? I had to know.

"Hey, Shep," I said, sauntering over to him.

"Hi, Willa. How's the shoulder and the noggin?" He rapped his head with his knuckles.

"My head's hard as ever and my shoulder's much better, thanks for asking. And thanks for going the extra mile for me last night." I didn't want to say the words *Harrington* or *stakeout* in case we were overheard.

"No problem. It's all a part of the job. I have to say, though, I haven't pulled an all-nighter since my partying days. It hits different after thirty, even without any alcohol involved. I slept most of the day today."

"I can imagine. I'm sorry it was for nothing."

"Not for nothing. Even nothing means something."

The conversation lapsed as I grappled with that. I'd rarely had occasion to interact with Shep outside of the investigations we were both involved in. There didn't seem any easy way to transition into asking him why he was here. "I didn't know you were on the decorating committee," I said. In fact, I knew he wasn't.

"I'm not. I'm here unofficially to keep a lookout in case anybody decides to steal another wallet." I saw him staring at the table of teenagers finishing up the veggie decorations with Lou.

"Any leads?"

"Not so far."

"You're not exactly undercover." He was in jeans and a long-sleeved shirt, but everybody knew Shep and he wasn't making an effort to blend in.

"If I only deter the thief tonight, that's okay too."

I quieted my voice, "How's the murder case going?" I instinctually looked over at Everett, now helping Baz with the speakers.

"I can't talk about the investigation," he said.

He'd been a little loose-lipped in the past with Baz and their friends, which had helped us out, but I obviously didn't fall into the *friends* category.

"I hope you've moved on from Roman as a person of interest by now." I looked around the room to see if I'd missed him, but he wasn't here.

"You know it's nothing personal, right? Roman's a buddy of mine," he said.

"I know you're just doing your job. I'm worried about him, though. I haven't seen him around much."

"I saw him at The Cellar with Gia before I came here. He seems good."

"Oh. Well, good then. I'm glad to hear it. I'm going to go see what I can help with." I walked away before he noticed the flush I felt spreading to my cheeks.

Yes, glad to hear it. Sooo glad. He's out to dinner with Gia and he's perfectly fine, which should make you very happy, Willa.

So why did I feel like I'd just swallowed a lump of coal? I wasn't sure of my feelings toward him either, not now. Still, did he have to move on so quickly?

I ended up near Baz and Everett and we exchanged hellos. I heard a third "hello" and saw Ginger squirming out from under the table. She dusted off the knees of her skinny jeans and wrestled her thick auburn hair away from her face. "It's plugged into the wall," she said to the guys.

"I don't get why this won't connect to the speakers," Everett said, tapping keys on the laptop keyboard.

"Everett offered his laptop for the music," Ginger explained.

"That's nice of you."

"Only if it works," he replied. "I'm going to be one of the town-center shop owners soon, like you all, so I figured I should start pulling my weight."

"We'll get it figured out," Baz said, checking the connections again.

"You've been going through a lot. None of us would expect you to help out under the circumstances. Are you planning to come still? Chloe told me the memorial is tomorrow night," Ginger said.

"I think I'll be able to do both. I'd like to, anyway.

Are you going to the dance with someone?" Everett asked her.

I looked at Baz. Had he asked her yet? I felt bad for forgetting to speak to him about Ginger.

Ginger held her answer, obviously waiting for Baz to intervene. He didn't. "Nobody's asked me," she said.

This finally triggered Baz to speak, "I didn't think we were supposed to couple up. That's kind of the point of it, right? So everyone feels included?"

"That's true," I agreed. I didn't want Everett to swoop in on Ginger and I didn't think she really wanted it either. Besides, we weren't sure Everett wasn't a murderer.

"Right, right." Everett nodded.

I took the first opportunity to extract myself from the uncomfortable trio. "I'm going to go see how I can be useful."

I went over to the table of teenagers. Mrs. Schultz, Frank, and Lou were standing nearby. Another love triangle.

The teens were using markers to decorate the white paper tablecloth. F.U.N. and *FRIENDS UNITING NEIGHBORS* in colorful graffiti lettering marked it up.

"This looks fantastic," I said to the group.

"It's for the buffet table. It was Frank's idea," Mrs. Schultz said with pride in her voice.

"Are your vegetable-flower centerpieces done, Lou?"

"Just finished them up a few minutes ago. Archie's putting them on the tables now," Lou said.

"They're really something, Lou," Mrs. Schultz said.

Lou's mouth tweaked upward. "The kids did most of them."

"It was your skill and talent that showed them how." Mrs. Schultz wasn't going to let him get away with not accepting the compliment.

"You're coming tomorrow night, right Lou?" I asked. He shrugged.

"You have to," Trace piped up from the table. "You said you'd bring those wings I tried at the market the other day. They were awesome."

"So was your shepherd's pie. We really enjoyed that," I said.

"Archie in particular," Mrs. Schultz added, giggling as she recalled how he snarfed it up in only a few bites. "I'm still deciding what to make for the dance."

"If you want to walk to the hall together, I can meet you at the shop and help you carry whatever it is," Lou offered. He stuck his hands deep in his pockets and suddenly looked like a school kid himself.

"That's a nice offer, Lou, but I'll be going home first to freshen up and change into my dress. Everyone from my poker group is meeting at my house so we can go to the dance together."

"I'll be making something cheesy, Mrs. Schultz. I'm happy to make enough to represent you and Archie too," I said, wanting to alleviate Lou's rejection.

"Make sure you put on your dancing shoes. You're saving the first dance for me, right, Ruthie?" Frank said to Mrs. Schultz.

Ruthie? I'd rarely heard anyone call Mrs. Schultz by her first name, Ruth, much less *Ruthie.*

"Of course I am," she replied, her blue eyes brightening. Frank looked at her adoringly.

Oh my. This was puppy love, and I couldn't be happier for Mrs. Schultz.

"Why did we decide to do a dance anyway? We should've organized something fun," Lou groused.

"Like what? Bingo?" one of the students ridiculed. Laughter bounced around the table of teens.

"Hey, don't crack wise to your elders," Frank scolded.

The laughing ceased, but Lou seemed more annoyed at being referred to as an "elder" than the kid shooting down his idea. And Lou was almost a decade younger than Frank, even though his demeanor made him seem older.

"A game night's not a bad idea for next time," I said.

"Just don't put poker on the list unless you want Ruthie to skunk everyone," Frank said, leaning in for a laugh with Mrs. Schultz.

"I think you let me win," she said to him with a toothy smile.

"No, you won fair and square," he insisted.

"Did Frank join your ladies' poker night?" I asked her. The Schultzes' regular poker nights had turned into ladies' poker nights after Mrs. Schultz's husband passed, she'd told me long ago. It was the one night she always hurried out of the shop, brewing with excitement.

"We made an exception Saturday to try out a co-ed night and invite friends and husbands. It worked out well, except the boys like to play with too much money," she insisted. "The girls and I prefer penny poker."

So much had gone on since Saturday that Mrs. Schultz hadn't shared this. I got the feeling she would've kept it to herself, regardless. Changing up her poker night for Frank was a bigger deal than she'd admit to.

"I don't think Archie's putting those on the tables right," Lou suddenly grumbled. I watched him stride over to Archie, who seemed just fine placing the veggie-flower centerpieces.

I left Frank and Mrs. Schultz to make googly eyes at each other and found the Melon sisters at a table separating name tags. Daisy seemed to be having a harder time of it, as she was reaching over the big daisy pocketbook on her lap. She must've heard about the wallet thefts and wanted to keep it as close as possible. I sat down and joined them.

"How are you doing, ladies?" I asked.

"Did I hear somebody yell 'Bingo'?" Daisy asked.

"Nobody yelled 'Bingo,' Daisy. You've got gambling on the brain," her sister Gemma said.

"Actually, someone did say 'Bingo,' but it's not because they're playing. Lou was suggesting that our next event be a game night."

"I'm in! Let's not wait too long, I'm on a winning streak. I won big at the casino yesterday," Daisy said, showing off a perfect row of white teeth, likely dentures, when she smiled.

"The casino?" I hadn't even realized there was one nearby.

"My grandson takes us every Thursday. He plays poker and we hit the slots," she said.

"Well congratulations! I hope your winnings are someplace safe."

"They are! Right here in my purse." She smiled and patted her large daisy purse.

This made Gemma shake her head. "It's no use trying to reason with her."

"How am I going to spend it if it's in a bank?" Daisy responded.

"See?" Gemma shrugged, resolved that she wouldn't change her sister's ways.

"There has been a rash of wallet thefts lately, so be extra careful," I warned her.

I heard my Eurythmics parody, *Sweet Dreams Are Made of Cheese,* coming from the purse at my hip. "Excuse me." I reached in to retrieve my phone. Everyone was here—who could be calling? Maybe Roman?

The screen read Olivia Harrington. I scrambled out of my chair and quickly hit the answer icon before it went to voicemail. I trotted away from the table to talk. "Olivia. Hi."

"Willa, I'd like to meet with you," she said directly.

"Uh, okay. When?"

"Now. My house."

"This might not be a good time."

"You'd be doing me such a favor," she said.

"Well . . ."

"Great. See you soon."

"I didn't say—" Her call vanished from my phone screen. She'd hung up.

Shep approached me. "Olivia Harrington called you?" He'd obviously overheard me.

"Yes. I've been summoned to her house."

"Do you want me to come with you? I'm free after this finishes up."

That wouldn't be for another hour, and Olivia Harrington didn't seem like the kind of person that took kindly to waiting.

"That's okay. She probably wants to make sure I don't sue her for falling off her horse. I'll run over now," I told him.

"You think that's a good idea?"

"I'll ask Baz to come with me."

I walked over to where Baz was still with Ginger, hovered around Everett in front of his laptop. Ginger was reading from the song list I'd seen on the Town Hall bulletin board. Over the weeks, residents were encouraged to add any songs they wanted played at the dance. The group no longer appeared frustrated.

"Looks like you figured it out," I said to them.

"We did," Baz answered. "Now we have to compile all the songs."

"Can I steal you for a sec?" I asked him. We stepped away and I kept my voice hushed. "Olivia Harrington just told me to come to her house."

"Why?" he asked.

"She didn't say."

"You told her you'd go?"

"She didn't give me the chance. She expects me to come."

"You don't have to do what she says, you know."

"What if Heath finds out that Chloe or Summer didn't kill Nelson? Olivia still runs the magazine and I'm sure to never get any good publicity in it if I ignore her. I think I should go. If I let her know I'm not pursuing any lawsuit or investigation into the horse incident, maybe it'll help smooth things over with her."

"I'm coming with you." Baz turned to Ginger, who'd apparently been watching us. "I have to do an errand with Willa. I don't think I'll be back to the hall tonight."

Ginger's face fell in disappointment. "Baz . . ."

I made an about-face. "I don't need you to come with me," I said to Baz. The last thing I wanted to do was get in the way of a blossoming relationship. Everett was already making enough inroads with Ginger, and we weren't so sure about him. I started to leave.

Baz put up a "wait a minute" finger to Ginger and followed me.

"You don't want me to come?" he said.

"We don't know if Everett killed Nelson. Do you really want him getting closer to Ginger? What if they decide to go out afterward and she's alone with him?"

"I hadn't thought of that."

"Shep knows I'm going too. I'll be sure to tell Olivia that you and Shep both know where I am. I'll call you later," I said, walking away.

As I left, I glimpsed Everett taking notice.

CHAPTER 33

Turning into the Harringtons' long driveway at night in the rain felt different than the other two times I'd been there. It reminded me once again of Rebecca driving up to Manderley—the house was beginning to feel ominous.

Olivia answered the door herself wearing a flowy caftan. She met me with a pleasant-enough "Willa" and a smile that didn't register in her eyes. I was grateful she was at least faking it for me, and I reciprocated so she'd know I came in peace.

She told me to hang my raincoat on the rack by the door and led me into the living room, where I sat on the familiar hard couch. I glanced around for any sign of Chloe or Summer, but we appeared to be alone. All I heard was the ticking of a clock. She sat in the wing chair, again like a queen on her throne, and I felt very much like one of her subjects.

"You look well. No concussion?" she said.

"No, I only bruised my arm. It's healing."

"Such an unfortunate accident."

Accident?

"Yes," I responded. She continued to stare at me, saying nothing, until my discomfort forced me to fill the silence with what I knew she wanted to hear. "I'm sorry about all that last night. It was entirely my fault."

"You and Chloe let your imaginations get the best of you."

"That must've been it. After what happened with Nelson, maybe we were a little spooked," I said, choking on my pride.

"Mm-hmm," she agreed. "How often do you ride?"

"I haven't had much experience on horses."

"So what was your reason for coming here yesterday?"

"Oh, uh, well Chloe invited me. She and Ginger are friends and I'm friends with Ginger, so . . ." It seemed simple enough.

"So you decided to leave your shop in the middle of a workday to go horseback riding, something you're obviously not comfortable doing, in order to spend the day with a friend of a friend?" She contorted her face to appear exceedingly confused.

I cleared my throat. "Ginger came too."

"And Marcos?"

Now *I* was confused. "Marcos wasn't here."

"No, I mean, how do you know him?"

"I don't really. I only just met him at the shower."

"Huh. How do you explain you and that newspaper editor meeting with him earlier today?"

Wow. How did she already know about that?

"It was nothing important. We ran into him at the inn. He's a friend of A. J.'s." I found myself wringing my hands and stuffed them under my thighs.

"So he's another friend of a friend?"

"Y-yes."

"Isn't it interesting that your friends of friends all seem to be connected to my family?"

"I wouldn't say *all*."

"I'm wondering what your interest is in us, Willa."

"I-I don't have one."

"Mm-hmm. Chloe doesn't seem to understand the problem that can occur with her strays."

"Her strays?"

"The friends she picks up along the way who aren't . . . well let's just say, they aren't in our social circles."

Was she comparing me to a feral cat?

"I don't quite know what you're trying to say, but I can assure you I'm not a *stray*. My business is well respected in Yarrow Glen and I'm an active member of our community." I no longer had an urge to wring my hands. Now I had to keep them from balling into fists.

Her perfectly pleasant expression suddenly snapped back into place. "I'm sorry, Willa. I wasn't implying otherwise. You must be working hard to keep a new business going."

"Yes, I do work hard. Very hard." I was still feeling defensive. She was getting at something, and I wished she'd spit it out already.

"It's always helpful to have the right people on your side, don't you think? People with connections?"

"I suppose."

"Of course it is. It's called being a savvy business-woman. Influential people can make you"—she paused—"or break you."

Was she threatening my shop? I worked to keep my voice steady. "I have a lot of good people who support me. Like Mayor Trumbull."

Her face hardened for a split second.

Uh-oh. I wasn't helping myself. I didn't mean to draw a line in the sand between her and the mayor. "It was so good of the mayor to recommend Curds and Whey for Summer's shower," I added.

"Kate was excited to have an ally in us, especially since we bought *All Things Sonoma*. Nelson's death won't change the fact that we'll keep the magazine's eye on Yarrow Glen. I know how much influence our magazine has. Controlling what readers hear about each business is a big responsibility." She looked down her long nose at me, making sure I understood her subtext. I understood it clearly, evidenced by the knot in my stomach. She could be an ally or an enemy. "Well, it was lovely getting to know you, Willa. I think we understand each other better, don't you?"

I nodded, not trusting my voice.

"Okay, then. Thanks for coming by. You can show yourself out?" She stood and walked through one of the archways and down the hall into her study without looking back, closing the door behind her.

What just happened?

I kicked myself out of my stupor and off the couch. With rapid steps, I raced to the front door and grabbed my raincoat. I wanted to leave this house even more than Olivia Harrington wanted me gone. I looked back only when I'd reached the front walkway, where I caught a figure watching me from an upstairs window. Was it Summer or Chloe? She hastened away when I saw her. I continued to my car and locked the doors as soon as I got in.

I was shaken and confused. At first, I believed what Mayor Trumbull told me and then I didn't, but she was obviously right about Olivia Harrington. I yelped when my ringtone played again. Relief flooded me when it was Heath's name on the screen. I answered immediately.

"Heath," I said. Darn it—my voice was still shaky.

"What's the matter? Are you still at the house? Shep just told me Olivia called you."

"I'm in her driveway. I need to get out of here."

"I'm not at the station. Do you remember how to get to my house?"

"Uh . . ." I tried to remember it from last year, but couldn't come up with it, especially not from here. "I don't think so."

"I'll text you my address."

"Are you sure?"

"Come to the house. I'll be waiting for you."

"Thanks."

I drove away from the hulking manor and waited until I was several miles down the road to pull over and put Heath's address into my GPS. My anxiety eased with each mile I drove closer to Heath's and farther from the Harringtons'.

CHAPTER 34

I'd gotten myself together by the time Heath welcomed me into his home, but the kind way he asked after me almost made me want to crumple into his arms. That was one thing about living alone with a fish, you didn't often get the hugs you needed. As we stood in the compact foyer face-to-face, I imagined the comfort of hugging Heath, his sweater soft on my cheek as I buried my face into his chest. Instead, I assured him I was fine and followed him into the living room, where there'd be plenty of space between us.

I was surprised when he took my raincoat and threw it over a dining chair in the kitchen, two steps up from the living room. It felt like it should have a place, like everything else in the room. His minimalist style highlighted the tidiness.

Even with the high ceilings and square-edged modern furniture, it was a warm room. The moody paintings of abstract figures brought life to it. He'd told me last time I was here that his deceased wife had painted them. I sat on the couch, firm underneath me. He sat on the matching chair, side-stepping the more comfortable-looking lounger.

He had a glass of water waiting for me, but offered me

what he was drinking, Malbec. I surprised myself by accepting. My nerves were shot, and since he hadn't offered cheese, a deep red wine would do.

He came back with the opened bottle of Malbec and poured me half a glass. "Since you're driving," he said.

I told him verbatim what Olivia had said to me, or at least what I could remember. The words themselves didn't sound threatening, and I wondered if I had made too much of it. Olivia was a formidable presence. She didn't have to come right out and say anything to make me feel threatened.

Heath said nothing.

"I'm sure you think I deserve it," I finished. I took a hefty sip, then focused on the inky hue of the purple-red wine in the glass so I wouldn't have to look into his eyes when he said so.

"No, I don't. Are you all right?"

Darn. Why did he have to be sweet?

"I'll be okay. It was just unexpected, although in hindsight it shouldn't have been."

"Why do you say that?"

"She makes sure she gets her way." I told him what we'd discovered about Mayor Trumbull's ex-husband and Chloe, and how Olivia had obviously contributed heavily to the mayor's campaign to keep it quiet. "I don't know if it has anything to do with Nelson's murder. It all depends on who's telling the truth and if Nelson was going to go back to Summer or to Chloe."

"What else do you know about Chloe?" he asked.

I broke Mayor Trumbull's confidence and told Heath all about our meetings. "There's just as much circumstantial evidence to point to Mayor Trumbull or Everett as there is to one of the Harringtons, so there was no point in me trying to find something on the Harringtons anymore. But Olivia's intimidation makes me feel like I must be getting closer to the truth. I can't help but think she must be covering for one of her daughters."

"I don't like the way she went about it or that you felt threatened, but I have to agree with her that you should stay away from this case."

"The last thing I want to do is tangle with her."

I hated giving into someone I considered a bully. I faced plenty of them during my school years as a farm girl who didn't like farming. I didn't fit in with the kids who weren't from farming families nor the ones who knew they'd be future farmers, thus I was an easy target for bullies. Once I grew up and found my voice, I was determined never to stay quiet in the face of a bully again. But this time there was more at stake than a lost cafeteria lunch. This was my shop, everything I'd worked for up until now. It was all the more reason to stand up to her, except for two things: Archie and Mrs. Schultz. The shop was something they relied on. They had both felt lost before working at Curds & Whey, same as I had but for different reasons. I was looking for the feeling of a real home, Mrs. Schultz was looking for a purpose, and Archie was looking for his passion. Could I chance taking that away from all of us?

I weighed my options, which included Heath sitting in front of me telling me to step aside. If I trusted anyone to fight my fight, it would be Heath.

I threw my hands up. "She wins. I'll stay out of it."

"You mean that?"

"I can't put my shop at risk. Besides, I have the same suspects I did from the beginning—everybody! Summer, Chloe, Olivia herself. Mayor Trumbull, Everett. Even Marcos could've done it. How do you do it? When there are so many possibilities, how do you know which one to focus on?"

Heath took a sip of wine and placed his glass on the coffee table. "Sometimes the simplest explanations are the right ones."

"You and Shep sound like fortune cookies," I said, trying to decipher this expression as I had Shep's back at the hall. "None of it's simple."

"So why don't you leave it up to me? Go back to your regular life."

"You won't say 'I told you so'?"

"Have I ever?"

"You don't have to. You have that look that says it for you."

Heath laughed, his sudden smile softening his chiseled features and evaporating my prior concerns, at least momentarily.

"Speaking of Shep, did he tell you if he saw anything suspicious at the hall tonight?" I asked, feeling a little lighter.

"Haven't gotten word yet, but we don't expect the pickpocket to be bold enough to do it while Shep's there. He's more of a deterrent. I'll make sure he's at the dance tomorrow too."

"What about you? Will you be there?"

"I'll just wrap up this murder real quick and head on over."

I squinted at him. "I get the feeling you're being sarcastic."

That smile was back. "Maybe I'll stop by. I see your arm's better just in time for it."

"It works perfectly." I brought the wineglass up to my mouth, then down, then to my mouth again to demonstrate.

He seemed to appreciate my humor. "You're all set then."

"Yup, even though I'll be feeling like everybody's third wheel. Archie and Hope will probably be going together. Ginger and Mrs. Schultz each have two men vying for a date. Even Lou and his dad have the Melon sisters."

Heath reached for his glass once more and finished it before asking, "That's not why Roman wanted to see you last night?"

"That's not how the night went. He explained what happened between him and Summer and why he left her at the altar."

"Ah, I can see how that might cool you on him."

"I know I have my trust issues, but I thought we were working past them. He didn't trust me enough to tell me, even when I told him all about my own broken engagement."

"You were engaged?" Heath sat back in the chair and crossed his ankle over his knee.

"Yeah. It was right after college. My fiancé and my best friend and I were going to open a cheese shop together. The three musketeers we called ourselves. But while I was getting in my hours for my cheesemonger certification, they were falling in love behind my back."

"Ouch."

"Yeah. I gave him back the ring and they used the money to open a chocolate shop."

"Double ouch."

"No kidding. They added insult to injury—now I can't even look at chocolate."

"I'm sorry."

"Me too. It's a bummer. I used to like a good chocolate molten lava cake."

Heath chuckled, then became serious. "Thanks for

sharing that with me. I'm glad I know that about you. I'm getting a little better idea of why you're so tough."

That wasn't my worst heartache. I thought about sharing my brother's death, but I figured I'd laid enough on him for one night. There was something I needed to say, though.

"Listen, I owe you a huge apology," I began.

"For trying to run your own investigation? I'm getting used to it."

"No, this is one that's long past due. It was that night last year when we danced together at The Cellar. Do you remember?"

"Dancing with you? Yes."

My feelings from that night came rushing back and I didn't dare look into his eyes. I took a last swig of wine for courage. "Afterward, I was upset with you, and I brought up your wife."

His right hand went to his left ring finger, although he no longer wore a band there. "You don't have to—"

"No, I do. Please, let me get this out. I've felt so horrible about it ever since I found out I was wrong about you being married and that she'd died. I didn't know. I thought . . . I mean, I know it was only a dance and you were just trying to keep an eye on me, but I felt . . ." No, I couldn't tell him that I'd felt an attraction to him. "That doesn't matter. I never meant to be so callous."

When I got it all out, I did look up at him. This time, he was the one who averted his eyes.

"Apology unnecessary but accepted," he said.

"Thank you."

"But I should say that what you were feeling when we were dancing . . . that wasn't all on you. I wasn't just keeping an eye on you. I wasn't married but you were a person of interest in an active investigation, and my better judgment left me when I let my feelings get the best of me."

"Your feelings got the best of you?" *Did I say that out loud?*

"Although I'm a police detective, contrary to popular belief, I *am* also human."

I laughed in relief that he broke the intense moment with humor, but I was also dying to ask him what type of feelings he'd been having. It brought up mine from that night and they fluttered around in my belly, excitement and anticipation colliding with nervousness and uncertainty.

I reached for my wineglass, but realized it was empty. "I guess I'd better go." I rose before I said something I might regret.

He got my coat and followed me to the door.

"Thanks for being here for me," I said. We faced each other in the small space, the same as when I'd entered.

"Anytime."

"Oh, don't say that. You might be sorry." I chuckled to cover up how appalled I was that I'd said it.

"Try me," he replied without laughing.

Time stood still. Or maybe it was just me, unable to break my gaze from Heath's eyes while my heart beat out of my chest.

"Okay," I said. That broke the spell. *"Okay"?* I needed a do-over.

Heath opened the front door. "Drive carefully."

"Will do," I responded lightly, walking to my car as if nothing had happened.

Had anything happened? I pondered that on the entire way home. It was sure better than thinking about veiled threats and murder.

CHAPTER 35

❧

Mrs. Schultz and Archie were in good spirits as we worked through a busy Friday, counting down the hours to the F.U.N. dance that evening. I didn't want to worry them about the shop, so, other than telling Baz last night when I got home, I kept what happened with Olivia to myself. Any developments between me and the handsome detective also stayed with me.

I caught Mrs. Schultz humming after she finished up with our last customer of the day and sent him on his way with a bag of cheese curds. After a full day, Archie still had quite a bit of pep in his step, although that wasn't unusual for him.

"You two sure are high energy today," I said. Luckily, my arm was out of its sling and almost at one hundred percent, so I was also feeling brighter.

"I'm looking forward to the F.U.N dance," Mrs. Schultz explained. She locked the shop's front door and flipped the sign over so that it read Closed through the door's paned glass.

"Hope said she'd go to the dance with me," Archie announced, unable to hide a grin as he circumnavigated the Aubusson rugs to dry mop the hardwood floors.

"That's great!" Unlike Archie, I wasn't surprised. "I'll

be going solo, but I don't mind. I plan to get to know some neighbors better."

"That's what it's all about," Mrs. Schultz said as we began the closing routine. "You're welcome to join me and my poker friends for pre-dance chocolate martinis. It's our signature drink. Except for Janet—she's the designated driver."

"I appreciate the invitation, Mrs. Schultz, but I think I'll need the extra time to make my dish for the dance. It's been so busy today, I haven't had the chance." Yesterday's heavy rains had subsided, which was reflected in the extra foot traffic we'd gotten.

They nodded in agreement and we hustled through the rest of our closing duties, all of us in a hurry to get home. I stuck Guernsey inside and locked the shop door from the sidewalk. Mrs. Schultz mounted her bicycle, clicked on the headlamp, and pedaled away. Archie kicked his skateboard to speed toward home. We shouted "See you at the dance!" at one another before I walked down the alley and upstairs to my apartment.

Baz's truck was in his parking space in the back lot, so I reached over the low rail between our shared deck and gave his door our three-rap knock before I let myself into my apartment. It was our way of saying "Hey!" to each other when we got home, with no obligation to chat.

"Hello, Loretta. How was your day?" I fed my fish as soon as I got inside—she gave me attitude otherwise—and turned on *Chopped*. She loved having dinner with Ted Allen. Who wouldn't?

I went straight to the kitchen to start making my Gruyère Gougères for the dance. I had to start them now or they wouldn't be cooled in time to pack them up. When I thought of something that would be easy to bring, easy to eat, taste good at room temperature, and everyone would love, it didn't take me long to remember the delicate cheese puffs I had in France. I'm not much of a baker, but I'd made a pâte â choux dough before. For this recipe, I added Gruyère cheese.

Baz walked into my apartment, knocking and saying hi as he entered. I said hello without turning around, as I was scooping out the dough like cookies onto baking sheets.

"Shouldn't you be getting ready?" he asked.

"I'm baking Gruyère Gougères for the dance."

"Groo what?"

"French cheese puffs."

He came over to get a closer look. My attention turned from the puffs to Baz, who looked spiffy in a jacket and tie over a collared shirt and jeans. Tennis shoes completed the outfit. My raised eyebrows and open mouth reflected my surprise.

"What? You think I should wear different shoes, don't you?"

"No. I think you look great. I've just never seen you dressed up."

"That's 'cause I never do it. It took me three times to get the tie right."

"I think Ginger will be very impressed. Did you end up asking her to go with you?"

"I tried to after I bungled it at the hall last night. I didn't want to ask her there in front of you and Everett. It was awkward."

"You *were* kind of put on the spot. It's not like you had *weeks* before to ask her." I looked at him pointedly.

"Okay, okay. I lost out anyway. She's going to the Harringtons' for Chloe's sake, so she's coming to the dance from there."

"Did you ask her if she'd like you to go with her?"

"To the Harringtons'? Was I supposed to?"

"She might prefer not to go alone. And if Everett still plans to go to the dance afterward, I bet he and Ginger will end up going together."

"I hadn't thought about that."

"Come on, text her."

Baz took out his phone. "What do you I say? *Do you want to go to the memorial party together?*"

"It's not a party."

"What's it called then?"

I thought for a second. "A reception, I guess? Gah. Give that to me." I took his phone and typed *Would you like me to go with you to the Harringtons'?* I tapped *send*.

"What did you write?" He read my message. "Okay. That's good." He stared at the screen for her response.

A moment later, it appeared: *That would've been nice but I'm already here.*

He texted back: *Sorry I didn't think of it earlier.*

"That's that then," he said, putting his phone away. "I was going to go to the hall early anyway to make sure the two teenagers we put in charge of DJing don't decide to make changes to the music."

"That would be quite the prank."

"Better than pickpocketing."

He had a point. "I wondered why you were dressed already. I didn't know if you were early or I was running late."

"Both. It's getting late."

I looked at the clock. "Ah, you're right. I gotta get a move on." I stuck the puffs in the oven and set the timer for thirty minutes.

"See you at the dance," Baz called as he let himself out.

CHAPTER 36

I showered, gave myself a high five for remembering to shave my legs, and changed three times. I wanted to wear something dressier than my usual outfits, but I wasn't a dressy kind of gal. I felt more comfortable slipping on a pair of jeans, but that wouldn't do for tonight. Looks like my little black dress would finally get a night out.

It wasn't exactly a cocktail dress. There was nothing frilly or shiny about it. In fact, I think I bought it for a job interview once. It was a simple fitted dress with a crew neck and short sleeves. I appraised myself in the mirror. I pulled on the hem trying to stretch it to my knees. It was shorter than I remembered, or maybe my hips filled it out a bit more nowadays.

The aroma of baked pastry and cheese seeped from the oven and made its way to the bedroom. The timer dinged, leading me into the kitchen. I took the trays of small round pastries out of the oven. They looked perfect, puffed to a crispy golden color and small enough to be eaten in a couple of bites—one bite if you were Baz or Archie. I transferred them to cooling racks and bit into the last one. It was light and airy, like eating a pillow of cheese. I popped the rest of it into my mouth—tight dress be darned.

After doing my hair and makeup, I checked the skies out my bedroom window. I was happy with my hair. I'd styled my bangs to the side and they were behaving— which meant the weather would surely be bad. To my surprise, it remained clear with a bright moon in the sky skirting the quick-moving clouds. I surveyed my shoe rack at the bottom of my closet and decided to take a page out of Baz's book. I bypassed the black pair of heels meant for this dress and chose a white pair of Keds that looked practically brand new. The better to dance with, right?

I'd been on my feet all day. Who was I going to kill my arches to impress? I had to face the hard facts that things weren't improving between Roman and me.

I walked out to the living room. "How do I look, Loretta? Be nice."

My fish tended to judge me a little for never looking as fabulous as she did, often swishing her red crown tail like a flamenco dancer's dress. This time she didn't try to show off. She wiggled her iridescent blue body in approval.

"Thank you. I'll leave *Chopped* on until I get home." I put on a thin white cropped cardigan with three-quarter-length sleeves before slipping the strap of a small black purse across myself. "See you later. Have fun with Ted," I told her as I *almost* walked out the door without my puffs.

Minutes later, with three containers of French cheese puffs and a couple of large bread baskets in tow, I drove to Main Street, where I considered passing Town Hall and continuing on to the Harringtons'. With all the people who would be there for the memorial, I could possibly stay out of sight of Olivia. This could be my last chance to talk to those involved in Nelson's murder. There had to be something new to discover.

No, Willa. Just take your freshly baked cheese puffs to the dance like you planned.

I forced myself to turn into the lot shared by the church and Town Hall, and was a little disappointed when I found a spot to park—my last excuse to go to the memorial was dashed.

As soon as I pulled on one of the heavy double doors of Town Hall, I could hear the muffled party noises of music and happy chatter. I was glad for my decision as I made my way to the decorated hall.

It looked every bit as festive as the committee hoped it would. The fairy lights twinkled against the backdrop of the night sky visible through the row of tall arched windows. The decorated buffet tables were mounded with casseroles, cakes, and cookies. Contributing to the potluck was voluntary, but it appeared everybody had brought their specialty. The friendly, party-going atmosphere was emulated by Sharice and Ginger's wall mural of happy dancers and linked hands.

The students from the committee—almost all but Trace—were at a table at the back, playfully throwing butter packets at each other, but looking bored. Having to spend their Friday night at this dance was probably more of a punishment than all those days of decorating.

I recognized many of the people mingling—Sharice, Constance, Deandra. I didn't see A. J. He was most likely at the Harringtons' covering the reception. I spotted Archie and Hope laughing with some friends. Hope's pixie-style blonde hair was freshly dyed a unicorn of colors to match her patterned dress. The Melon sisters, wearing an abundance of sequins, were seated at a table in the corner on either side of Lou's dad, Cyrus, who looked pleased at the seating arrangement. Baz was at the DJ table overseeing a couple of the teens like he'd said. It looked like Mrs. Schultz kept her promise to Frank—they were already tearing up the dance floor, which made my heart dance too.

I brought my contribution to the buffet table and said hi to Lou and Trace, who were helping folks dish up their food. I took out my baskets and draped cheese-decorated tea towels over the bottoms, then filled them with the French cheese puffs until they were in jeopardy of toppling over.

My eyes feasted on the food. I tugged on the hem of my dress again. How much could I eat in this thing? I should've worn something flowy, like Deandra.

"Are you going to guard the food all night or eat?" Lou said to me.

I came out of my thoughts to see the buffet line had trickled away. Trace had left his post behind the table.

Lou held out a marker and a miniature paper tent. "To label your rolls," he said before leaving, as well.

I wrote "French cheese puffs" on the card and placed it in front of my baskets. I took a plate to finally feed myself, but there were almost too many choices. Which ones would be least likely to end up dribbled on the front of my dress?

I spooned an assortment of food onto my plate and looked around the room to see where I should sit. I noticed that Daisy Melon's large yellow pocketbook with the daisy applique was left on a chair at her table. Daisy, Gemma, and Cyrus were no longer there. Where was Shep? Heath said he'd make sure Shep was here tonight. Maybe they caught the thief last night after all. I kept an eye on Daisy's purse, just in case.

Richie—or Richie Muscles, as I'd nicknamed him—came over. He was the guy police relied on to tow cars involved in criminal cases, which is how we'd crossed paths. He was a bit of a meathead, but nonetheless was well-liked around town. Richie's tight shirt pulled at the buttons, as if his Incredible Hulk–like body was going to rip it open at any moment. He looked me up and down, as he tended to do.

"Hey, beautiful. You clean up nice. I like your kicks with the dress." He pointed to my Keds.

"Thanks, Richie. You look nice too," I said.

His expression told me he already knew this.

"Up for a dance?" he asked.

"I'm going to eat first. Maybe later?"

"There might be a line for me by then. You snooze, you lose!" He laughed. "Just kidding. I'll save one for you." As he walked away, I heard, "Hey, Caroline. Look at you. You clean up nice."

I laughed and forked the goulash on my plate.

The bang of a chair hitting the floor grabbed my attention, as it did everyone else's. A commotion had broken out at the corner table where I'd seen Daisy's pocketbook.

Someone yelled, "It's him! It's him!"

I saw Lou standing over the table, yelling, "We got him!"

The music stopped. I pushed my way through the crowd that had closed in around the table.

"What's going on?" someone asked.

"He stole Daisy's wallet," Lou said, pointing to the floor where Trace and Frank were untangling themselves.

"Trace?" I said, disappointment weighing heavy on my heart.

"Not Trace. Frank!" Lou announced.

My gaze searched for Mrs. Schultz, who was on the other side of the scuffle, looking on in horror. Her friends swooped in to surround her.

Please, let this be a mistake.

CHAPTER 37

"What's going on?" Shep called out, entering the hall. The crowd parted as he pushed to the center of the action. He was dressed in his police uniform.

"He stole Miss Melon's wallet!" Trace told Shep.

"Mr. Coogan?" one of the high schoolers said incredulously.

"I did no such thing," Frank declared. He straightened his tie and retucked his shirt over his doughy middle, smoothing his mussed hair afterward.

"It's right there," Trace said, pointing to the ground at Frank's feet where a bright magenta wallet lay near the overturned large daisy pocketbook that belonged to Daisy Melon.

"They're trying to frame me," Frank said to Shep. "Trace was the one who tried to take the wallet. Not me."

"That's not true!"

"I can vouch for Trace. It's not true," Lou broke in.

"How can you be sure, Lou?" Mrs. Schultz asked skeptically. Her poker friends surrounded her, each with an arm or a hand on her in protection.

"I can tell you." Daisy Melon stepped forward, a twinkle in her eye. Everyone was silent. "It was all planned out."

Everyone's attention was on Daisy.

"My son likes to play poker at the casinos," Daisy said dramatically now that she had a rapt audience.

Glances went around.

"Excuse me, Daisy, but what does that have to do with what happened here tonight?" Shep asked gently.

"I'm trying to tell you. Trace works in Cyrus's market and Cyrus is a very good judge of character, aren't you, Cyrus?" Her bright eyes turned toward Cyrus, who'd come forward in the crowd.

"I am. I've never hired a thief in all my years owning Lou's," he said definitively.

"You're trying to say he couldn't do it? It's not like Trace has a spotless record. Come on now, Shep." Frank forced a laugh that fell flat.

Shep turned patiently to Daisy. "Is there anything else, Daisy?"

"I won big at the slots the day before yesterday," she answered.

"Yes?" Shep nodded, obviously hoping to spur on Daisy's storytelling.

"Well, there it is," Daisy said triumphantly, as if she'd explained everything.

"You think I took your bag because I knew you won money?" Frank guffawed. "Everybody on the committee knew you won. You told everybody when we were decorating here last night." Frank's voice rose to a crescendo.

Now it was Gemma's turn. She stood beside her sister. "That's true, Frank, but Daisy and I were the only ones who knew you lost big at the poker table a couple months ago at the casino. So when the buzz went around about the wallet thefts, we had an idea of who the thief might be. But we knew we had to have proof. So we put our heads together—"

"And pulled off the big sting," Daisy finished in delight. She put a finger to the side of her nose and brushed it, just like Robert Redford and Paul Newman had in the classic con movie *The Sting*.

Lou took it from there. "We decided Daisy should bring her bag with an empty wallet as bait. We had Trace hide under the table hidden by the tablecloth, and then Daisy purposely left the pocketbook alone on the chair where Trace could see it."

"As soon as I saw a hand go into it, I jumped out to catch who it was," Trace said. "It was Frank."

Frank continued to brush off his navy-blue blazer. "That's preposterous. Trace knocked over the chair. I just happened to be standing here. I'm afraid it's my word against yours, young man."

I could see panic begin to color Trace's face and so could Frank.

Frank's flustered demeanor calmed to smugness now that he had the upper hand. "I never touched that wallet and you can't prove otherwise."

"Can't we?" Gemma said. "What's that on your hands, Frank?"

Frank looked at his hands, as did the rest of us. He turned them over to see his fingers and palms were smudged a bright magenta, the same color as the wallet. Confused, he tried to wipe the color off, but it remained.

"Daisy and I took it upon ourselves to dye her wallet right before we came here. We made sure it would rub off on whoever touched it."

The panic left Trace's face as he threw his palms up to show they were dye-free.

"I might've tried to pick it up when it fell out of her purse, I-I can't remember," Frank said, stuffing his hands into his pockets.

Shep intervened. "Thank you all for filling in the blanks, although you should leave police work to the police. I happen to know who's telling the truth." He pointed to two corners of the ceiling. "We installed cameras in the room to see if we could catch the thief tonight. I was in the custodian's closet next door, watching. The video is right here on my phone." Shep lifted his cell phone so everyone could see it. "Should I hit *play*, Frank?"

Realization that he was caught washed over Frank. He slumped down in the chair that had been uprighted.

"Frank?" Mrs. Schultz cried in a small voice. Her friends held her steady.

Frank's explanation poured out of him. His voice carried none of the earlier bravado. "I've been gambling too much since my divorce. Like Daisy said, I lost big at the tables a couple of months ago and I didn't have the funds to recover. I couldn't keep using my retirement savings. I just needed a few extra bucks so I could win my money back, you know? I didn't think anybody would miss a little cash." He looked at Mrs. Schultz. "I'm sorry. I thought you might still have your poker winnings in your purse the night of the Paint and Snack. Some of it *was* mine. I hope you can forgive me."

Mrs. Schultz tutted and snapped her profile at Frank, refusing to look at him. Her friends, however, glared at him with death stares.

"I think it's time to bring you to the station," Shep said to Frank.

Frank stood and hung his head. The room was in shocked silence as Shep led him out of the hall.

Trace's classmates, who'd previously ignored him, now

clapped him on the back and gave him high fives, pulling him over to their group. I watched Mrs. Schultz's friends coax her to another table. The music started up again.

"It just goes to show, never underestimate a good tea," Daisy Melon said as the crowd began to disperse.

"Daisy, you talk in riddles," Lou said, but he was smiling.

"What do you mean?" I asked her.

"It was our inspiration for the dye. We were over at Lorna's the other day trying to get some secondhand scoop about that murder, you see, since her daughter, Polly, is the Harringtons' housekeeper. She's just not enough of a gossip, that Lorna," Daisy said with a disappointed shake of her head.

"The dye, Daisy." Gemma brought the story back on track. "Lorna brought in a tray of her famous tea the day we were there, but the dog came by and knocked the tray over. The tea spilled everywhere, all over her rug. It turned it a beautiful magenta color, but oh what a stain. That's where we got the idea."

"It was such a shame, though. I hadn't even taken a sip and I so love her hibiscus tea," Daisy lamented.

Hibiscus tea. Polly made her mother's hibiscus tea. The recollection of the housekeeper coming down the stairs with a tray of hibiscus tea now appeared blindingly bright in my memory. It was the day of the murder. Possibly the time of the murder. She'd gone up to give Olivia and Summer her famous hibiscus tea—something they never turned down—yet she came down with one of the glasses completely untouched, which means only one of them drank it. Did the other turn it down or was only one of them upstairs? According to their alibis, they were upstairs together the entire time. But maybe they weren't. Maybe one of them was at the stable murdering Nelson.

This could be the final clue I'd been searching for. Powerful Olivia Harrington might be the culprit. This time I wouldn't step aside. I had to talk to Polly and find out.

CHAPTER 38

But first, I hurried over to Mrs. Schultz, who was still being tended to by her poker friends. Archie, Hope, and Baz were also standing by. I gave her a hug.

"Mrs. Schultz, are you going to be all right?" I asked.

"Of course, I am. You can all stop fussing over me," she said.

I could tell she was putting on a brave face. It had to hurt, but she was a lot like me and hated the attention.

"Do they have a blender here? If any occasion calls for chocolate martinis, this one does," one of her friends announced. The others laughed.

I walked away from the group satisfied that Mrs. Schultz was in good hands, and waved Baz over. "I'm going to go to the reception at the Harringtons'. I just remembered something about the case." I explained what I recalled about the tea at the time of Nelson's murder. "It could explain why Polly was so nervous to talk to the police."

"I'm coming with you," Baz said. "Let's go."

I drove to the Harringtons', admittedly above the speed limit. I was more convinced than ever that either Olivia or Summer weren't where they claimed to be at the time of the murder and that Polly knew it. She was covering for them, afraid for her job. But I had to be sure.

We were still a couple of hundred yards from the Harringtons' when I began to see cars lining the road. It must've been packed inside. I was lucky to find a newly vacated spot not too far from the house. We used the flashlights on our phones to navigate our way to the lighted driveway. Up ahead, I recognized A. J.'s mop of curly hair before his face appeared from the shadows as he walked toward us. He had his canvas satchel slung over his shoulder.

"Willa, is that you?" he called.

Baz and I met up with him.

"Keep it moving," said a large man in a suit who'd been walking several feet behind him.

"I am, I am!" A. J. snapped. He lowered his voice to us, "You're going to have to walk with me."

We turned and accompanied him back down the driveway.

"What's going on?" Baz asked.

I looked back to see that the imposing guy with the commands had now halted in the middle of the driveway, standing with his arms crossed, keeping guard.

"I got thrown out," A. J. said.

"Why? Overdressed?" I asked, eyeing his signature Salvation Army jacket, T-shirt, and jeans attire.

A. J. ignored my sarcasm. "It was Olivia. As soon as she saw me, she called over her thug to personally escort me out."

"She didn't say why?" Baz asked.

"Not to me. I was being respectful, just observing and taking some notes. I spoke with Mayor Trumbull a few days ago to make sure it was all right that I cover it for the paper. She gave me the okay."

"I bet it has to do with us talking to Marcos at the inn yesterday," I guessed. "She made it clear she wasn't too happy with me either."

"How would she know about that? Marcos wouldn't have said anything."

"I think his assistant might've inadvertently told her when she called during our chat with him." I filled A. J. in with the short version of what happened when she summoned me to her home.

"But I saw Marcos inside. If she's mad at me and you, why isn't *he* in hot water?"

"Good question, but right now I have bigger things to work out."

"Like what? What do you have cookin', Willa?" Even in the shadows, I could see A. J.'s eyes light up at the prospect of a new lead.

"I'll tell you afterward if I find out what I think I'm going to," I answered.

"You'd better hope Olivia doesn't see you."

"Thanks for the heads-up."

"I'll expect to be paid back for the favor. Call you tomorrow."

A. J. left, but I kept Baz from continuing to the house until Olivia's bouncer turned and went back inside. I didn't want him to fix us on his radar from the get-go.

We continued up the driveway of parked cars and entered the house's grand foyer, which was teeming with subdued guests, as we'd suspected. All the better to go unnoticed. I scanned their faces as we walked through the rooms, keeping an eye out for Polly—hoping to see her—and for Olivia—hoping to dodge her. I peeked into the kitchen while Baz kept a lookout, but Polly wasn't among the workers hustling to replenish silver trays of finger foods to be passed around. We continued to the living room, where most of the guests congregated, spread out between this formal room and the more casual family room at the back of the house. I saw a few guests in the side garden but the chilly evening weather wasn't bidding anyone to come outside. Polly wouldn't be out there.

I spotted Chloe with a drink in her hand, leaning over the grand piano, chatting with Marcos. I agreed with A. J.—I couldn't imagine Olivia not being upset with him too.

I discarded my questions about Marcos to stay focused on Polly. "I don't see her. Maybe she's not working tonight since they've hired so much outside help," I said to Baz.

"Isn't that her?" Baz said, thwarting my rising disappointment.

I followed the direction he pointed and saw her walking across the room with an empty tray.

"Excellent. I bet she's headed to the kitchen." I tapped Baz to join me as I followed her. From the entrance to the dining room, I saw her go into the butler's pantry. "Keep a watch out here for Olivia. I don't want her to see me talking to Polly."

"Sneaking around this big house, I feel like I'm in one of those spy movies. Should we have a code name for Olivia?" Baz asked, straightening his tie.

"Just keep a lookout."

I walked into the dining room then dipped into the butler's pantry. I lucked out—Polly was alone, putting an assortment of empty wine bottles into a recycle bin.

"Polly, hi. Nice to see you again," I said with a smile.

"Hi, Willa. Did you need a drink?" She moved from the empty bottles to new ones and began uncorking.

"No, thanks. I just popped in to see how you're doing."

"That's nice of you. I'm fine. I feel terrible for the Harringtons and the Trumbulls, though. It's such a sad day.

How are you? I heard about your accident on one of the horses."

"Just a sore arm. It's fine now, thanks." I didn't know how much time I'd have, so I wanted to get right to the point. "I also have a quick question for you. Remember when I talked to you in the kitchen after the shower was called off? After you'd brought drinks up to Olivia and Summer?"

"Yes," she replied cautiously.

"I couldn't help but remember that it looked like only one of the glasses had been used. Which one of them wasn't upstairs?"

"I-I don't know why you're asking. I'm very busy." Her hand was shaking now as she poured wine into half a dozen stemmed glasses.

"It's a simple question," I pushed.

Baz stuck his head in. "The eagle is circling," he pronounced, and left swiftly.

It took me a second to compute what he was trying to say, but as soon as I did, I quickly shuffled around Polly into the connecting kitchen just in time for a near-miss with Olivia. I heard her speak to Polly.

"All hands on deck, Polly. Let's not dillydally," she said.

"Yes, ma'am," Polly replied.

I scurried through the kitchen to exit via the doorway farthest from the butler's pantry. There'd be no way to blend in if Olivia found me in the kitchen. I made my way through the front hall and back to the living room, where Baz and I reunited.

"Sorry I couldn't give you more time, she came out of nowhere. Did you get any intel?" Double O Baz asked.

"No, except she inadvertently confirmed she'd brought tea up to both of them and she was nervous about the question, which tells me she's been covering for one of them. But I still need to know which one, and if she also saw or overheard anything incriminating. I need more time with Polly. We have to make sure we know where Olivia is. We can't be spotted."

"Sorry, I lost her," Baz said, scanning the room. Then he leaned over to me. "Big Bird. Ten o'clock."

"What?"

"Mayor Trumbull. She's at the ten-o'clock position. You really need to improve your spy game, Wil."

I sighed and looked to the left side of the room, where Mayor Trumbull stood with a small group, her back to us.

"I'll have to give her my condolences later," I said, keeping my eyes peeled. I picked out Marcos from the back, his arm entwined with Summer's as they crossed the room. "There's Marcos and Summer." Her thick hair was pulled back in a neat ponytail and her conservative black dress skimmed her petite figure. "That's weird. Marcos said Summer would never give him the time of day. I don't trust her, and neither should Marcos, especially not now that they know he was talking to me and A. J. Why hasn't he been warned off the family like we were?"

"If he knows Chloe's big secret, they're not gonna fire him and chance him telling it to his newspaper contacts."

"Hmm. They don't seem like a family that would let someone have the upper hand." I thought of how Olivia had low-key threatened my shop. "If one of them is a killer, what would keep her from doing it again?"

"You think they'd do something here at Nelson's reception?"

"Why not? One of them killed Nelson at Summer's shower. There'd be a lot of reasonable doubt tonight with hundreds of people who have opportunity."

"What would Summer have against Marcos? It's Chloe's secret he knows."

"Maybe that's not the only Harrington secret he's keeping. Maybe he knows something much bigger and more damaging."

"Like who killed Nelson?" Baz asked.

I shrugged. "He was out of sight at the time of the murder. He was on the phone with A. J. but only for part of the time. He says he was looking for Chloe, which means he may have gone to the stable and seen something he shouldn't have. Let's keep an eye on him."

We walked to the family room, but didn't see them.

"Where did they go?" I wondered.

"Outside by the pool?" Baz suggested.

We looked out the slider doors, but the reflected lights on the glass made it impossible to see anyone outside.

"Baz!" Ginger walked over to us, with a wide grin. "I didn't think you'd come just because I was here," she said to him.

"I came with Willa," he said, extinguishing her smile. "I mean, I didn't remember how to get here, so I drove with Willa. But I came here for you," he corrected. "Sorry we're so late."

"That's okay. I was getting ready to go to the dance. Would you like to come back with me?" she asked him. She most definitely didn't look at me when she asked.

"Well, uh . . ." I could tell Baz was torn between wanting to go with her and wanting to spy with me.

I helped him out. "You guys go on. I'm going to give my condolences to Mayor Trumbull and Everett before I head back."

"I know he plans to leave for the dance soon too," Ginger said, her smile returned.

Baz looked back at me as they walked off, questioning

if he should go. I shooed him away and mouthed, "I'll be fine."

Okay, so I'd have to do the rest of this alone. This was my last chance to be in this house to find out what secrets it might hold. If I could continue to go unnoticed amidst strangers, I might not have to rely solely on Polly. I casually made my way to the closed door of the study and tried the door handle. It was locked, no big surprise. There was another room at the back of the house I had yet to be in—Chloe's art room, as I recalled Olivia telling Heath. Chloe didn't want anyone in there that day. Maybe there'd been a good reason.

I strolled across the family room to the opposite hallway, glancing to see if anyone took notice. The arch between the hall and the family room afforded me some privacy as I approached the door to the art room. This knob turned in my hand and I slipped into the room.

CHAPTER 39

❧

The room had a lot to tell me—Summer and Marcos were inside. She had one of Chloe's canvases in her hands. Marcos stood behind her.

Several easels were scattered around the room, all with Chloe's horse paintings on them. More paintings lay against the walls on the floor, three or four canvases deep. A wood table stained with paints held art supplies. Standing out from the rest of the room was an antique-looking Edwardian couch in its own corner that reminded me of the iconic one from *Titanic*.

"What are *you* doing here?" Summer said.

I cleared my throat. "I came to pay my respects."

"I mean, here. In the art room."

I thought fast. "The same reason. I saw you come in."

"Oh. Did Roman come with you?" Her voice sounded hopeful. She looked over my shoulder at the door.

"No. Did you invite him?"

"No. Mother wouldn't have approved, but I thought maybe . . ."

She thought he'd come for her sake, the person who may have set him up for the murder of her fiancé and the one who may have shot at me.

She carelessly put the canvas back on its easel and

walked over to another. Another horse. She seemed unsatisfied with her discoveries.

"Maybe we should go back out," Marcos said to her. He shifted from one foot to the other. He didn't look comfortable being in here.

"There's got to be more," Summer said. She sifted through the paintings on the floor resting against the wall.

"More what?" Marcos asked.

"More portraits of Nelson?" I ventured.

Summer stopped her search. "How did you know? Have you seen them?"

"No. I saw the one in her bedroom. The one you slashed," I took a guess.

Summer walked over to the satiny, leaf-patterned antique couch and slumped onto it. "I didn't know they'd done it for *me*. I thought Chloe . . ." She trailed off and started crying. Marcos sat next to her and put a comforting arm around her.

"You thought Chloe had painted it for herself." I dug into my purse for a pack of tissues. I offered them to Summer. She accepted.

"I always hated that they were together first. Nelson would sometimes compare me to her. He knew how mad that would make me. I'd take it out on Chloe. So when I saw the portrait that day, I realized they'd spent time together behind my back. I went nuts and ruined the painting—the only painting I had of Nelson and now it's gone." She blotted away a tear streaming down her cheek, which was perfectly kissed with pink blush.

"Were you still in a rage when you tried to shoot me?" I asked. Maybe it was insensitive, but I had to know.

The door opened. It was Chloe with a drink in hand. She closed the door behind her. "What are you all doing in here? Mother really needs to let me put a lock on this door." She put her drink to her lips as she drifted over to us. She was drinking something stronger than wine, and I could tell it was far from her first.

Now that I had everybody together, I wanted answers. "Summer was just explaining about the other day when she tried to shoot me."

"I didn't try to shoot you," Summer barked. Her eyes suddenly dried up.

"She really didn't. She thought you were me," Chloe said with a little laugh and a shrug. She took another swig of her drink.

"Wait, so you *did* shoot a gun at me?" I said to Summer.

"It was a simple mistake," Chloe said. "And I just told you—she thought you were me."

"So you're okay with your sister trying to shoot you?" Why was I the only one who found this crazy? "Did you know about this, Marcos?"

Marcos threw his hands in the air in innocence and leaned back on the couch to let their explanation unfold.

"I wasn't trying to shoot anybody. I just wanted to ruin Chloe's ride. I'd just found the portrait and I was still mad. I used my skeet gun. I even pointed it into the air away from you to make sure nobody would get hit," Summer explained.

"So that's why you weren't worried the police would find anything near the tree."

"I'm sorry you got hurt," Summer said. "I really am. I thought it was Chloe riding Dash. She would've been able to control him. I just wanted to give her a little scare, that's all."

I recalled that Summer mistook me for Chloe in the mudroom when I was taking Chloe's boots off. She could be telling the truth.

"You're not going to go back and tell that detective, are you?" Summer said. "I saw him skulking around here earlier."

"Detective Heath is here?" I wasn't sure whether I was relieved he was here too, or nervous that he'd see me.

"There's nothing to tell," Chloe responded, ignoring my question about Heath. "She shot her own skeet gun on her own property. End of story."

I wasn't used to seeing Chloe come to her sister's defense, but I wasn't prepared to let Summer off the hook as easily.

"But you lied to the police about it," I said.

"Because Mother was right there. She was so mad the police were at our house again. She would've been furious with me." Summer nervously shredded the tissues in her hands.

It all made sense. Frankly, I was relieved they were, literally, gunning for each other and not me.

"I'm bored. Can we move on?" Chloe said, realizing her drink was empty.

"I agree, let's move on. Explain to me your excuse for lying to the police about the text you sent to Roman," I said to Summer.

"I didn't lie about that. I told the police I asked Roman to meet me before the shower," Summer said.

"I mean the other text. The one you sent after you called off the shower, telling Roman to come back."

"I don't know why Roman said that I sent him another one. I didn't even have my phone most of the afternoon. I forgot to bring it with me when I went to meet him, that's why I lost track of time. I went looking for it when I got back to the house so I could call Nelson, but I couldn't find it. Not until later. I was so upset about the fight, I must've just looked right past it on my dresser."

She looked down at her hands and realized she'd shredded the tissues. She balled them up and tossed the wad on the couch. "Maybe if I'd had my phone and called Nelson, things would've turned out differently."

"You can't blame yourself, Summer," Chloe said. The impatience in her tone superseded the kindness of the sentiment.

"No, but I *can* blame you," Summer shot back. "You're the reason Nelson saw Roman and got so mad."

"I wasn't the one who invited Roman to the house in the first place!"

"All right, all right." Marcos stood up. "We've been through this before. Nobody can change anything now. Neither of you is to blame for Nelson's death."

Marcos was more certain of that than I was, but I couldn't totally dismiss Summer's excuse. Just this evening, I'd texted Ginger using Baz's phone. Someone else could've used Summer's phone to text Roman. It would be easy enough to do.

"Were you upstairs the whole time afterward?" I asked Summer.

She paused, taking control of herself again. "Yes. Upstairs with mother. Polly can vouch for that. She brought us our favorite tea." It sounded to me like a rehearsed answer, the one she'd likely given Detective Heath. "I have to go fix my makeup." Summer stood and strode past us out of the room before I could ask her more.

"You need to go easier on her, Chloe. She's having a hard time," Marcos said.

Chloe rolled her eyes. "Not you too, Marcos."

"What? I'm just saying to give the girl a break. Today of all days."

Chloe sighed and looked up at the ceiling. "Fine. I'll go find her. But has anybody thought that maybe *I'm* having a hard time?" She stomped out of the room after Summer.

"Keeping those two from catfighting is going to be my second full-time job," he said.

"You seem pretty tight with them."

"I guess so."

"Have they confided anything to you this week about the day Nelson was murdered?"

"Like what? We know as much as everybody else. Jeez, no wonder A. J. chose you as his sidekick. You go after a story like a dog with a bone."

I swallowed the remark I wanted to make and kept myself focused on getting answers. "You're sure you didn't see anything that day?"

"I already told you and A. J. where I was." He crossed the room to leave, but I matched his stride.

I spoke quickly. "I'm not accusing you of anything, I promise. A. J. explained your phone call."

"So then what are you trying to get at?"

I stood between him and the doorway to prevent him from leaving. "I know some of the Harringtons' secrets too, Marcos. I know Chloe talked to Nelson at the stable."

His eyebrows shot up. "You *are* good. So then you know Everett Trumbull was there too. My money's on him."

"What makes him more likely than Chloe?"

"Because I saw Chloe in here after. She wouldn't have been chilling in her art room. She didn't kill anybody."

"Look, I sort of have proof that Summer and her mother might not have been upstairs together the entire time as they claim."

"*Sort of* have proof?"

"Yes, just trust me. I'm not buying that she and her mother were together the whole time."

"Well, Chloe did tell me that Summer destroyed her closet that day."

"What do you mean?"

"Summer threw all of Chloe's clothes off the racks, her shoes off the shelves, stuff like that. She was mad at her for convincing Roman to come back to the house. It's not the first time she's messed with her stuff, apparently."

"Summer's got a temper?"

"More like she's impulsive and dramatic. Chloe's complained about her doing this before. The point is, if Summer was doing that, she wasn't off stabbing Nelson with a pitchfork. I know you and A. J. have this murdery history together, but I think you're looking at the wrong family."

There were a lot of reasons to suspect Everett, but now I had even more reason to believe Summer and Olivia provided false alibis for each other. "First I need to talk to Polly, but she's afraid to talk to me."

"The housekeeper?"

"That's right, you would know Polly. You've spent time here at the house." Maybe Marcos could help me. "Could you use your charm to help me talk to her?"

"What do you need to talk to her about?"

"She's Summer and Olivia's alibi. She brought their special hibiscus iced tea up to them that afternoon. But I saw her coming down the stairs with two glasses, one of them untouched. She only gave the tea to one of them."

"So what? Maybe the other one didn't want it."

"Or maybe only one of them was up there. I tried to talk to her about it before, and she got nervous. I think she lied to the police about it to cover for one of them."

"So you want me to ask Polly if she lied about Olivia or Summer being upstairs?"

"Yes."

Marcos burst out laughing, surprising me. "Willa, you're something else. There's no way I'm asking Polly anything. Listen, I've got a good gig here. I'm not ruining it by crossing the Harringtons. Chloe already saved my butt for talking to A. J. yesterday and smoothed things over with her mother. I paid my debt to him and now I'm done. You can do your little sleuthing by yourself. I'd concentrate on Everett Trumbull if I were you." Marcos walked out still shaking his head at my request.

Looked like I was on my own.

CHAPTER 40

I left the art room behind and made it my mission to find Polly. It was getting late. Was I wasting my evening on a wild-goose chase when I could be at the dance? I gave a second look to every person dressed in black and white like Polly was, which, unfortunately, was all the staff and a lot of the guests, as well. No Polly.

As my gaze continued to bounce from person to person, hoping it would land on Polly, I found Everett, who spotted me at the same time. He came over and we hugged politely.

"Rough day?" I asked.

"For Mom more than me. For her, it brings back the pain of losing her only brother."

"I'm so sorry," I said.

"Everett! There you are." It was Chloe, hanging on Marcos. "We were looking for you."

"What's up?" Everett said, not looking quite as happy to see them as they were to see him.

"Help us get Summer to stop bawling. You seem to be the only one she doesn't get mad at."

"Maybe she just needs some time alone."

"No, she needs to have some fun. Mother sent Polly in the golf cart to bring back more wine from the delivery

guy. I say we take the cart there before she does and get
first dibs on all that wine. That'll loosen up my sister."

I perked up at the mention of Polly.

"Uh, I'm actually headed out," Everett said. "See you
at the dance, Willa?"

"Yup. See you later." We smiled goodbye before he
walked off.

"You can never have any fun at these funeral things,"
Chloe complained.

Marcos put an arm around her, and they walked off,
presumably in search of fun.

This could be perfect. All I needed to figure out was
where Polly would be meeting the wine delivery guy and
I could talk to her without being interrupted by Olivia.
Chloe mentioned taking the cart, so it had to be at one of
their parking lots. Would I have time to get to my car and
try to catch her at the garden shed lot?

It was then that I spotted Polly. She was walking briskly
toward the mudroom hallway, no tray in hand. She must've
been leaving just now. I was in luck!

"Excuse me. Pardon me," I said as I wove through clus-
ters of people. I kept my head down. Now was not the
time to be noticed by Mayor Trumbull or any of the Harringtons.

I opened the side door, but the cart was gone, its red
taillights bumping along the trail toward the stable. If she
was meeting him at the stable parking lot, I could get
there in no time.

I walked carefully down the dark path. Any light from
the house diminished with each step. The moon guided
me the rest of the way. By the time I caught up to the cart,
it was empty. The lot was empty too. No delivery truck
yet. Where was Polly?

I turned back and saw a glow illuminating the open

doorway of the stable. The whinny of a horse carried outside. If Polly was hanging out in the stable, we'd have time to talk since she'd have nowhere to be until the truck came. *Please bide me some time, Mr. Wine-Delivery Guy.*

I walked into the stable. "Polly?"

Halfway in, I stopped in my tracks. Polly lay on the floor, not moving. I started toward her when something raced toward my head.

I shielded myself with my arms and felt a stinging whack that took me down. I fell hard, the smell of manure filling my nose as I face-planted onto the hay floor. I shook my head of the fog that tried to engulf it and willed my sore body to move. It railed against me as I turned over and sat myself up, only to face the sharp tines of a pitchfork mere inches from my chest. I froze as my gaze traced the handle to the person holding it.

Olivia.

CHAPTER 41

I scrambled backward on all fours until my back met the wall of the stall. I used it as leverage to pull myself to a standing position as Olivia stood her ground, the pitchfork still pointed at me. My arms had taken the brunt of whatever it was that came at me, but the rest of my body still felt the repercussions of hitting the ground.

"I should've known you'd follow her here," Olivia said. "You couldn't leave it alone. She was willing to keep it a secret. No one else had to be killed."

My brain bounced from *How do I keep myself alive?* to processing that Olivia was the killer. "You're right, no one else has to be killed, Olivia. I-I'm sure you can explain to Detective Heath what happened with Nelson. It was . . . self-defense?"

"It was in defense of my family. Nelson was playing games with my daughters, thinking he could go from one to the other. He'd already caused damage to their relationship. I wasn't going to let him humiliate our family."

"So you were protecting your daughters. Understandable."

"I was protecting our family name. I came here that day to tell him to stop humiliating Summer with those public outbursts."

"But instead, you saw him with Chloe." I filled in the blank to keep her talking.

"I heard you in the art room telling Marcos you knew Chloe had been here with Nelson. You seem to know everything."

I swallowed. "Not everything." How best to save myself? Play dumb from here on out or keep her talking and hope I could somehow get to the phone in my purse?

She continued, "How did you know about Chloe? Was it my *loyal* friend Kate Trumbull who told you?" She said *loyal* sarcastically.

I was never good at playing dumb. "It was actually Chloe who told me."

Olivia rolled her eyes in exasperation. "That girl and her mouth! She blabs about everything."

"So who killed him, you or Chloe? Or both of you?"

"Don't be ridiculous. Chloe didn't even know I was there. As soon as I heard Nelson proclaim his love for her, I hid in one of the stalls and waited."

"You could get the police to understand why you did it. I could help you. I know Detective Heath."

"I don't think our fine mayor would back you up." She soured her lips. "She's too much of a straight shooter. She and that son of hers, always so virtuous. Nelson told Everett to leave when he came to the stable and saw them kiss. If only he hadn't been there, I might've been able to convince Chloe not to tell the police she was there. Thank goodness he didn't stick around for the worst of it, Nelson asking *Chloe* to marry him. We didn't need the police knowing that. My older daughter has such a hold over men and my poor Summer can't keep one. Why does Summer always have to choose men who can't make up their minds?" She still had a strong grip on the pitchfork, but the tines were now lowered to the floor.

I took quick glances around the stall, hoping a weapon would present itself. All I saw was hay. There was no way she'd take her eyes off me long enough for me to unzip my purse and get my phone. I let Olivia continue to moan about Nelson. Maybe she'd lose steam and rethink what she was doing.

She continued, "One thing about Chloe, she goes through men quickly and doesn't look back. She wasn't having it. She told him to stop being stupid. When she left, it was my turn to tell him how I felt about him. He wasn't going to get away with treating Summer like that. He was pitting my girls against each other. How dare he?"

"So you were upset with him. Anyone would understand that."

"I told him to get his act together and apologize to Summer so we could get on with the shower and the wedding. The Harringtons were not going to be humiliated again. But thanks to Chloe's blabbing, he knew we didn't have the money we once had and needed his money to secure Summer's future. He said *he'd* decide whether to marry Chloe or Summer." She scoffed. "I was furious, so I grabbed the shovel and smacked him in the head with it. All it did was knock him to the ground. It wasn't meant to kill him." Olivia paused. "He'd still be alive today if only he hadn't laughed. Lying on the ground, laughing at me." She looked at the floor of the stall, as if reliving it in her mind. "The pitchfork put an end to that. He thought too highly of himself. He may have had new money, but *I* still have the Harrington name. This was my chance to get back at him *and* Roman."

"Get back at Roman?" Did this mean Roman's life was at stake too?

She was picking up steam, not running out of it. "I wasn't allowed to take revenge on Roman when he humiliated us. My husband and his mother wouldn't hear of badmouthing the Masseys. We had too much history with his family, they said. But our history with the Trumbulls? I knew that could be broken. Roman might've done me a favor by showing up at the shower the way he did. He made for an easy scapegoat, and my mother-in-law in her state will never know about it. If this investigation goes the way I intend it to, I'll have gotten rid of both Summer's horrible fiancés."

So it was Olivia who used Summer's phone to text Roman to return to the garden shed so she could set him up for Nelson's murder. Olivia did it all, all by herself to save her family's reputation. *Sometimes the simplest explanations are the right ones.* Hadn't Heath told me that?

She stood up straighter and lifted the pitchfork with strong hands. "I was saving my daughters when I killed Nelson and I'll continue to do what I have to."

I tensed, ready to juke and run.

"What are you saying, Mother?" Summer's shocked voice resounded through the stable.

Olivia jerked around. Summer came into view, then a moment later, Chloe and Marcos. I nearly cried in relief.

"Mother, what are you doing with that pitchfork? Who are you talking—" Chloe's voice hitched when she saw me in the stall. "Willa! What's going on? Why are you here?"

"Is that Polly lying over there?" Marcos said. I glimpsed him hurry past the stall toward Polly. "We have to call an ambulance."

"Yes," Olivia said. "I saw Willa knock Polly out with that shovel. I was holding her here until help arrived. Thank goodness you came."

"That's not true." I found my voice. My fingers scrambled to unzip my purse. "I'm calling the police."

"I heard you, Mother. Right when I came in, I heard you say you killed Nelson," Summer said.

"Summer, dear. That's not what you heard," Olivia said, attempting to make her voice sound soothing yet commanding, the way I'd often heard her speak to Summer.

"You killed Nelson?" Chloe repeated. She seemed to be sobering up by the second.

"Of course not. I didn't say that. Tell them I didn't say that, Summer." Olivia delivered a withering stare that had always worked on Summer before.

Summer looked at me then back at her mother. I froze. Would Summer do the right thing?

"You said you killed Nelson. I heard you," Summer said with conviction. "And you weren't upstairs at the time of his murder. You made me lie about it. You made Polly lie about it. And now you've hurt her."

A moaning came from Polly. I felt giddy at the sound. Olivia hadn't killed her.

"Nine-one-one. State your emergency," the voice from Marcos's phone rang out in the stable.

"We need police and an ambulance right away at the Harrington stable," he said.

Olivia put the pitchfork down. She said to Summer and Chloe, "Someday you'll have daughters of your own and you'll understand."

CHAPTER 42

The next half hour was a blur of police and paramedics. Heath was the first one to check on me before leaving me with an EMT. I'd have given anything for him not to go, but I knew he had a job to do. I was relieved to see Polly sitting up and talking before she was put on a stretcher.

An efficient paramedic checked me over. I watched as Summer and Chloe stood huddled together, draped in mylar blankets, clutching their mother's hands before she was finally led away by police. The reality of what their mother was now facing must've sunk in. Marcos took her place to try to comfort them, but they ignored him and clung to each other as if they were sharing a life raft on rough seas. I guess in a way, they were. After all that had happened—fighting over Nelson, Chloe ruining Summer's wedding shower, Summer's attempt to scare Chloe on horseback, and Olivia murdering Nelson—the Harringtons still deeply loved one another. I had no doubt the sisters would ultimately decide to stand by their mother during the ordeal to come. Olivia had killed Nelson to protect her family. If only she'd had faith that they could weather anything together.

I rejected a trip in an ambulance after the paramedic confirmed nothing more than bruises and a renewed sore shoulder. I walked out of the stable on my own accord for some fresh air.

Mayor Trumbull had been alerted to the commotion and strode toward the two police officers escorting Olivia to the patrol car.

"Olivia?" Mayor Trumbull said, her voice coated in shock at seeing her in handcuffs.

Olivia paused. "I told you, Kate. I rely on myself to get things done right. I did what I had to do to protect my children." She continued walking with her chin in the air.

Mayor Trumbull saw me next. "Willa, are you okay? What happened?"

"I'm okay. It's all over," I told her.

Heath came from the stable. "I'm sorry, Mayor Trumbull, this is a crime scene and an active investigation. I'm going to have to ask you to step back."

With a nod of Heath's head, an officer darted over to the mayor and led her away.

Heath and I were alone.

I hated this part. "I'm sorry. I didn't come here to confront her, I swear. I—"

He put a gentle hand on each of my shoulders, stopping me mid-sentence. "Are you okay?"

"Oh." I thought about it for a second. "Yeah, I'm okay. Relieved, actually."

"When I heard the call, somehow I knew I'd find you here. I'm glad you weren't hurt."

"I just came out here to talk to Polly. I feel terrible that she was almost killed because of me. I'd put together that only one of them—Olivia or Summer—was upstairs when Nelson was killed. They weren't together like they claimed. I had a strong hunch Polly was covering for them. Olivia overheard me talking to Marcos about it. That's why she lured Polly out here on her own."

"In the end, you saved her."

"I suppose. And Summer saved me. I didn't see *that* coming."

"Do you know why they were here?"

"Chloe had said something about intercepting the wine Polly was getting. They obviously didn't know it was a ruse by Olivia to get Polly out here. Olivia confessed everything to me, you know."

"Are you up for giving your statement?"

"Yes. I want to get this over with."

"We'll make sure you get to the station safely." He trapped my gaze with his. "Make sure you take extra care of yourself in the next few days. I'm sure you know this by now, but going through something like this doesn't always hit you right away."

I used to try to shoo away Heath's concerns like a gnat. Now they wrapped me in comfort like a warm blanket. "As long as I don't have to hang around any horses, I should be okay."

Heath reached out his hand to my hair. I felt his gentle fingers move between the strands, igniting a flutter in my chest.

"Heath—" I began, finally ready to give in to a wave of attraction.

"Got it." He pulled out a stray piece of hay from my hair.

All fluttering ceased and awkwardness took its place. "Oh. Thanks."

"I think you'll be okay," he said.

He was right, I'd be okay. I survived going solo to the dance, being confronted by a murderer, and coming very close to embarrassing myself with Heath all in one night.

CHAPTER 43

A. J. awaited me like a game-show host whose contestant had just won the big prize as I walked out of the station after my police interview.

"How did you manage this? Tell me everything." He stuck his hand in his bag and pulled out his recorder.

"I'll tell you all about it tomorrow." I was in no mood to recount it for a second time.

"Tomorrow?"

"Marcos was a witness, along with Summer and Chloe. Stick around. I'm sure he'll be out next."

"All right, but you promise. Tomorrow!"

"I promise."

"Hey," he said as I began to walk past him to leave the security complex.

"What?"

"Good work."

"Thanks, A. J. I appreciate that."

"But next time, call me first."

I walked away, chuckling. A. J. would always be A. J.

I stood outside the complex, inhaling the chilly winter air. I always had this same feeling when a case was finally over—relief mixed with inexplicable sadness. I wasn't particularly sad about the perpetrator this time.

Olivia Harrington would get what she deserved. No, I
think it was because the case wasn't the only thing that
was over. I sensed Roman and I were over before we had
a chance to get started.

I saw three people hurrying down the wide steps of
Town Hall. I was surprised to see plenty of cars at the Town
Hall lot—the dance must've still been hopping. The trio
didn't walk to the parking lot. Instead, they headed to the
sidewalk and across the street toward me. Under the street-
lights, I realized who it was. Baz, Archie, and Mrs. Schultz
strode toward me and gathered me in a hug.

"Ginger was with Everett when Mayor Trumbull called
him about what happened," Baz said. "Before they left
the dance, they told us Olivia was arrested and you were
there too."

"Are you okay?" Mrs. Schultz asked, looking me over.

"We had a scuffle at the stable, but I'm fine," I assured
them. I was, now that they were all with me. "At least I
didn't injure anything new. Summer, Chloe, and Marcos,
of all people, saved me."

"I'm sorry I didn't stay with you at the Harringtons,"
Baz said.

"Come on, don't be feeling guilty. I told you to go."
I punched him gently in the arm to knock him out of it.
"It's all over with now. Olivia confessed to killing Nel-
son."

"Told you she was scary," Archie said.

I agreed. "I don't know why I never stayed focused on
her for long. She had the most obvious motive—protecting
the Harrington family image. She'd just bought an entire magazine to make her family look picture-perfect
to all of Sonoma Valley. I knew she was concerned with
what everyone thought of them, but I didn't connect the
dots. She wouldn't even admit to drinking during the

day because of how it might look in her social circles. I should've realized when she used her resources to keep Chloe's involvement with the mayor's ex-husband quiet, she'd do whatever it takes to keep any family humiliation from reaching the light of day."

"It's such a relief to have the case solved," Mrs. Schultz said. "And that you're all right."

"I better go explain to Hope. I left her in kind of a hurry," Archie said.

"I suppose I should round up the gals," Mrs. Schultz said.

"Nobody needs to cut their night short. Let's all go back to the dance and have some fun." I wasn't sure I was up for it, but I refused to ruin anybody's good time, especially not Archie and Hope's first date. "We can finish this Team Cheese meeting tomorrow. Nobody else needs to know what happened tonight."

We gladly left the security complex and the murder case behind and headed back to the dance.

EPILOGUE

Once back inside, Archie found Hope right away, and Baz walked off, I presumed to find Ginger.

"Are you okay after what happened with Frank?" I asked Mrs. Schultz now that we were alone.

"I have to admit, it shook me up. It's not like we were dating or anything, but . . ."

"I know. Still, it's sad when the man you set your heart on turns out not to be who you thought he was." I looked for Roman and found him sitting beside Gia.

"I feel pretty foolish," Mrs. Schultz said.

"Don't you dare. You couldn't have known. Everyone was shocked."

"I'm glad I took it slow."

A new song came on. A bunch of the teenagers had taken over the DJ duties and were getting a kick out of playing some oldies. I was happy to see Trace among them. They seemed to want to bury the hatchet with him now that he was the hero of the night.

Mrs. Schultz's friends called her out onto the dance floor.

"Come with me, Willa," she said.

"In a minute," I promised, insisting that she go.

She joined the group, which included Lou in the mix. Tonight was full of surprises. I wasn't going to be the one to tell Lou that it would take a lot more than dancing "Y.M.C.A." together for him to win over Mrs. Schultz.

I realized I was starving, so I took myself over to the buffet table to see what was left. Baz was there and offered me a shortbread cookie.

"I need something to fill me up," I said.

"I'll get us a table," he offered, leaving with a tower of cookies.

I was glad my French cheese puffs had been a hit but bummed I wouldn't get one. I loaded my plate with tortellini salad. Most dishes looked pretty picked over. This would have to do.

I couldn't wait to eat. I stabbed at the salad and took my first forkful before I even left the buffet table. It was a much bigger bite than I'd intended. Like a chipmunk who's overfilled its cheeks, I attempted to chew the pasta in my mouth in a halfway-ladylike way, when I saw Roman walking over.

He was in the same blazer he wore the night he was supposed to take me to Apricot Grille only a week ago, causing the excited feeling I'd had about our date to briefly wash over me. The last few months together flipped through my memory like a slideshow: the nervous way he asked me on our first date to the harvest festival, drinking too much mead and laughing all night while we made holiday cheese and mead baskets, long talks over dinners at The Cellar, our first kiss at my door . . . *Sigh.* Maybe it was that simple.

I didn't look away quickly enough. He'd caught my eye. I chewed faster and swallowed the pasta down.

"Hi, Willa." Roman was by my side, smelling of fresh soap.

I threw the plate in the trash can behind me and surreptitiously wiped my teeth with my tongue before I spoke. "Good to see you. I'm glad you came." *Please don't let me have anything stuck in my teeth.*

"I've been lying low for a while, but Gia convinced me I should get back to the living."

Gia.

"She's right," I said. "Hey, I have some good news. Olivia confessed to Nelson's murder."

"What? You're kidding. How do you know?"

"I was there."

"Is that why you're so late?" He looked me up and down. "Are you okay? Were you in any danger?"

"I'm fine. It's a long story. I don't want to go into it right now. But you should know, Summer and Chloe came to my rescue."

"Wow. I hope they're all right. What a blow." He shook his head in disbelief. "Olivia. I would've never thought."

"At least you're out of the woods."

"True. That feels good. Do I have you to thank?"

"There were a lot of us involved."

He stuck his hand in his jacket pocket. "This *really* doesn't seem like enough now." He pulled out a small white box and handed it to me.

"Filled chocolate candies" was spelled out on it in flowing gold letters.

"Chocolates." Another surprise tonight.

"I know they're not very original but it's almost Valentine's Day and, uh, I'd already bought them for you, so . . ."

"Thanks." *Chocolates, Roman? Really?* I could tell white lies to virtual strangers, but when it came to people I cared about, I never pulled it off as smoothly. My expression must've tipped him off.

He cringed. "Ohhh, right, chocolates aren't your favorite, are they? Sorry."

"No, that's okay." I tried extra hard to smile. It *was* sweet of him to think of me. "It was nice of you to get me something for Valentine's Day." *Even if it was the one thing I despised.*

"I'd planned to do more if we'd still been . . ." He cleared his throat. "I know we won't be spending Valentine's Day the way either of us thought we would."

"That's for sure." I stared at the box of chocolates, feeling the irony of that idiom about life being like it. *You never know what you're going to get.*

"Listen, Willa, I know we were just getting started, but . . . can we start over? Is it too late to fix things?" He looked vulnerable, afraid of my response.

The part of me that missed how it was with Roman wanted to forget everything that had happened and have a great time with him tonight. But over this past week, I'd come to a slow realization. "I don't think there's anything *to* be fixed, Roman. I am who I am, and you are who you are, and there's nothing wrong with that. You're not a bad guy, not at all. I just don't think you're the guy for me."

He cast his eyes away from mine, then nodded and looked at me again. "I hope we can at least get back to being good friends. I'd hate to lose that too."

"I don't think we've lost that. Have we?" I said, hoping to reassure both of us.

He smiled at me, that crooked one that put a dimple in his cheek and always ended in a mischievous twinkle in his eye. This time I detected a hint of sadness there. It was hard to know if things would be good between us. We'd always had the "what if" in front of us, and now that was gone. Did we have enough of a friendship without the flirty banter? I smiled back, this time genuinely. We could try.

"Maybe a dance later?" he said, falling back into his confident, chill self.

"You bet," I replied.

He cuffed me on the chin and walked away. He joined a group that included Gia. Now that she was standing, I saw that she also wore a little black dress, hers decidedly slinkier than mine, along with a strappy pair of her usual sky-high heels.

I looked down at my comfortable Keds, now spattered with dried mud and a few stray pieces of hay, and wiggled my toes inside. The pasta sat heavy in my stomach, so I skipped any more buffet food and found Baz's table. He was by himself when I sat beside him.

"Why aren't you with Ginger?" I asked.

"Didn't I tell you? She went to the police station to support Everett."

"Oh. I'm sorry. Maybe she was just being nice?"

"Nah, they were into each other all night. I'm okay with it now that we know he's not a murderer." Baz shrugged. "She's a little intense for me and we don't have that much in common. And I couldn't pretend anymore to like that vegan stuff."

I laughed. "Not even for love?"

"I can't help it. I grew up with a mother who made meat pies and English puddings. I need someone who loves food. Regular food. Maybe a nice Italian girl."

"Like her?" I pointed toward Gia, now dancing like no one was watching. Or like everyone was watching, which they were.

"She looks too high maintenance for me. I need someone more down to earth."

"It looks like she's got her eye on someone, anyway."

She shimmied over to Roman and pulled him onto the dance floor.

"Look at us sitting here. Me in this stupid tie and you smelling like a horse barn. Aren't we pathetic?" Baz said.

"Hey! Being single isn't pathetic. It's perfectly fine." I put my sleeve up to my nose and sniffed. He was right about the horse-barn part. "Here." I tossed my box of fancy chocolates on the table in front of him.

"You bought chocolates for me?"

"No. I'm regifting. Roman gave them to me."

"*Chocolates*? Of all things, he gave you *chocolates*?"

"I know. Why do we have to try so hard? Why can't we just meet people who get us, you know?"

"Well, we've got Team Cheese," Baz said.

I smiled. "You're right."

The music switched up and a conga line started. Before we knew it, it was passing by our table, led by Mrs. Schultz. "Come on!" she called to us.

Baz and I looked at each other and laughed. Archie broke off to come and grab us. We rose from our chairs and cut in line between Hope and the Melon sisters. We conga'd our way around the hall and danced the rest of the night.

RECIPES

Goat Cheese Breakfast Quesadilla

This crunchy, sweet, and savory treat makes for a quick and delicious breakfast.

Start to Finish Time: Approximately 10 minutes

Serves: 1

Ingredients:
- 2 ounces fresh goat cheese (honey/cranberry walnut goat cheese optional)
- 1 tortilla
- ½ sweet, crispy apple (like Fuji), thinly sliced
- 1 tablespoon honey

Instructions:
1. Spread thin layer of goat cheese on half of tortilla, top with apple slices, and drizzle with the honey.
2. Fold tortilla in half.
3. Place quesadilla in a buttered, heated skillet and cook on each side for 2–3 minutes, until tortilla is lightly browned.

Savory Oven Pancake (Dutch Baby)

When the members of Team Cheese gather to figure out method and motive, we need an easy cheesy meal to help us think. This savory Dutch Baby does the trick.

Start to Finish Time: Approximately 25 minutes
Serves: 4–6

Ingredients:
- 4 eggs
- 1 cup milk
- 1 cup of cheddar cheese (or use cheeses of your choice) plus 2 tablespoons more
- 1 cup flour
- Pinch of salt
- 2 tablespoons butter
- ½ cup of ham, chopped

Instructions:
1. Preheat oven to 425 degrees
2. Combine eggs, milk, and 1 cup of cheese.
3. Sift flour and salt, then combine with the wet ingredients, whisking vigorously.
4. Put 1 tablespoon butter in a 10-inch heavy (cast iron, preferably) skillet on stove over medium heat. Add ham and cook until it becomes crisp, about 2 minutes.
5. Melt rest of butter into the pan and turn off stovetop. Add the batter and top with 2 tablespoons cheese.
6. Put pan in the oven and bake for approximately 15 minutes, until the pancake is puffed and golden.
7. Remove skillet from oven. Serve hot from skillet.

Spicy Snack on a Stick

Mrs. Schultz, Archie, and I sure wake up our taste-buds with this spicy appetizer!
Start to Finish Time: Approximately 10 minutes
Serves: 8–10

Ingredients:
- 2 red apples (like Gala), peeled
- 4 ounces Coppa salami
- 8 ounces Spicy Jack cheese
- 1 tablespoon honey (optional)

Instructions:
1. Dice the apples and the cheese into 1-inch cubes, so you have an even amount
2. Break Coppa salami into same number of pieces as apple and cheese.
3. Roll up a piece of salami and skewer onto a cocktail stick. Follow it with an apple cube and cheese cube.
4. Drizzle with honey if desired.